To a dear classmate,
Many blessing, Edna.
Candace

Tangled Affairs

Singing Tree
PUBLISHING

ISBN: 0-9827-8810-X
ISBN-13: 9780982788103

Library of Congress Control Number: 2012912103

Singing Tree Publishing
www.candacemurrow.com

Cover design by Julie Zaballos

Printed in the United States of America

Tangled Affairs

sequel to *Rose from the Grave*

Candace Murrow

Singing Tree Publishing
2012

For Sue

Acknowledgments

Heartfelt thanks to all the people who contributed to the success of this book: To Sue Atwood and Victoria Tennant for their excellent input. My editor, Barbara Fandrich, for her superb editing skills. My mother, Frances Clogston, and my sister, JoAnn Ableman, for their continuing support. And to my loving husband, Gary, for his extraordinary help and his kind and caring nature. As always, to the constancy of the Creative Spirit within.

CHAPTER 1

Seattle's weather forecast for August 1 promised temperatures skyrocketing into the 90s, but the heat was no match for Kat Summers's fiery-hot temper. She pulled the brush through her auburn hair and glared at Chance Eliason, her lover for the past nine months, nearly searing him in two.

Wearing white slacks and a short-sleeved silk blouse, she could have been dressed for church on this Sunday morning, but instead she was preparing to show a house to a new real estate client. She flipped the brush in Chance's direction, which he caught, and stomped out of the bedroom of her 100-year-old Craftsman style home.

By the time she reached the back door, he had her by the arm, stopping her in her tracks, his eyes as set as hers. "I know you don't have to leave for another hour, so you can just come back here and talk this out."

Her five-foot ten-inch height was a good four inches below his, but she rose on tiptoes, trying to equal out the difference, and looked at him straight on. "There's nothing to talk about. You like your women barefoot and pregnant, and that about says it all."

She yanked her arm to free herself but lost her balance, giving him the opportunity he needed to steer her into the living room, away from the door leading to her car. "We're going to have this out once and for all if it takes all day."

"Haven't we said it all? You want me to quit my job, the career I've built up over the years, just to move to Timbuktu to spend the rest of my days with you, and doing what? Sitting on the porch in rocking chairs until we die? I can't live like that." She jerked her arm, but he held tight.

"I can't live like this either, Kat. I drive here every weekend to be with you, and what do you do? You work. Not just Saturdays, but Sundays too."

"Well, that's what realtors do. I can't help that. I have to be available. That's how I make my sales."

"But you haven't even driven to Rosswood to spend time with me on my ranch. Not once."

She agreed, but she had no intention of changing. "What happens when a client wants to look at a house or is ready to buy and I'm three hours away? It won't work."

"Have Maggie handle it."

"I can't do that, not after she was so good to me after what happened. I can't ask her to do any more than she already has." Kat's voice faltered.

Chance lifted her chin. "Is that what this is all about? Brianna? Are you afraid to come to Rosswood because it will bring up all those horrific memories?" His tone had lost its fire.

Kat glanced from Chance to the fireplace to the floor, anywhere other than to meet his gaze. He'd hit a tender spot. After all this time, the memories still haunted her. She didn't want to admit that to Chance; she'd told him on numerous occasions everything was fine. If she stared into his dotingly intense eyes, she'd break down, just as she'd done many times before in the privacy of her bathroom in the middle of the night when he was sound asleep.

During the momentary pause, he'd let go of her arm, and she bolted away from him. He followed her to the kitchen, and while she snatched her purse from the counter, he blocked the door. "Kat, tell me. Are you afraid to go back to Rosswood? Is that why you've kept yourself so busy on the weekends?"

"Get away from the door, Chance."

"Not until you answer my question."

"Get away from the door."

"No."

Kat spun in the direction of the bedroom, strode through the doorway into the master bath, and locked herself inside. The scent of his minty aftershave engulfed her, and it was as if his whole presence filled the room, reminding her of the passionate night she'd spent in his warm, caring arms. Tears welled up.

Chance pounded the door. "Kat, talk to me."

"Go away."

"I'm not going anywhere until we have this out."

At times Chance could be relentless, stubborn, so incredibly suffocating. And this was one of those times. She felt the air in her lungs dissipate; she couldn't breathe. The walls in the room were closing in on her. She wanted out. "Get away from the door, Chance."

"Are you coming out?"

"Would you just leave?"

He rattled the doorknob. "Kat?"

A phone sounded and stopped after three rings. He'd answered the cell he'd left on the nightstand. After a short pause, he said sternly to the caller, "This is not a good time, Monique. I don't care what you want." The phone snapped shut and clanked on the wooden nightstand. He banged on the door, loud enough for Kat to draw back. "Kat? Come out and let's talk."

"When will that woman ever stop bothering you," she yelled back, "and when is the firm ever going to leave you alone?" She unlocked the door and pushed past him. "I have to go."

He caught up to her and grasped her upper arm. In a fit of frustration, she swung around and gave his face a hard slap. They both froze.

Until now, she hadn't realized how brittle her emotions were. Shaken and embarrassed for what she'd done, she fought for a way to explain the inexplicable, but she couldn't think at all. She couldn't speak.

In the midst of no explanation, no apology, no words out of Kat's mouth, his expression changed from hurt to blistering anger. She felt her own anger rise. She strode across the kitchen, but he was right behind her and jammed his palm against the door, holding it shut tight.

Her pulse pounded in her ears, and her breathing accelerated until she was on the verge of hyperventilating. "Get away from the door, Chance. I mean it."

He stood firm, his hot breath skimming the top of her head.

With her hand on the doorknob, she took a deep breath to calm herself and said in a steady monotone, "This isn't working for me, Chance. Let me out, and when I get home, I want you gone." Her throat constricted until she couldn't swallow.

She didn't see him step away, but she felt the rush of cool air around her. Without looking back, she turned the knob and slipped outside. A blinding numbness washed over her.

CHAPTER 2

The glint off a chrome bumper woke Chance to the realization he'd nearly rear-ended the Silverado in front of him, woke him to the realization his mind was focused elsewhere. He released the pressure on the gas pedal and backed off to a safe distance.

The east side of the mountains was hotter and drier than the Seattle side. The sun baked the truck cab. Waves of heat rose from the pavement. The warm breeze from the opened windows kept the air circulating, but provided little relief in a truck with no air-conditioning.

He was almost home now, but all the way over Snoqualmie Pass he'd been thinking about Kat. After their argument, he'd packed his belongings and left. What else could he do? She said it was over between them. But he didn't buy it. He loved the woman, and he knew she loved him. Maybe he should have stayed, should have fought harder for what they had together, which was a chemistry beyond anything he'd ever had with a woman. The thought of her body melding with his was enough to make him want to turn the truck around and drive the three hours back to Seattle. But he wouldn't do that. She needed time to cool off. Still, the silkiness of her skin, the feel of her hair between his fingers, and the sweet scent of her perfume were etched in his mind. For now that would have to do.

He sped down the straight stretch of highway, nearing Rosswood, by grassy fields, parched from summer's sun, by the fenced property owned by a money-grabbing developer. Lost in thought, he automatically turned off Randall Road and continued down his private drive, the dust swirling behind him. The wheels hit every pothole, lurching the truck from side to side. As he approached his ranch house, he slowed the truck to a crawl. A black SUV was parked out front. Zeke, the rambunctious pup he'd expected to rush the truck with tail wagging, was nowhere in sight.

He parked alongside the unfamiliar car and cut the engine, grabbed his cowboy hat and stepped outside. He wiped the sweat from his brow. The wind whirled dirt in the driveway. He waited a moment for Rusty, his hired hand, to greet him, but there was no movement around the barn, save for the burros crowding the wooden fence and braying in trumpet-like wails upon seeing Chance.

A sickening feeling gripped his stomach. Turning his attention toward the house, he bounded up the porch steps and opened the unlocked door, the powerful scent of Chanel No. 5 giving him an immediate clue to his visitor's identity. At the table sat Monique Bouvier, the woman from his best-forgotten past, the past he'd tried to bury for the last six years.

Not just a former colleague, Monique was a woman he'd known better than any other woman. Their minds were finessed within the same framework of the shady organization they'd worked for, as were their bodies. She knew every nuance of his personality, as he knew hers.

She sat with legs crossed and feet bare. Her toenails were painted a soft pink. He followed the lines of her tanned legs to the hem of her dress, hiked above her knees, then to the V of her low-cut bodice and up to her remarkable face.

"Chance, darling."

Her accent was unmistakable. And despite a few age lines burrowing the outer corners of her eyes, she seemed ageless, looked as young as when they'd first met: a petite, dark-haired, irresistible temptress. He couldn't deny that. The last time he'd seen her was a year ago when she'd visited him unannounced. By that time Kat had come into the picture, and he'd fought hard to steer clear of Monique's advances.

On the table next to an opened bottle of Cabernet Sauvignon and an unwrapped dark chocolate bar were two half-filled wine glasses. She held up a square of chocolate and pushed a glass in his direction as an invitation for him to sit down.

He tossed his hat and keys on the kitchen counter. "How did you know I'd be home today?" As soon as he asked the question, he knew he'd wasted his words. The organization knew his every move. With Monique keeping tabs on him, he felt as though there was always a private investigator lurking in the background.

"Please, sit with me, Chance. I have a proposition for you."

From his pocket he retrieved his cell phone and placed it next to his keys, then ran his hand through his silver-tinged hair. "You're wasting your time. I've told you before I'm not interested in returning to the company."

"Maybe not, but perhaps I can convince you. You see, Chance, they need your help, and they are willing to pay you double whatever you ask. Just one last time."

"I'm not interested."

She patted the tabletop. "Then sit with me a moment, please, and we will drink before I go."

He barked a laugh. "Am I to believe you'd give up that easily? What's the ruse?"

"No ruse, as you say. I promised them I would come and ask you this. That is all."

Chance opened the front door, the hot air rushing in like the heat from an opened oven. Still no sign of Rusty or Zeke. He stalked through the house, checking every room, and made a pass through the attached garage before facing her.

"There is no one here besides me." Her lips curved into a slight grin.

"That SUV is not your style."

"It was the only car available."

"I doubt that." He went to the door and double-checked outside. Clear to the barn was an eerie emptiness.

"Your man, Rusty, he let me in, if you must know," she said. "Come away from the door and talk to me."

Chance had an itch, a sense something was off-kilter, but his instincts were bruised from his argument with Kat. All he could think of was Kat. His thoughts were jumbled. His senses weren't as sharp as they normally would be. After what he'd been through with the woman he cared for most in this world, after the lashing she'd given him, he figured he could use a drink. "One drink and you're gone, Monique." He sat, slid the glass closest to him toward her, and picked up her glass for his own.

"You do not trust me, Chance?"

"Why should I?"

"I would do nothing ever to harm you. I love you too much. You know that. I always have." She held her glass in the air. "To the love that we once shared."

"As long as you're with the firm..." He clinked glasses with her. "To the end of our friendship." From the tears in her eyes, his comment had made its mark. His thoughts immediately drifted to Kat and the anguish he felt in his gut from their last encounter. Monique's presence here was an unwanted distraction. He took a long sip of wine from the glass he'd switched with her.

"Oh...we were so close, you and I, do you not remember?"

Though he protested with a wave of a hand and another guzzle of wine, she proceeded to chatter about the prior times they'd spent together, a pet subject of hers. The more she went on about their first meeting in a London hotel room where they'd consummated their relationship and then continued to gush about their various escapades around the world, the more his eyelids grew heavy.

"Yes, Chance, we were like honeymooners. It was like magic between you and me, no?"

His head felt light and cottony. The smell of her perfume swirled in his head.

"Do you recall the time we promised never to be apart from one another no matter what Philip said? Do you, darling?"

He strained to pay attention, but her words were filtering in and out, in and out. He squeezed his eyes shut, opened them again, but her face kept blurring. To clear his brain, he gave his head a quick shaking, but it was too late. Drowsiness had overwhelmed him. In a split second he knew he'd been duped before he slumped over the table, reached out to her, and hit the wine glass. A clink and a scraping of chair legs on tile was all he heard before he passed out.

***

Monique had pushed back from the table as a precaution in case the wine from Chance's knocked-over glass spilled on her dress. The red liquid seeped toward the table's edge. She righted the glass and grabbed some napkins to stop the flow, then dumped the sopping mass in the trashcan. She retrieved a cell phone from her purse and made a quick call. "It is time," she whispered into the mouthpiece.

She shoved the phone away and hurried to Chance's side. While hugging him, she kissed the top of his head. "I am sorry. I am so sorry. I have no choice."

The door burst open. Two men—one burly, square-jawed with a head of tight blond curls, the other short and wiry with head shaved, both in jeans and polo shirts—rushed in and hefted Chance under the arms.

Monique pointed toward the hallway. "Last door to the right. Be careful with him." Conflicted, she kept telling herself she had no option but to do the firm's bidding. Still, it was like a knife to her heart.

As they dragged Chance's limp body across the living room rug, another man, thin and slickly dressed in slacks and a pinstriped shirt, his black hair greased back off his forehead, came through the doorway holding a smartphone. "Where to?"

"This way." Monique led him to Chance's bedroom.

The two men had dumped Chance on the bed and were removing his shirt. When they finished, they laid him on his back.

"Leave me a minute," Monique said. "I will call you when I am ready."

After the men left the room and closed the door, Monique removed her dress and undergarments, crawled under the covers, and lay face down on top of Chance. She kissed his lips, savoring the intimate moment. "If you knew how good this feels to me. I wish it was forever. Forgive me." With the smell of his aftershave filling her with memories of times past when Chance willingly held her in his arms, she lay still, the tears trickling onto his chest. A rap on the door forced her to grab a corner of sheet and hastily dry her eyes. "I am ready," she said loud enough for them to hear, though her voice wavered.

The men filed in. The short wiry man peeled the covers down a little below Monique's waist, exposing her bare back, and tucked the sheet inward to hide Chance's jeans. He then propped Chance's arms over her back. Monique held Chance's head between her hands and placed her lips on his, making it look as if they were in a passionate embrace. The well-dressed man took pictures from several angles.

Monique shifted her body sideways, rolling away and exposing her breasts, then curled up next to Chance and closed her eyes, making it appear as if they were cuddled together asleep. She laid her arm across his chest. The man snapping the shots adjusted Chance's arms and moved his head to the side to make the pose look more natural. Again, several pictures were taken.

When he'd finished shooting, Monique asked the men to turn their backs to her. She slipped out of bed and into her clothes and pulled the covers over Chance's body. One of the men offered to zip up her dress, but she refused. The men left the room. Before joining the others, Monique stood in the doorway and gave Chance a parting look.

***

Fighting to wake up, Chance vaguely heard voices drifting in from another room, voices of a man and a woman. He shook his head to clear the cobwebs and recognized the lilt of Monique's accent.

The room had taken on a purplish tone. Outside, dusk was settling in.

He tried sitting up. His head pounded like the thump of his heart. He lay back down and waited for his head to quit spinning. The perfume scent was as powerful as smelling salts, but no one was lying beside him.

He threw off the covers and realized his chest was bare, his shirt taken off and thrown in a heap on the floor. He took a few deep breaths and forced his legs to move off the bed. With a groan he bent over to seize his shirt and held his forehead as he straightened up. He threaded his arms through the shirtsleeves.

Using the mattress for leverage, he pushed to a standing position and felt the blood pool in his calves. He slogged forward one step at a time, his body as heavy as cement.

Relying on the walls for support, he staggered down the hallway until it opened into the living room and he could see the hazy forms of three or four people around the dining room table, a coffee aroma filtering into his brain. Everything was hazy. He fought to stay awake. Someone was coming toward him.

"Chance." Monique's voice sounded as if it were echoing in a tunnel. She was racing to his side. She held him up under one arm.

Another blast of perfume made him queasy. He tried to shake off her assistance when a man came after her and held him under his other arm. They walked him to the table and lowered him into a chair. Someone shoved a cup in his direction.

"Drink this," came a gruff voice.

Chance gripped the cup's handle, but his hand was shaking so badly Monique sat beside him and steadied the cup. It felt as if he were floating through space. Someone kept the cup filled at all times. He drank the lukewarm liquid until he couldn't swallow another sip and the fog began lifting.

He stared at Monique. "What?" He glanced at the men. "Who?"

She touched his cheek with her palm. "Darling, you must listen to me."

"I'll take it from here, Monique," said the man with the slicked-back hair.

"Who the fu...?" Chance forced his eyes to focus on the man who looked young enough to be his son.

"Let's just say Philip sent me. He needs you to come back to the company to do a job, and we're here to make that happen."

That was enough to burn out the cobwebs. "Like hell you will. I'm done..." His head throbbed from the violent sound of his own voice. "I'm done with the whole goddamn business."

"I don't think you are."

The man's tone was so cocky Chance reached out for whatever part of him he could grab, but the pain in his head drove him to sit back down.

"Take it easy, Chance." Monique grasped his shoulders. "Listen to Derek."

"You should've hauled me off in the car drugged, because I'm not going with you."

"Yeah, well, we needed a little insurance you'd go easily and not fight us later on."

"Yeah, and what...?" He glanced at Monique, who quickly rose and hugged her arms to her chest. He flashed to the bedroom scene where he'd woken half naked, surrounded by her favorite fragrance. "Monique?"

Derek twitched his head toward the two men in polo shirts. Before Chance could move, they pinned both his arms back while Derek picked up his phone nearby and proceeded to show Chance all the compromising shots he'd taken of Chance and Monique in bed together.

Infuriated, Chance tried to wrestle free, but they had a firm grip on him. "You bitch," he shouted at Monique.

"I am so sorry, Chance."

"You're just like the rest of them."

"Let's not waste any more of our time. We've got a plane to catch." Derek slid the phone in his pocket. "Now, here's the deal.

Philip wants you back for one more job. You'll be back in Rosswood in a couple of weeks, four tops. If you come with us willingly and fulfill your duty to the company, these pictures will get destroyed. But if you don't, they'll be sent directly to the Summers woman. Shall we go?"

Chance couldn't believe this was happening. Normally, he'd have no reason to believe Kat would question the pictures. However, after their recent blow-up, which was the worst they'd ever had, after the way they'd parted company, and considering Kat's emotional state, which he'd totally misjudged, he wasn't sure what her reaction would be. He couldn't risk it. If he did what they asked, maybe that would give her enough time apart from him to reevaluate their relationship and ask him back. That was a chance he would have to take.

All of this was going through his mind when the two men pulled him to his feet. "I'll go on my own accord," he said, "but I want to call Kat and my daughter, so they won't worry about me."

Derek nodded. "Make it brief. Tell them you'll be out of touch for a while, getting some R and R, and you'll contact them later."

The two men stood by while Chance picked up his cell phone and made the calls. He couldn't reach either of the women and had to leave messages on their answering machines. Afterward, Derek yanked the phone from him and set it back on the counter.

"I have to pack and talk to my hired hand before I go."

"That will not be necessary," Monique said, her voice taking on a business-like tone. "You will have everything you need where you are going, and your hired man has been informed of your departure. He will take care of the ranch and your dog."

Chance frowned contemptuously. "You've thought of everything, haven't you? You know my size, my tastes. You're a real asset to them."

"I am sorry, Chance. I have no choice."

"Yeah, right. Then let's get this over with." Chance started for the door, and the two men grabbed his arms. He tried to elbow them. "Call off the dogs."

"Let him go," Derek said.

The men gave Chance room to step outside, but stayed close. Derek and Monique followed them and got into the front seat of the SUV. Chance slid into the backseat, and the two men took their places on either side of him. As Derek backed the car around, Chance glanced in the direction of the barn where Rusty had emerged from his cabin, holding Zeke by the collar. Rusty's face was stricken with fear.

CHAPTER 3

While she was with a client, Kat had worked at keeping her emotions in check, but when she was alone in the car driving home, the tears wouldn't stop. She was losing her edge. Ever since Chance had come into her life, she'd found herself leaning on him more than she wanted to. Now he was gone. She hadn't realized how much she'd relied on him for support, how much she needed him. In all her forty-one years, she'd never met anyone like Chance.

Today was a lousy day all around. Not only was Chance gone, but one of her clients backed out of a deal. She wished she could talk to Chance, tell him about her day. If she could, she'd probably break down and let it all out. He was right. She was afraid to go back to Rosswood, back to Brianna's house.

As soon as she slowed through the alley, through a narrow gauntlet of wooden fences and back alley garages, and parked her car at the rear of her house, she checked her cell phone. There were no missed calls from Chance.

The neighbor's kitten was sitting on the back step, waiting for an affectionate greeting, but Kat was in no mood to pet her. Besides, every time she ran her hand over the creature's soft furry body, it reminded her of Tiger, the kitten who had adopted her in Rosswood, the one she gave to the strange girl who lived down the road from Brianna's old house. In Kat's vulnerable state of mind, just looking at the kitten brought up all the miserable memories: the haunting visions, the strange phone calls, hunting down the truth about her sister's suicide, all that, plus Kat's own brush with death. Kat slipped into the house and closed the door, shutting the kitten out.

Though the interior was warm, she felt the chill from Chance's absence. His loving presence had always filled the rooms. She had to admit that. But why was it so damn hard to let him into her inner world? From the start, she'd warned him about her inability to commit. She half expected him to be here, to work it out. The sting of disappointment hurt.

She wandered toward the bedroom and stopped in the doorway. An inner tug made her turn around and go back to the kitchen phone, the landline she'd meant to have removed but never had. She hardly ever used it or received any incoming calls, except for all those disturbing crank calls after Brianna died. Shuddering, she shooed the memory away.

The light was blinking on the answering machine she'd had installed. She punched the button. The voice talking back to her was flat, monotone, not the animated voice of the man she knew. No anger or sorrow, not even an inflection of forgiveness was present. Chance was telling her he was going away for some R and R and would contact her later. That was all.

She'd really done it now. Her hopes of repairing the relationship were replaced with agonizing regret. She'd driven him away, and who knew for how long? This was the price she paid for letting him into her heart. The pain of losing him was unbearable—an aching reminder of why in the past she would never commit to a long-term relationship. She always drove men away.

She tried calling Chance, but he didn't answer. The sinking feeling deepened inside her. She hadn't eaten all day, yet felt no hunger except for Chance and the feel of his powerful embrace. Crying wouldn't solve anything, so she headed for the bedroom in hopes sleep would ease the hurt, but the doorbell rang.

She rushed to the foyer, thinking he might have had second thoughts and decided to surprise her. But on the porch Maggie Loggins and Jim Gavin, co-owners of Loggins Realty, stood side by side to greet her. Jim mirrored Maggie's concern, not a smile between them.

"What is this, an intervention?"

"Aren't you going to ask us in? From the looks of that downhearted expression, you were expecting someone else?"

"Sorry, Maggie. Both of you, come in."

Maggie, Kat's friend and mentor, stepped in ahead of Jim, ushering in her characteristic lilac fragrance. She was in her sixties, wore hats and suits, and had been widowed for many years. Jim, a lanky, wavy-haired man in his mid-fifties, was in a twenty-year relationship with a man. He breezed in, carrying with him a strong musky scent. They were like family to Kat. They marched to the chairs by the fireplace.

It was clear they were here to stay, so Kat settled on the couch and cuddled a satiny decorator pillow. "What are you doing here this late?"

Maggie glanced toward the kitchen and back. "So where's Chance? Doesn't he usually leave on Monday mornings?"

"We didn't see his truck, did we?" Jim nimbly rose, parted the curtains, and sat down again.

"He's not here," Kat offered.

"Obviously." Jim exchanged a perceptive look with Maggie.

"I kicked him out, if you must know." Kat took a deep breath in, fighting to remain stoic.

"I figured something like that happened," Jim said. "You were obviously distraught when I saw you today."

"So you called Maggie and tattled."

"Kat, don't blame Jim. I've noticed other times these last few months ever since the Rosswood incident. You haven't kept your promise to see Dr. Rosen."

"I don't need a shrink." Kat tightened her grip on the pillow.

"You're still not functioning like you used to," Maggie said. "You're not yourself. I think you're still suffering the effects of post-traumatic stress. You need help after what that madman did."

"I have Chance." Kat averted her eyes, knowing full well that wasn't necessarily true.

"See? You've ruined that, too."

"He was the best, Kat."

"Don't you think I know that?" Kat scowled, and Jim fisted his hips and scowled back.

"All right, you two," Maggie said. "Kat, we think you should take some time off."

"Again? I've already done that."

"That was nine months ago."

"I need to work."

"You need to get your life together," Maggie said. "Make nice with Chance."

"How can I? He's gone away, probably for good, and he hasn't even told me where I can reach him."

"He loves you, Kat," Jim said a bit softer. "I know he'll come back to you."

"In the meantime," Maggie added, "take your own vacation, see Dr. Rosen if nothing else. You've got to de-stress before you can come back to work. You can't go this alone."

Kat felt as if her whole world were falling apart. With no Chance and no work to occupy her, she was at a loss. "I need to work, Maggie. I do. The real estate market is bad enough as it is. I can't *not* work."

"After the Rosswood incident, you never went to that spa I arranged for you. You've been working every weekend. You can afford this time off. Jim and I will take over for you like we did before, and it will all work out." Maggie stood and adjusted the hem of her jacket. "Rest, see Dr. Rosen, then call me in a couple of weeks. We'll go from there." She removed a document from her briefcase and handed Kat a pen. "Sign and date this commission agreement like you did last time in case a deal goes through in your absence."

Kat signed and gave back the papers. "This feels like tough love."

Maggie held her in a warm embrace. "If you've driven Chance away, maybe you're driving your clients away. Did you ever think of that?"

Kat glanced at Jim, who was nodding in agreement.

On the way out, Maggie turned to Kat. "I'll call you, my darling."

Jim blew Kat a kiss. "Love you."

Kat closed the door, leaned her back against the hard wood, and shut her eyes. Maggie was right. Things weren't going so well at work lately. And now Chance was gone. She longed to see him. Until now, she hadn't realized how much.

She tried calling him, but again no answer. Hoping sleep would clear her mind, she fell into bed exhausted and turned out the lights at quarter to nine.

At times like these, without Chance around, when she felt the most thin-skinned, she'd think of her sister, their miserable childhood, and how she had abandoned Brianna to years of abuse by an uncle, which only added to Brianna's misery. As much as Kat tried to get over it, she still felt responsible for not helping Brianna more. Kat sensed a subtle tangerine fragrance in the air, another reminder of Brianna.

Wide awake, Kat had the distinct impression the phone was about to ring. Ten seconds later it rang. She jumped up and nearly stumbled over the scatter rug on her way to the kitchen. Wishing it were Chance, but deep down knowing it wasn't, she reached for the phone just before it switched to the answering machine. She recognized the voice of Stella, Chance's daughter, a soon-to-be junior at the University of Washington.

"Kat, I'm sorry to call you this late, but I just got back from a hiking trip with my friends, and I had a message waiting from my dad. Did you get one, too? Do you know where he went?" Her voice was higher than normal and shaky.

Kat snapped on the overhead light, giving her a better view of the stove clock. It was after eleven. "I did get a message, but I don't know where he went. He said he'd call." She tried to remain positive for Stella's sake, but she wasn't sure she'd pulled it off.

"You're worried, too. I can hear it in your voice. Why isn't he with you? Doesn't he usually stay till Monday?"

"Yes, but…we had an argument."

"I know it's late, but I'm coming over."

"Stella, I'm sure—"

She'd hung up. She was as determined as her father.

Kat splashed cold water on her face, waking herself fully. She rescued her robe from behind the bathroom door, and while she waited she fixed a pot of hot chocolate. As she stirred the rich sweet liquid, she reflected on hers and Chance's quarrel and the message he'd left, curious over Stella's apprehension. When Stella arrived, Kat had set two mugs on the table.

Resembling her mother, who'd died of cancer when she was fifteen, Stella had the same classic beauty, plus eyes as aqua blue and as intense as Chance's. A red bandana covered most of her short blond hair that normally spiked in places like baby porcupine quills. She came in wearing a flannel shirt over a tank top and cutoffs. When she began to untie her hiking boots, Kat told her she could leave them on. Stella sat and took a cautious sip of the hot liquid.

"You didn't have to come over," Kat said. "We could have talked on the phone."

"Aren't you worried about him?"

Of course she was worried about him, but not in the same way. "To be honest with you, Stella, your dad and I had a terrible argument. It didn't end well, and it wouldn't surprise me if he wanted to get as far away from me as possible."

"You guys have had fights before. Dad told me. But he never sounded this way."

"Yes, well, I never told him it was over between us." Looking at Stella's shocked expression, Kat was certain she'd delivered too much information.

"You really said that?"

"Pretty much."

"What happened? You guys were in love, weren't you? How could you say that to him? He's crazy about you."

Kat's confidence at explaining herself catapulted into sorrow and guilt. Her commanding posture settled into a slouch. She grasped her mug with both hands, glad for the warmth. "Stella, sometimes you say things in the heat of an argument you don't really mean. Believe me, this was one of those times. So you see, that's probably why he sounded the way he did." The way Stella sat with woeful eyes quietly sipping her drink made Kat regret starting this conversation with Chance's only child.

Kat left to fetch the pot of chocolate. Before she could return to top off Stella's cup, Stella appeared in the doorway staring at Kat, her face contorting into looks of anxiety mixed with misery, as if she were about to strike out at Kat for causing all this trouble for her father. Kat was fully prepared to take the blame. "I tried to call him to patch things up, but he didn't, or wouldn't, answer." Kat hoped this would diffuse Stella's anger.

"It wasn't the argument," Stella said.

Kat was taken aback. "Really, Stella, what else could it be?"

"Dad would have told me about it. He tells me everything. Well, just about everything." Stella drifted closer to Kat. "Remember how he confided in me when he first met you and how he wanted me to get your phone number? And he's always telling me how much he loves you, and he gets sad when you have fights. He's always telling me those things. This time he barely said anything to me and nothing about you. It's not like him, Kat, to go anywhere without letting me know where he's going. He always gives me a phone number where I can reach him." She paused to take a breath.

"Maybe he was too upset. He said he'd call, didn't he?" But Kat's own unsettling feelings were bubbling up.

"He hardly ever calls my landline," Stella continued. "He knows he can reach me on my cell phone. And he didn't sound like himself. Even when he's upset, he never sounds like he's half dead. His voice was weird. It was boring. He never sounds boring."

"What are you suggesting?"

"Something's totally bogus, Kat. I know it. He always starts our conversations in a cheerful way even when there's something bothering him. He always says something like 'Hey, Spike' because of my hair. He never said that. I'm totally worried about him."

"I'm sure he'll call us."

Stella's shoulders slumped, and a moment later she shook with tears.

Kat embraced her, inhaling the woodsy odor coming off Stella's shirt. "What can I do to make you feel better? Would you like to stay here tonight?"

Stella nodded. "Can I sleep with you?"

Kat agreed, though this request from a self-confident, independent young woman seemed out of character. Kat loaned her a nightgown, and when she was curled up asleep in bed next to Kat, Kat realized for the first time how truly fragile Stella was. She'd lost her mother in her teenage years, and previous to that had not known her father all that well. His job had taken him all over the world. She was strong, yet vulnerable, and deep down scared as a little girl.

Kat lay awake, thinking about Stella's fears, which were gradually becoming her own. Trying to think rationally, she conjured up different scenarios, places Chance could have gone to be by himself to reflect on the situation, such as camping. Sitting under the stars by a crackling fire, listening to the owls and nighthawks, fishing in a lake or a fast-running stream made perfect sense for a man like Chance. But what if he'd done the opposite and had gone to a splashy resort? She pictured him having a pampering massage and afterward meeting any available woman in a darkened lounge and drowning his troubles in wine and sex.

Stella's purr-like snores shook Kat into the present, out of her wild imaginings. She turned on her side and looked at Stella's profile, lit by the comforting nightlight Kat had installed after her Rosswood ordeal. Setting her imagination aside, Kat was beginning to feel Stella's instincts were right. Something wasn't adding up.

Before sunrise and without waking Stella, Kat slipped out of bed and called Chance. Again, the phone switched to voice mail. Sitting with a cup of coffee, she tried making sense of the message he'd left. Thinking more clearly now, she knew he would never have left like this.

Kat heard sounds coming from the bedroom. Soon, Stella, dressed for the day, stopped in the doorway to tie her boot laces. Her hair was twisted in all directions.

"Coffee's brewed."

Stella poured herself a cup. "Thanks for letting me stay the night, but I'm still weirded-out about Dad. It's just not like him."

"Would it make you feel any better if we drove to Rosswood to see for ourselves? Maybe Rusty knows something."

"Then you're worried about Dad, too."

"I've been thinking about it all night, and you're right. He didn't sound like himself. He would have put up a fight. He wouldn't back off like this, not even after what I said to him."

"Yeah, Dad's a fighter, not a quitter."

"He's definitely not a quitter." Kat could think of a number of occasions Chance wouldn't back down. Though he had a softer side, he could also be stubborn and aggressive, but that was what she liked about him, his multifaceted nature. He was definitely not a boring man. In the worst way, she wanted him back. "I've got the time off. Can you get away from your job for a day?"

"I'm not worth anything until I know what's up with Dad."

"Okay, then, why don't you go home and get cleaned up and check in at work."

"I'll call in sick. I'm too wiped out to work anyway."

"Whatever you have to do. Meet me back here when you're ready. We'll go in my car."

Stella draped her arms over Kat and gave her a hug. "You're the best."

Kat smiled and patted her hand. "Can I make you breakfast first?"

"No, thanks." Stella dug into her jeans pocket and pulled out her car keys. "I'm not a breakfast person."

"Besides having your dad in common, we have that in common, too. Go on then. I'll see you soon."

Now all Kat had to do, besides readying herself to go, was tame her own fears about returning to Rosswood where she'd spent one of the most terrifying times of her life. But for Chance, she would do anything.

CHAPTER 4

Kat thought she could do anything for Chance, but when she and Stella were over the mountain pass and she motored off the freeway toward Rosswood, her stomach erupted into waves of nausea. In the bottom of her purse, she felt around for a stray mint and popped it into her mouth. For a while the sharp peppermint flavor distracted her.

For most of the three-hour trip Stella had remained quiet and wasn't her normal chatty self. She would fiddle with the radio from time to time. Kat was unconcerned because she knew Stella was anxious to get to the ranch.

On the eastern side of the mountains, the cooler coastal air gave way to a dry but intense heat. They both wore light summer clothing and although the wooded road and its intermittent shadows helped cool the SUV, Kat eventually turned on the air-conditioning.

Rounding the last curve before the long stretch toward town, Kat willed her stomach to settle down. Up ahead on the left side of the road was the Wheeler Resort site. The barbed-wire chain-link fence surrounded the property, and a newly constructed sign replaced the bullet-riddled one. So far, the citizens of Rosswood had delayed Nate Wheeler from moving ahead with his building project. After the way he'd treated Brianna, Kat was glad his proposed development had never gotten off the ground.

As a distraction, Kat pointed to the right side of the road. "Somewhere around here is where I first met your dad." She shared the story about Chance coming to her rescue after her car had broken down. "I wasn't very nice to him. But he was very patient with me."

"He told me all about that," Stella said. "He told me you were like a tiger, all claws that day. He just about got back in his truck and left you there."

"I wouldn't have blamed him," Kat said. "It's just that my bladder was about to burst and I wanted him to hurry, but he was taking his own sweet time. We sort of locked horns that first day."

Stella laughed. "You guys were meant to be together. You're so much alike. Mom was pretty tough, but she'd usually back down. She never challenged him the way you do. He loves it. He tells me that."

"Maybe I challenged him one time too many," Kat said. "I hope not."

As they approached Pine Road, Kat purposely kept her gaze straight ahead. Still, her moist palms gripped the steering wheel, and her throat tightened so much she could barely swallow. To stave off a flood of nightmarish memories, she focused hard on a less painful recollection about Rosswood, though that could have been debated: the woman in the black dress, whom Kat had passed on this very road, the woman who had stayed overnight with Chance, Monique Bouvier. By placing her attention on Monique, along with the ire it stirred up, Kat successfully dissipated her fear.

Leaving the main road behind, she gladly swung right onto the dirt drive leading to Chance's house. As she slowed, approaching the red brick rambler, a cloud of dust settled behind the SUV.

The tension in Kat's body eased from being within the safety of Chance's property but also from seeing his old scratched and dented pickup. "There, you see? Your father's truck is here. That's a good sign." Except now Kat would have to face Chance. Her stomach fluttered again. "He must be home licking the wounds I inflicted."

"But why would he lie to me about leaving?"

"That's a good question, Stella. Maybe I drew too much blood, and he wanted to keep to himself for a while."

"I don't buy it. He's not like that."

Kat turned the car key, shutting down the engine. "Let's go find out."

Stella had already opened the door and was on the porch before Kat had dropped her keys in her purse. Since Kat was unsure what kind of a reception she'd get from Chance, she held back and let Stella take the lead.

Some of the burros he'd rescued over the years were gathering at the fence near the barn, curious. Rusty was nowhere in sight, nor was Zeke.

Stella hammered on the door. "Dad, are you in there? Open up. It's me."

Kat stood near the bottom step. "He's not answering? Maybe he's out somewhere on the property with Rusty. Why don't we check the barn to see if the horses are gone?"

"Or I could use my key."

"Let's check the barn first."

Stella rapped one more time, then caught up with Kat. One of the old jacks started braying, and Stella ran ahead to give him a friendly pat.

Kat glanced in the barn. No sound, no movement, only dusty hay and manure odors. Grazing peacefully in the pasture were the two horses she and Chance had ridden the last time she was here. She had mixed feelings about that refreshing ride around his pasture, considering the startling discovery they'd made.

Stella walked up beside her, rubbing her palms over her cut-offs. "No sign of Rusty or Zeke." She motioned toward Rusty's cabin. "Looks like his truck's gone. Dad must be somewhere with him."

"Or your dad could have borrowed his truck and left him taking a nap. Let's make sure Rusty's not here." Kat led the way to the cabin and knocked on the door. No one stirred.

Stella turned the doorknob and stepped inside. "Rusty, are you here?"

Kat stayed in the doorway and surveyed the one-room abode that held a mingling of cigarette and body odors, tinged with the smell of fried eggs. The twin bed, which hugged the far wall next to the bathroom enclosure, was haphazardly made, and the sink was stacked with dirty dishes. A soiled plate remained on a corner table.

With the dark paneled walls and the curtains drawn, the interior had a gloomy feel.

Kat backed out but stayed in the shadow of the porch. "It's so hot. It must be 100 degrees in the shade."

Stella closed the cabin door. "Why don't we wait in Dad's house. He won't mind."

Though Kat was struggling with the actuality of facing Chance, the thought of going into town was even worse. All the reminders—the townspeople, the post office, even the Grill—would definitely be triggers. She didn't want to relive the experience. "Yes, let's do. I could use a drink of water."

"I can make us peanut butter sandwiches."

Food sounded like a good idea, but with her stomach in a turmoil at the thought of seeing Chance, Kat wasn't so sure she could eat anything right now.

Stella used her key to let them inside. Upon entering, Kat cradled her arms. The temperature was frigid compared to the outside air.

Stella aimed for the living room to adjust the thermostat to a more comfortable temperature. "This is weird. Dad wouldn't leave without turning the air-conditioning down. It's almost like it was left on all night. Sometimes he goes overboard trying to save energy. Before I leave a room, he's always telling me to turn the lights off."

Kat pointed to the kitchen counter where his cell phone, key ring, and hat were sitting. "He wouldn't go off without those either. He must be here somewhere."

Stella's eyebrows lifted. "He doesn't go anywhere without his cowboy hat. Oh my gosh, what if something's wrong? What if Rusty had to take him to the hospital?"

Kat placed a hand on Stella's shoulder. "If that were the case, I'm sure Rusty would have called you. There has to be a better explanation."

"What if he didn't want us to know how bad it is?"

"Now you're letting your imagination run wild." Kat remained calm, surprised at her own steadiness. "Maybe he's napping and didn't hear us drive in."

"But I shouted loud enough for the whole town to hear."

"Let's check the bedroom anyway, just to be sure." Kat followed her down the hallway.

Stella barged through the doorway. The bedcovers were flipped back, and the sheets were wrinkled. It appeared as if the bed had been slept in.

"He's not here, Kat, and he always makes his bed. Something is definitely wrong."

Kat picked up the pillow. Something *was* wrong. It held a faint, yet powdery feminine scent. She kept her expression restrained and tossed the pillow back on the mattress. Inside she was seething. She and Chance hadn't been apart more than two nights and already he'd taken up with someone else. That could explain the odd phone calls, the unusual tone in his voice, and why he wouldn't elaborate on anything. That could very well explain why his truck was here. He was with someone besides Rusty, someone who had a vehicle: another woman.

Kat's jaw was clenched tight. She wanted to flee from the house, but Stella's eyes were intent on hers. "Well, as you can see, your dad has slept here, so he must be all right. He must have a good reason for his behavior. He'd better have a good reason. Perhaps we should go back to Seattle and let him call like he said he would."

Stella stared at her, surprised. "We can't leave now. I have to make sure he's okay. That's why we came here in the first place, isn't it? Maybe we should call the hospital in Benton to see if he's been admitted."

If he wasn't in the hospital already, he would be soon if Kat had anything to do with it. She had to find a way to herd Stella out of the house before Chance came back with whomever accompanied him. "Let's go back to Benton and see for ourselves." She linked arms with Stella and ushered her from the room. "I'm sure he's all right."

On impulse, Kat pushed open the door to Chance's study and stopped cold. Stella gasped at the room's condition. Books and papers were strewn on the floor. Everything on his desktop was scattered. Drawers were left opened.

Kat stood in the entrance while Stella circled the room examining everything. The framed photo of Stella and her mother lay on its side. Stella set it upright. "This isn't like Dad. Even in a rage, he wouldn't do this." She turned toward the desk. "His laptop's missing."

Kat checked the bottom desk drawer, which was empty. "So is his manuscript. He kept it right here." She shook her head. "This doesn't make sense."

A persistent pounding startled both of them. Kat glanced at Stella, then charged ahead to the front door.

Rusty, Chance's hired hand, stood on the porch, holding Zeke by the collar. Zeke wiggled and whined to get to Kat. Rusty tugged on the dog's collar to settle him down. "I seen your car when I drove up." He looked intently at Kat, his usual relaxed smile missing.

Stella stepped to the forefront. "Where's Dad?"

Rusty stood with an agonized expression on his face, deepening the wrinkles in his cheeks.

"Is he in the hospital? Was there an accident?" Stella's voice pitched higher with each question.

"Can't say."

"Rusty!"

"Let me handle this, Stella." Kat wormed her way forward and got a whiff of an overpowering tobacco odor. "Rusty, I don't know what's wrong with you, but you have to tell us what's going on here."

Zeke started barking, excited by the agitated voices. Kat motioned for Rusty to come inside. He commanded Zeke to stay put, then slipped through the doorway and closed the door.

"Tell us what's happened to Chance," Kat said.

Rusty, short and stocky with graying hair and stubble on his chin, made a sweeping look around the house, taking in the dining, living, and kitchen areas that were combined in one great room. He removed his hat and fidgeted with the rim.

Kat wondered if his obvious discomfort had to do with being inside the house in Chance's absence. "Why don't you sit down and tell us what's wrong?"

"Rather stand if you don't mind."

"Where's my dad, Rusty? Just tell us."

"Not supposed to say, or they'll…" He peered at the floor.

"What are you talking about? Just tell me where my dad is."

"Look, Rusty, we know something happened here. Chance's computer is gone. His study is a mess. You didn't do that, did you?"

Rusty's head shot up. "Oh, no, ma'am. Wouldn't do such a thing. But they said if I told anyone, they'd kill me and Zeke."

"Kill you."

"Yes, ma'am."

Kat thought about Chance's past and the unscrupulous people he used to work for. They were certainly capable of administering such threats.

"Rusty, come on. If Dad's in trouble, you've got to tell us."

"Wait a second, Stella. Rusty, was there a woman involved?"

Rusty looked down at his hat while twisting the rim.

"If you don't describe her, I will. Did she have an accent?"

Rusty stared at Kat as if she were a mind reader. "Yes, ma'am. It was that French lady." He sighed with the relief of having the facts coaxed out of him.

"You might as well tell us everything. They threatened you because they didn't want you to go to the authorities, but now they're gone. They can't harm you." Kat was uncertain of that, but she needed to get to the truth.

Rusty hesitated, looking from Stella to Kat. "I guess it won't hurt then." He swiped his mouth with the back of his hand. "Well, me and Zeke, we was minding our own business down by the barn when that black car come barreling up the driveway. One of those big black SUVs. The boss, he was gone to Seattle, and that French lady come and asked if I could let her inside the house. She ain't even knocked on the door, but she tells me the boss says it's okay. She says real sweet-like that she left her diamond watch the last time she was here and come to get it. She hands me a phone and says I can call the boss if I want to." He hung his head. "Shoulda done it, I know." He shrugged and looked at Kat.

"Go on."

"Like I said, she hands me a phone, and I figure she was telling me the truth, so I let her in with the spare key the boss left me. Then I hear doors open and close behind me and before I can turn around, these two fellas got me by the arms and are dragging me back to my cabin. Zeke's a-barking and growling. I have to calm him down. Then a third fella pulls a gun on me, and says they was gonna kill me if I said anything. Well, then I hear the boss's truck drive up. After a while these fellas get a phone call and tell me to stay in the cabin till I hear their car leave. Saw the boss get in the back seat with two of the fellas. That French lady and the other fella was in the front."

"Did Chance say anything to you?"

"No, ma'am. He just give me a sorrowful look from that big black car. They tell me to watch the house and the dog, and then the boss, he'll be back in a couple of weeks."

Kat draped an arm around Stella, who'd been sniffling in the background. "Don't worry, honey. We'll get to the bottom of this."

"I'm right sorry, Stella."

Kat searched her purse and handed Rusty a business card with her personal number written on the back. "We'll be returning to Seattle in a little while, so look after this place, make sure it's locked up after we leave. Call if you hear anything from Chance."

"I'll surely do that." Rusty seated his hat on his head and left to tend to a pawing, whining Zeke.

"What are we going to do now? I know those are the same people Dad used to work for. Who knows what they'll do to him."

Kat paced the floor, trying to figure out what to do next. From reading Chance's novel, which reflected his past, she had a good sense of the gravity of the situation.

Six years ago he'd worked for a firm that fronted several corporations. The firm illegally offered money to politicians, heads of state, and other leaders in exchange for contracts for weapons and other services directed to their corporations. Chance's job was to seek out these officials for bribery purposes. Uncooperative politicians would find the money for their campaigns withdrawn. In the global arena an uncooperative leader might be driven out of office, or, worst-case scenario, assassinated. Chance had abruptly left the firm to take care of his ailing ex-wife and in the process began to question his life's purpose. He never returned to the firm. Since then, they'd been hounding him to come back. In the past they'd had problems with a whistleblower, whom they'd handily silenced. They didn't want their secrets told.

In the hands of the firm, Kat knew full well what could happen to Chance. She worried he might never come back. "Do you remember the company's name your dad worked for?"

"He never really talked about it much. He may have told me, but I forgot."

"Let's go back to his room and see if we can find something, anything that might give us a clue."

"Why? What are you going to do? Do you think Dad's in real trouble?"

With no proof of her suspicions, Kat didn't want to unnecessarily upset Stella. "I don't think so, Stella, but we can't sit here and do nothing. Perhaps we can at least find out where he is. Come on." Kat led the way to Chance's study, her mind working to come up with a plan. "Let's see if we can find a name on anything."

Stella sat on the rug and began gathering up papers. "These are just receipts and paid bills."

On the desk, Kat picked up a sheet of paper with the words "Black Cash" centered on the page, reminding her of Chance's manuscript. "What was the name of the firm in his novel? I can't recall."

"I'm not sure, but I think it started with the letter V, something like that. But he wouldn't have used the real name."

"Maybe it's close to the real name." The letter of the alphabet Stella had tossed out jogged Kat's memory. "Let's look in your dad's bedroom for a T-shirt with a name on it. I saw him wear one jogging once. You take the dresser, and I'll take the closet." She jetted into the master bedroom with Stella on her heels.

"What name?"

"I don't know for sure, but it may be a company name. It's a long shot."

While Stella rummaged through the dresser, Kat sifted through slacks, shirts, jeans, sport jackets, looking for a logo or initials. She pulled a stack of T-shirts from the closet shelf, laid them on the bed and sorted through, but no names were evident.

As Kat returned the shirts to their proper place, Chance's very distinct masculine scent, so familiar to her, which brought back memories of their passionate embraces, caught her by surprise. How she wished they hadn't argued, and how she wished she hadn't been so miserably bent on ruining the best thing that had ever happened to her.

"I didn't find anything," Stella said from across the room. "Did you?"

Kat tore herself away. "Let's look in the laundry room. Maybe there's something there."

Stella ran ahead of her to the room close to the kitchen and started sorting through the hamper. "This is so weird, going through Dad's stuff."

"I know." Kat checked the washer and dryer, and they looked at each other at the same time.

Stella shrugged. "Now what?"

Kat eyed a pile of clothes in the corner. "What's that over there?"

Stella picked up a wool shirt with a hole in the sleeve. "He must be throwing these out."

"I recognize this." From the clothing heap Kat captured a faded blue T-shirt. On the upper left side, written in small black letters, were the words "Topping Ventures." She filed the name in the back of her mind and turned the shirt around so Stella could see. "I'm not sure this name means anything." She tossed the shirt in the rag pile and leaned against the washing machine. "If we had the novel, we might find something there, but we don't even have that."

Stella brightened. "Yes, we do. Dad burned a copy on a memory stick and had me put it in my safe deposit box at my bank. It's a rough draft, but basically it's all there. He told me if anything happened to him, I was to take it to his lawyer."

That last comment gave Kat a menacing chill. Her gut instinct told her indeed Chance was in trouble.

Stella slumped against the wall. "Do you think he'll come back?"

"Of course he will," Kat replied, though she couldn't guarantee it. "Let's stay positive. We'll go back to Seattle, get the memory stick from your safe deposit box, and we'll do our own investigation."

"But what can we do?"

"I don't know, Stella, but we can't just sit around and wait." Kat was careful not to voice her last thought: that she couldn't wait for a call that might never come.

***

When Kat and Stella returned home Monday, it was too late to visit the bank to retrieve the memory stick. Stella left for home in preparation for work the next day, though she would have rather stayed with Kat. Kat convinced her that work would keep her mind off the situation. Kat promised she would research the name she found on the T-shirt and stay at the house in case Chance called.

By the time Kat took a soothing bath and laid her head on the pillow, the hot summer day had segued into a stuffy summer evening. She cracked the window and slid under a light cotton sheet. Both the long drive home and the intensity of thinking about Chance had exhausted her, and she fell into a deep sleep, into a dream.

Through a hazy scene Kat could make out high-rise buildings and skyscrapers. The sun cast shadows on the pavement. A woman, vaguely familiar to Kat, at least in stature and hair color, exited a glassed building and hurried down a crowded sidewalk. Suddenly, out of the mist Brianna appeared and urged Kat to follow the woman. As Kat took a step forward, the dream faded.

Kat woke in a sweat and sat up in the darkness. Prickling shivers crawled up her spine. She felt her sister's presence, the tangerine scent of her perfume permeating the room. It had been months since Brianna had come around in a dream or had appeared to her in spirit. Kat had hoped the visitations had ended, that her own psychic nature had gone underground again. At least now Brianna's presence didn't frighten her; Kat sensed her sister was at peace. But who was the woman in the dream and why was Brianna there?

The house was still, but outside the chirping crickets competed with the distant hum of the freeway. To deaden the noise, Kat got up and closed the window, but she was too stimulated to sleep.

She slipped her robe over her nude body. In the predawn hours she settled in at the dining room table with a mug of coffee and her laptop. On her Googled attempt, a Web address for Topping Ventures popped up first on the list. She linked to the site. Underneath the name of the company were the words "An Asset Management Firm."

Kat skimmed through the website and learned in general terms that a huge percentage of their clients were from the aerospace/ defense industries and the mining industry. It all looked legitimate, but if Chance was right, the site whitewashed the firm's real purpose.

She jotted down the street address, which was in Boston's Financial District, and the phone number, then linked to the names of the management team. The CEO was Philip Topping. Kat recalled Chance mentioning the name Philip once. This had to be the right company.

She linked back to the Googled listings. Though her eyes were blurring from fatigue, she skimmed down the list and was about to give up when she spotted the name "Morningstar" within the same citation as the name "Topping Ventures." She brought up a short commentary from a political blog about the death of Gerald Morningstar, a former employee of the firm. The text said, "It was rumored Morningstar was on his way to speak to a journalist about his work at Topping Ventures when his car skidded off an icy rural road and rolled over an embankment, killing him instantly. No one knew if he could be taken seriously because a piece of broken glass with a Smirnoff label was found on the floor, and traces of cocaine were discovered on the driver's seat." The rest was unimportant to Kat.

Because of what she already knew about Chance's former life, she didn't buy the implication that Morningstar had caused his own death. A wave of panic gripped Kat. The firm had confiscated the novel, the laptop, and now they had Chance. For Stella's sake, Kat needed to tame her own fears. She had to think about what to do, but it would have to be something that didn't directly involve Stella.

CHAPTER 5

While Kat and Stella searched for clues about Chance's disappearance, Chance had been whisked away overnight via Topping Ventures's private jet to a small airport in Maine. From there he was driven deep into the Maine woods. At gunpoint he had been escorted inside the five-bedroom log cabin lodge owned by Philip Topping. Not only was the lodge used for entertaining Philip's hunting buddies, but also for the unconventional coaxing of uncooperative employees or clientele. It provided seclusion away from curious onlookers.

All day Monday and Monday night, Chance had hidden away in his room upstairs, refusing to fraternize with Monique or the men who had brought him here. Nor would he eat the food left on a tray outside his door. Monique hadn't dared enter. Going into his room, as agitated as he was, would have been like stepping into a hornet's nest.

Chance spent the time either raging inside or thinking about Kat. By Tuesday morning hunger had finally driven him downstairs. He paced the floor from the kitchen into the living area, skirting the leather sofa and easy chairs and the round oak dining table. He double backed to the north wall and stood next to the massive stone fireplace: a dusty gray, hollowed-out cave.

To keep intruders from breaking in and to keep him from breaking out, the downstairs windows were barred and not easily opened. A whirring overhead fan was enough to keep the summer's muggy heat from becoming unbearable, as were the balsam firs, birch, and red maples surrounding the building.

Chance was a caged tiger behind a locked door. The two men who had escorted him all the way to Maine on the company's plane were on the porch. He could hear their muffled laughs. Two hours ago Monique had left in the company's SUV, which was similar to the vehicle she'd rented in Seattle. She wouldn't tell him where she was going, but he had a pretty good idea.

He had no access to a phone; the firm had seen to that. Kat's anger would have prevented her from catching on to the subtle way he'd tried to communicate his predicament to her, but Stella would have figured it out right away, though thinking it over, he had second thoughts about worrying his daughter.

When he glanced toward the window, he caught a glimpse of the black SUV pulling up to the lodge. From the passenger's side emerged Philip, the CEO of Topping Ventures. He'd aged somewhat since the last time Chance had seen him six years ago. Though he was still physically fit, his hair had turned completely white, and his cheeks sagged a little. But there was no mistaking his mink brown, penetrating eyes. Even in the wilderness in summer, he wore a Ralph Lauren light gray suit. He stayed on the stone walkway, careful not to dirty his Ferragamo loafers. He carried a thick manila envelope. The bald man escorted Philip inside, then closed the door behind him on his way out.

Purposely avoiding Chance's stare, Monique strode into the kitchen area and poured the coffee she'd made earlier that morning into three mugs. Philip and Chance locked eyes.

"Well, well, my friend, we finally meet again." Philip held out his hand for Chance to shake, but Chance, hostility gripping him, made no move toward Philip. "If that's the way it is," Philip said, "we might as well get down to business." He took off his jacket and laid it across the back of a chair. "Sit down," he said, but Chance remained standing.

Monique set two mugs on the coffee table and went back for her own. She was dressed in a tight skirt and halter top, and when she settled on one end of the sofa and crossed her legs, her skirt hiked up mid-thigh. Philip picked up his mug and took one of the easy chairs. She looked at Chance and patted the spot next to her. Chance reluctantly sat, but picked the chair opposite Philip.

Philip tossed the envelope on the coffee table. "Your assignment. You have two weeks to familiarize yourself with the corporation, what their mission is, what their needs are. In case you've forgotten, you need to familiarize yourself with the government official you'll be bribing. It's all in there—his likes, his dislikes, his perversions, especially his perversions. The corporation is RBK, and you'll be traveling to a Russian state. It involves mineral rights. It's all in the dossier. You'll need to brush up on the language. That's one reason Monique is here. She can help you with that."

Chance's shoulders bunched in anger. He clenched his fists to keep from ranting at both of them. "Why do you need me for this? You have a capable stable of young bucks."

"This is a sensitive matter. It concerns uranium. You have the experience and the finesse to see this through."

"That's bullshit. I know for a fact Larry Vore and Mike Targee have handled these kinds of assignments. Even Banks could do it."

Philip cocked his head, as if pondering Chance's remark. "Oh, so you *are* keeping abreast of what's going on at the firm. Very well." He set his mug down and faced Chance with a fierce stare. "I read your book. Did you think you'd get away with exposing the firm?"

"I don't name names."

"Close enough," Philip snapped. "The assignment we're sending you on is quite dangerous. The country is volatile. If you don't handle it right, you may not come back alive."

Chance had been in precarious situations before, but six years in the little town of Rosswood was a far cry from his life in the firm. Intentionally, he hadn't kept up with the politics of it. He wasn't sure how the detailed operations were done these days. Asking him to step into an assignment like this could be as good as a death sentence. He was smart enough to know it was payback for writing the book. "And what if I refuse?"

"As you already know, we have pictures ready to deliver to Ms. Summers, which would ruin your relationship, no doubt." He paused, as if he were waiting for Chance to absorb the impact of what he'd told him, then his lips turned into a calculated grin. "And then there's Stella."

At the mention of his daughter's name, Chance rushed at Philip and grabbed his shirt at the neck, "You sonovabitch. You lay a hand on her, and I'll personally break every bone in your body."

Monique leapt to her feet, shouting, "Sit down, Chance. Do not make this any worse for you than it is."

The door burst open. The bald man clamped onto Chance's shoulders and pulled him off Philip. Chance shoved away from the man. Philip rose and waved the man out.

"Why are you doing this, Philip? We were friends once. You were my mentor, for chrissakes."

Philip adjusted his collar and looked Chance in the eye. "You don't cross me or my firm, or you pay, just like Morningstar. You remember Gerald, don't you? Turns out he had a drinking problem. Talked to the wrong people." He laid his jacket across his arm. "Monique will be going with you. She knows what to do. If we take the official's predilections into consideration, her services will come in handy. It's all in there." He gave the envelope a nod. "We'll talk again when you return for your next assignment, that is, *if* you return." He kissed Monique's cheek. "I'll see you tomorrow afternoon, my dear." He edged toward the door. "Take care of him."

Chance was astute enough to know that meant: don't let him out of your sight and offer him sex if need be. And Philip's last comment concerning Chance's next assignment tipped him off that the firm had no intentions of releasing their hold on him.

He watched out the window as one of the men got into the SUV with Philip and revved up the engine. After they'd driven off, he remained where he was. The bald man stepped off the porch. It was then that Chance noticed the gun tucked in at his waist.

In the far distance, the sunlight sparkled off a pond where wood ducks swam near the shoreline. The forest was thick close to the edges, and the trees were like feathered spears reflected in the water. Near the lodge a warbler lit on a maple branch.

The anger Chance had vented at Philip mellowed him somewhat. His heart had slowed to its normal rhythm, though it wouldn't take much to set him off again. His nerves were primed.

Monique tried to hand him the envelope, but he made no effort to take it from her. "We must make the best of it, Chance." She inched into the space between him and the window and clasped her hands around his neck, letting the envelope fall to the floor. "We will be together, no? Make the best of it, darling. Make the best of it."

His eyes gradually narrowed into a defiant stare. His chest tightened with frustration, bitterness, and a deep sense of longing for the freedom he'd held for the past six years. In that moment striking her would have come easy, and pushing her away would have been the appropriate thing to do. Instead, he held her tight and kissed her hard on the mouth until she made whimpering sounds and squirmed to get free. He swept her up in his arms and headed for the stairwell.

"Chance, what are you doing?"

"Making the best of it."

Halfway upstairs she struggled to free herself. "Not like this, Chance."

"Then how would you like it? Downstairs? On the couch? In the kitchen? Do you want it easy or do you want it rough?"

"Stop it, Chance!"

He tightened his hold on her and continued up the stairs. "You'll take it wherever and however I want to give it, so make the best of it."

***

The light in the north bedroom was naturally dim, and the lamp had not been turned on. Chance sat on the edge of the bed, elbows resting on his thighs, his head lowered in his hands. Monique's delicate Chanel perfumed scent permeated his skin, his hair, his clothing.

Monique stood at the full-length mirror, repositioning the halter top that had been yanked down and adjusting the skirt that had been hiked up during her and Chance's tussle. She finger-combed her hair. "I understand your frustration, but you do not have to treat me like a sack of potatoes."

Chance stood and tucked in his shirt. "I apologize."

"I know I am not *her*, but I have feelings, too, despite what you think of me."

"I said I was sorry." He wandered to the window and looked beyond the backyard into the forest. Even if he found a means of escaping the house, the dense growth of trees would offer its own kind of confinement. They'd surely track him down.

Attuned to the slightest sound, he heard her approach him from behind. When she embraced him and laid her head against his back, he stayed facing the window and crossed his arms.

"I know you are mad at me right now," she said, "but we have no choice but to be together in this. Can we not be pleasant to one another? You know how I feel about you, how I have always felt about you." She clung to him. "Why can you not make love to me as before?"

Chance broke her hold and began straightening the rumpled bedspread, and she took hold of it from the opposite side, helping him complete the task. "You remember how it was with us once, how when we worked together, we could not be apart. You remember, do you not? You remember our last time together?"

"Those days are long gone."

"But we will be together again, as Philip wants it to be. We must work closely, and we must act as if we care for each other, or this work will fail."

"The key word is *act*, Monique, and that's exactly what it will be, an act on my part. And I don't know why Philip would want me on such a sensitive project as this. Isn't he afraid my attitude alone will make it fail? How can he trust I won't blow the whole thing apart?"

She rounded the corner of the bed, held and kissed his hand. "You heard what he said. You have the experience he seeks, and he trusts you will not do anything to jeopardize your family."

Chance faced the window again. In this moment he resented Philip with an intensity that stung like acid.

"Come, and we will look over the assignment. Tomorrow I must report to Philip for further instruction. So please." She walked away, and with his daughter's safety in mind he trailed Monique downstairs. She picked up the envelope and handed it to him. "We must begin."

***

By noon Kat had showered, dressed in a summer pant suit, and made a few phone calls. While she was waiting for Stella to arrive, the phone rang. Maggie came on the line.

"And how are you today?"

"Oh, it's you," Kat said.

"Normally, I'd be insulted by that remark, but I take it you haven't heard from Chance."

"Sorry, no. I'm really glad you called, though. I have a few minutes before Stella gets here. Then I'm leaving for Boston."

"Boston. What's in Boston?"

"Long story short, Stella received the same kind of phone call from Chance, so we went to Rosswood."

"Rosswood! Why would you go back there? You're not ready for that."

"I had no choice. We wanted to see if he was there, which he wasn't. We have a good reason to believe he's in Boston."

"So, why don't you wait for him to come back?"

"I can't tell you the details, Maggie, but it's important that I go. I'll only be gone a couple of days."

"You shouldn't be traipsing across the country. You should be seeing Dr. Rosen. You promised you would. I'm not happy about this."

"I don't have a choice."

"You always have a choice. I'm disappointed, Kat."

Maggie's disapproving tone hit Kat hard. She knew she was pushing the limits of their friendship, let alone their working relationship. "Please, Maggie, you'll have to trust me on this."

"Where have I heard that before? Like I trusted you when you chose to stay in Rosswood so long? Look where that got you."

Feeling let down by Maggie's attitude, Kat paused, hesitating to answer.

"All right," Maggie said. "Call me when you get back."

"I wouldn't do this if it weren't important."

"I know, I know. Goodbye, Kat."

Kat hung up, weary. Not having Maggie's support was like trying to walk without legs. She took a deep breath to clear her mind and focused on finding something for Stella to eat for lunch.

Later, when Stella walked into Kat's house on her lunch hour, Kat had already made her plans. "How's work?" Kat set a tuna sandwich on the table, trying to keep things normal for Stella's sake.

"I had to shelve books all morning long. It was kind of a drag."

"At least you have a job, even if it's boring at times. Sit down and eat."

Stella dug in her backpack and produced the memory stick. "I'm not really hungry."

Kat could tell by Stella's red-rimmed eyes she'd either been crying or hadn't slept, or both. "You need to keep your strength up."

"I'd rather check out Dad's manuscript. Can we do it now?"

"I want you to take that straight back to the bank and put it in the safety deposit box, safe and sound. Do it before you go back to work. I won't be needing it."

"Why not? Did you hear from Dad?"

"No, but I did some digging on the Net, and with what I remembered from my conversations with Chance, I think I have all the information I need."

"To do what?" Stella stared at Kat, then glanced at the carry-on bag near the sofa. "Are you going somewhere? Kat, you're not leaving, are you? Not now."

Kat considered easing Stella's panic by soft-pedaling her answer but couldn't think of anything but the truth. "I'm going to Boston for a couple of days to see if I can find out where they took your father. From my research, I know the firm he worked for is in Boston."

"That's where he lived. He used to send me letters from there. Can I come?"

"I don't think that would be wise. Chance wouldn't want you involved, and besides, someone needs to be here in case he calls or comes back while I'm gone. I won't be away that long."

"But Kat..." Stella's eyes welled up.

"I know this will be hard on you with both of us away, but it will only be for two days at the most. I'll keep in touch by phone. You can always call me." When Stella didn't respond, Kat wrapped her arms around her. "Everything will be all right, honey. You're father will come home. I'll see to it. Now why don't you sit down and have some lunch."

"I'm not hungry."

"Then take it with you. You might get hungry later." Kat packaged up the sandwich and saw Stella to the door.

"Will you call me when you get to your hotel?"

"Of course. Now, take the memory stick back to the bank immediately."

"Do you think we'll have to call Dad's lawyer?"

"I certainly hope not. But at this point, anything is possible."

CHAPTER 6

An attractive gentleman around Chance's age, but not nearly as appealing as Chance, squeezed into the cabin seat next to Kat. Though it was a late afternoon flight, the plane was completely filled. In no mood to chitchat, she absentmindedly thumbed through the airline magazine and was grateful the man next to her, after exchanging pleasantries, opened his briefcase and got lost in paperwork. To relieve the stuffiness, she adjusted the nozzle overhead to release a steadier stream of cool air.

All she could think of was Chance and what she might discover in Boston. Her mind skimmed over the last few days, and she shuddered at the thought of their needless argument, which had started this whole fiasco. In Kat's view, Chance's troubling absence was totally her fault.

She closed her eyes and visualized him driving away in the black SUV. She thought about the men who had taken him and then her thoughts lit on the woman with the shaggy dark hair, the ivory skin, and the petite, but very alluring body. With a sudden stab in the gut she had an unsettling feeling Chance was with the woman now.

By the time Kat was secured in the Boston Airport Hilton after a short layover in Denver and after boarding a different airline, the only available flight, it was midnight. The room was exceptionally clean with a hint of floral scent. She made a quick call to Stella and took a shower before she collapsed on the bed, exhausted.

She'd asked the desk for a wake-up call at 8:30 a.m., but when she woke and checked the time, it was 11:00. Either the clerk had forgotten, or she'd slept through the call. The flashing red button told the story. Whenever she slept that hard, a train could have gone through the room unnoticed.

At 1:00 p.m. she took a cab to the Financial District and was dropped off in front of a high-rise with a glassed entrance that housed Topping Ventures. Her choice of attire—a short-sleeved blouse tucked into linen slacks—felt incredibly warm for this sweltering day. The cool air of the lobby rescued her from the heat.

Stationed near the entryway was an S-shaped reception desk, surrounded by a wall of muted grays and pinks. The sun, filtering through the glass, created rectangles of light across the tiled floor.

Kat bypassed the desk, manned by a young woman with a headset fielding phone calls, and aimed for the elevators and the directory of offices. Scanning the board, she found nothing remotely close to the name of the firm.

A steady stream of businesspeople, mostly men, were boarding the elevators. As she headed back toward the entrance, her mind focused on discovering the location of the company, a white-haired gentleman in a navy blue suit strode past her. A whiff of cigar smoke made her take notice of a man who bore a striking resemblance to Philip Topping, the CEO whose picture she'd seen on the website. She rushed to catch up with him, but didn't make it in time. Four elevators ascending left too many choices.

Undaunted, she approached the reception desk and waited for the woman with short, mousy-blond hair and too much make-up to end her conversation. "Can you tell me what floor Topping Ventures is on? I didn't see their name on the directory, but I know they're here."

"Do you have an appointment?"

"My name is Kat Summers. I'm sure if you call them, someone will want to see me." Kat waited while the woman made the call. If they wouldn't allow her to come up to the office, Kat wondered how long it would take to find it on her own. Could she search every floor? Would she? For Chance, of course she would.

The receptionist, who had been put on hold, finally hung up and said, "You can go up now. It's on the fourteenth floor."

"What's the office number?"

"When you get off the elevator, you can't miss it."

Once Kat was in the stale-smelling elevator with two men staring at her, the full impact of what she was about to do gave her pause, and the sensation of rising at high speed added to her anxiety. But when the elevator bounced to a light stop at Floor 14, the thought of Chance buoyed her resolve to see this through.

When the doors opened, there was no mistaking where she was. The name "Topping Ventures" was plastered in bold, black letters on the wall in front of her. The firm took up the whole floor with an array of corridors and offices, some glassed-in and some walled-off. On a wall behind the receptionist's desk was a world map with markers on various countries.

Glancing around, Kat noticed several men straining to get a look at her. She fought the urge to bolt. She brought her attention to the fashionably attired woman at the desk. "I'm here to see Philip Topping."

"You must be Ms. Summers. If you'll just sit down, please."

Kat's attention shifted to several pictures above the world map, pictures of the company's executives, and spotted the man who had passed her in the lobby. She was about to tell the woman she insisted on seeing the CEO when a man in his forties approached her. His ebony hair was combed forward, and he was wearing rimless glasses.

"Kat Summers? I'm Carl Banks. Come with me, please."

Kat followed him halfway down the corridor into a private office. He gestured toward a small leather couch, set apart from an empty desk and two chairs. She sat while he pulled one of the chairs close to her. He offered her M&Ms from the candy dish on a coffee table. She refused. The situation she found herself in was unbearably cozy. Even in the chill of the air-conditioned room, she felt the heat of anger rise.

"Do you want to do business with our firm?"

"I think you know I came here to see Philip Topping."

"That's not possible, Ms. Summers. Mr. Topping is a very busy man, and even if he would see you, he's not even in today. In fact, he won't be in the rest of the week. What can I do for you?"

Ever since Kat had met Banks, his face was a mask, showing no emotion, no smile, no rise of the eyebrows. Even in a lie, his eyes were sharply focused on her. She thought of the characters in Chance's novel, the men in the firm being ex-CIA types. No doubt Banks was one of them. The man was lying. She'd just seen Philip Topping.

"All right, then. I want to see Chance Eliason."

Without a twitch of an eyelid, he said, "There's no one by that name working here."

"He used to work here, and I have reason to believe your company knows where he is now."

"I'm sorry, but you're wrong, and even if he were here, you wouldn't be privy to that information."

"Then I want to see your manager or whomever you answer to."

He stared at her with hawk eyes and wouldn't reply.

Her temper rising, Kat had had enough. "This is bullshit and you know it." She glared at him. "I'm not leaving until I see Topping."

He stood, lengthening his six-foot frame. "I think it's time for you to leave."

"I know for a fact Chance was taken from his home by three of your thugs and a woman named Monique. I know the woman works here, so tell me where Chance is."

"You're mistaken, Ms. Summers. No one by the name of Monique works here." Maintaining his calm, cool demeanor, he tapped on the door.

Two security guards in black uniforms swiftly entered the room, took Kat by the arms, and accompanied her through the doorway. She struggled against them but was no match for the tall, well-muscled men.

As she was escorted into the hallway, she glanced over her shoulder and yelled, "I demand to see Philip Topping." Before she faced forward, she caught a glimpse of the petite woman with the shaggy hair ducking into an office.

But the guards had her in the elevator and wouldn't let go until they'd walked her through the lobby and out the door of the building. They hung around the entrance, and there was no way she could get back inside—not in a long shot.

To calm herself down and gather her resolve, she strode down the sidewalk and paced back and forth in the hot sun, dodging passersby. Her hot-blooded temper had flared up at the wrong time. With more control and better judgment, the situation might have ended differently. Now what was she going to do? Obviously, they were lying. She had seen both Philip Topping and Monique.

Just as Kat made a turn toward the entrance, the woman who had last been seen with Chance exited the building and looked Kat's way. Upon making eye contact, the woman took off in the opposite direction.

The adrenalin shot through Kat, and she bounded after Monique. Excusing herself, she elbowed around a couple and had to squeeze over to avoid colliding with an overweight woman coming toward her. She snaked in and round the other walkers. At the end of the block the light turned green, and the traffic started up again. Monique had already crossed the street. Kat edged to the front of the waiting crowd and watched Monique's progression, then lost sight of her.

When the light changed, Kat surged into the crosswalk and increased her stride, her feet aching in her pointy heels, definitely the wrong shoes for an all-out chase. Up ahead, Monique had stopped, as if she were waiting for Kat to follow.

Kat had almost caught up with her when she jetted across a side street and entered Post Office Park, an oasis in the middle of concrete. Kat followed along the red brick walkway into the lush green foliage and spotted Monique standing by the round fountain.

She glanced at Kat, then headed for a trellis that had an open dome and several columns covered in leaves. It was as if all along she'd been leading Kat there. Kat sat next to her on a wooden bench set back between two of the columns, glad to get off her feet. Even in the outdoors, Kat recognized the distinct scent of Chanel.

Monique held up the newspaper she'd been carrying and pretended to read. "It was not a wise thing of you to do, *mon ami.*" She kept her voice low.

Kat stared at her. "Where's Chance?"

"That is not for you to know. Look straight ahead, please. It is not wise for me to be seen talking to you."

Kat ignored her. "Then why *are* you talking to me?"

"I want to warn you, you must go home. Face forward, please, and keep your voice down."

"Fine, but this is ridiculous." Kat gazed at the criss-crossed pattern on the bricks created by the sun shining through the open dome. "I won't go until I know where he is and if he's safe."

"I can assure you he is safe, but you must leave now."

"Not until you tell me where he is."

"That, I cannot do."

"Then I'll go to the police."

"And tell them what? You have no proof of anything." Monique turned a page of the newspaper and propped it up again.

Frustrated, Kat watched a man in slacks and a short-sleeved shirt walk by with a coffee cup in his hand, the roasted aroma drifting her way. "I'll go back to your office and camp out until I see Topping."

"You are not very smart to think he will ever speak to you."

"We'll see."

"Listen, Ms. Kat Summers. You have no hold on Chance. He came here willingly."

"That's a lie. He would never leave his ranch the way he did, or his daughter."

"Or you?" Shielding her face with the paper, Monique peered at Kat and said very pointedly, "I am telling you, you must go home. It is in your best interest. Do not make it harder for yourself, or for Chance. He has a job to do. Go home, and he will call you in twenty-four hours. He will tell you everything you need to know."

"Why can't he call me now? I have my cell phone. I want to hear his voice. I want to know he's all right."

"He will call you on your landline. If you do not leave now, you will miss his call. I am going now. Do not follow me, and if you do not leave here, there will be dire consequences for Chance."

"How do you know I have a landline?"

In a hasty move Monique crumpled the paper together, stalked off, and left Kat with unanswered questions. Kat trailed her movements around the fountain and down the red brick path until she disappeared from the park, along with the click of her high heels.

Following wouldn't do any good. Kat was sure the security guards would block her from entering the building. The firm was like a firewall, offering no way into its deepest secrets, leaving her with no clues to finding Chance. If Monique was telling her the truth, Kat didn't want to make it hard on him. The only thing left to do was to fly back home as soon as possible in time to get his call.

**

Monique took the elevator to Floor 14, sweat beading across her forehead and trickling down her chest, her heart still pounding from rushing in the heat of the day. Up close, Kat Summers was more striking than Monique had anticipated, her hair as bold as her facial features, laid out in a beautiful pattern. She was a force to be reckoned with when it came to Chance.

Philip Topping appeared in the reception area and motioned Monique to follow. She tagged along and veered left at the end of the hallway. He ushered her into his posh corner office where she sat in a chair facing his massive glass desk. The decor was done in black and white, accented with splashes of red and gold in a Chinese vase that was as tall as Monique. The light, streaming in through the windows, gleamed off the desk.

Philip stood over her. Monique prepared to be grilled, not always an easy position to find oneself in when dealing with the head of the firm.

"So, do you think the woman fell for the bit about the phone call?"

"As I was leaving, she questioned me about the landline and how we knew about it."

"What did you tell her?"

"I left. I did not say anything."

"Hmm…Tell me about your conversation."

Monique grabbed a tissue from a table nearby and dabbed her forehead. She unfastened the top button of her blouse and blotted her upper chest to dry the accumulated moisture. Philip handed her a bottle of Perrier from a small refrigerator. After closing the door, he took the chair next to her and crossed his legs, the smell of cigar smoke lingering on his suit jacket.

"She is a persistent one, as you have witnessed, Philip. She wanted to know if Chance is safe and where he is. She threatened to go to the police."

"And what did you say?"

"I told her she would make it hard on Chance if she continued to make demands. I told her to go home and he would call in twenty-four hours."

"And how did she react?"

"She argued with me about wanting him to call her on her cell phone, but I told her Chance would suffer the consequences if she did not go home."

"Excellent," he said. "She's being tailed until she gets through airport security. And when she gets home, there will be a little surprise for her, the one we talked about."

"Will I go back to the lodge tonight?"

Philip rose and walked to the window, his hands clasped behind his back. Without turning around, he said, "How's he doing now? Has he calmed any?"

"Maybe a tiny bit, Philip. At least he was looking at the dossier when I left."

"Good. Good." Philip stood silent for a while, then faced her. "I want you to go back tonight, and I want you to stay there for the duration and use every trick you've ever learned in this business to make him forget he ever cared about this Summers woman."

"That is not so simple, Philip. He is, as you say, smitten with her."

"Come on, Monique. You've worked your feminine wiles on more difficult cases than Chance."

"Yes, but…"

"No buts. Just do it. And report back to me."

CHAPTER 7

When Kat arrived home after flying most of the night, her house was stuffy with the lingering fish odor from the sandwich she'd prepared for Stella before she left town. In her haste to get to the airport, she'd forgotten to toss the empty tuna can in the garbage receptacle outside. Typical of Kat's slack cleaning efforts, she'd left it in the sink. Much tidier than Kat, Chance would have made sure it was thrown out. Kat wrapped the can in newspaper and set it in the mudroom to deal with in the morning.

She hadn't slept on the plane because she kept hashing over her conversation with Monique. Kat thought it ludicrous the way Monique shielded her face with the newspaper and ordered Kat not to look at her, like some spy out of a James Bond movie. As if that were enough to scare Kat from prying into the company's affairs. They were everything Chance had written about—cold, devious, and liars to boot. They undoubtedly had something to hide. Her pending conversation with Chance should clear the cloud of mystery.

On her way to the bedroom to catch a few hours of sleep before sunrise, she checked her answering machine in case she'd missed a call, in case Chance had called earlier than she was told he would. No blinking light.

Despite the musty airplane smell that clung to her clothes and hair like a second skin, she was too exhausted to take a shower. She slipped on a T-shirt and climbed into bed.

No sooner had she fallen asleep when Chance appeared to her in a dream. Similar to her previous dream, Brianna beckoned her through a fog and led her to a scene where Chance stood with his back to her inside a rustic dwelling. As soon as she took a step in his direction, she saw the shadow of a woman draping her arms around him.

Kat woke with a start. She closed her eyes again and tried to recapture the details, all of which had vanished in an instant. Then sleep overtook her, and in the morning she stirred to the chirping of robins and the sunlight shining through the window she'd forgotten to cover. All she could remember about the dream was Chance, a cabin of sorts, and the feeling of dread.

In the middle of a shower with her face drenched in the spray of the warm water, snippets of the dream rushed into her mind, and she almost choked on the memory of another woman with Chance. No wonder the dreadful sensation. Her only consolation was that Chance's call would clear up everything.

The phone rang, and Kat grabbed her robe and strode barefoot into the kitchen, leaving a trail of wet footmarks, her heart thumping double-time. Hearing Stella's voice, she couldn't help feeling a little let down. After explaining she was waiting for a call from Chance on the landline, Stella agreed to stop by on her lunch hour and hung up right away to keep the line free.

Kat dressed in shorts and a tank top and surveyed the kitchen cupboards and the fridge for something to feed Stella. The pickings were grim. Though the twenty-four hours hadn't elapsed, she wouldn't risk leaving the house for groceries for fear of missing his call. She found another can of tuna and hoped Stella wouldn't mind another sandwich on toasted, slightly stale bread.

All she could do now was kill time, something her high-strung nature wasn't equipped for. Waiting for the phone to ring was like waiting for a pot to boil. She didn't dare lie down for fear of falling asleep. She thought of calling Maggie, but decided to hold off since Maggie would only harp at her about seeing Dr. Rosen.

As if on cue, her cell phone rang. She wrestled it from her purse. Maggie was on the line, asking her if she'd seen Chance.

"Aren't you even going to say hello? And no I didn't see him."

"And why not? He wasn't in Boston?"

Kat cautiously decided to leave out the details. "He wasn't available."

"What do you mean he wasn't available?"

"I can tell you more later. He's going to call and explain everything."

"This all sounds very cryptic."

"I know, Maggie, but everything should get cleared up soon." Too antsy to talk about Chance, Kat said, "How's work going? Are you sure you don't want me to come in?" The doorbell rang, and she coasted across the room with the phone to her ear. "Hang on, Maggie, I have to answer the door."

The postman thrust a clipboard at her, and she juggled the cell phone and signed for the registered mailing. He handed her the express envelope. She closed the door and brought it to the table. "Maggie, are you still there?"

"What was all that rustling?"

"I was signing for a registered letter. Actually, it's a large envelope. Can you hold on while I see what's in it? It's from Boston. It might be from Chance."

"I'll wait."

Kat shifted the phone to the table, ripped open the envelope, and pulled out a stack of eight-by-ten photographs, the first showing Monique, naked, lying on top of Chance. Shocked, Kat grabbed the table's edge and lowered herself into a chair. On the table, she laid out all four shots of Chance and Monique in various intimate poses, the last with Monique snuggling up against him, her breasts in full view.

Maggie's voice pierced through the line. "Kat, are you there?"

Kat held the phone to her ear. "I have to go." Her voice was soft and shaky, but she couldn't force it to sound otherwise.

"What's the matter, Kat? You sound like someone just punched the wind out of you. What was in the envelope?"

"I have to go." Kat snapped the phone shut, as if that would exclude the world. She needed time to process her feelings.

She sat in a daze, staring at the pictures like a person drawn to the scene of a shooting, curious to see what happened yet shaken at the sight of the carnage. The wall clock ticked away the hour until her despair shifted to a rage so fiery it mushroomed in her chest and swarmed her whole body. "Damn you, Chance. Damn you to hell!"

She broke down and shook with sobs. The last time she'd felt this miserably sad was when she was in the Rosswood cemetery, crying over the loss of her sister. If these photos were authentic, and Kat had no reason to believe they weren't, wasn't she losing Chance?

After Kat was all cried out, she fled to the bathroom to blow her nose and wash her face. Seeing her image in the mirror, she flushed with anger at herself. "You're a stupid, stubborn woman, Kat Summers. You drove him to it. If you hadn't argued with him and told him to get out of your life, this never would have happened."

The patter of footsteps on the porch alerted her to Stella's arrival. Before Kat could think clearly, Stella had knocked twice, then called Kat's name from the foyer. For once, Kat wished she'd locked the door. She dashed to the dining room, gathered up the photos, and haphazardly shoved them into the envelope, just as Stella approached the table.

Stella eyed her with a look of concern. "What's wrong, Kat? I can tell you've been crying. Did something bad happen to Dad?"

"No, no, it's not that. Are you hungry? Is tuna all right?" In a daze, Kat wandered into the kitchen and went through the motions of collecting the tuna, the bread, and the mayonnaise, her hands shaking all the while.

"I just want to know about Dad." Stella grasped Kat's arm before Kat could run the can opener. "Something's wrong, isn't it?"

The feel of Stella's touch brought Kat into the moment. Stella deserved an explanation. "Let's sit down." After they were seated at the table, Kat moved the envelope to the seat next to her, out of Stella's sight.

"Did you even see Dad?"

"They wouldn't let me near him, but they have him somewhere. All they would tell me was he had a job to do." Though Kat tried hard to stay in control of her emotions, her eyes flooded with tears.

"What's the matter, Kat? What aren't you telling me?"

In Kat's vulnerable state, she didn't have the strength to protect Stella's feelings. "I didn't want to burden you with this, but you're going to find out sooner or later that I've ruined everything. I'm not sure your father is *ever* coming back. They sent me pictures of him with a woman. Pictures I can't show you. They're very real, and it's all my fault."

"What pictures?"

"I drove your dad to go back to the firm. If I hadn't kicked him out, he'd still be here."

"Dad would never go back there unless he was forced to. And we both know he was forced into it. Rusty said so."

"It's my fault. The pictures say it all."

"Dad would never hook up with just anyone. He's not like that anymore. Plus, they can do anything with pictures these days. Let me see them."

"Absolutely not. They're not the kind of pictures a daughter should see."

"Oh." Stella wrinkled her nose in disgust. "*Those* kind of pictures. But I still want to know where Dad is. You said he was going to call."

"In twenty-four hours. That should be early this afternoon, our time."

"Maybe I should phone work and tell them I'm not coming in, although I know my boss won't be happy."

"No, you go back to work. I'll call you later and let you know what I find out."

"I want to stay here. Please? I want to talk to Dad."

Too strung-out to entertain anyone, Kat picked up Stella's backpack and wandered toward the door, Stella finally following along. "Trust me," Kat said. "I'll call you as soon as I hear anything."

Stella swung her backpack over her shoulder. "There's no way Dad would run off like this and take up with some woman. Besides, why would he call you to tell you he was going? He loves you, Kat."

"Thanks for your vote of confidence, but I'm not so sure." Kat gave Stella a quick hug. "Go on, now. I'll call you as soon as I hear from him." She watched as Stella reluctantly walked down the sidewalk and got into her Civic.

Relieved to be alone with her own misery, Kat backed against the wall with an urge to sink to the floor. But instead of giving in to that impulse, she sought out the photos. Call it masochistic, but she studied everything about them: the way Chance held Monique; the ardent way she was kissing him; even the curve of the woman's body, so sleek and petite.

With pure loathing, Kat slammed the pictures into the envelope. In this moment she despised Chance for having left her and taken up with the same woman Kat had actually sat with yesterday. How could he? How could both of them be so cruel? Maybe Maggie was intuitive to push Kat to see Dr. Rosen. After everything that had happened, she could surely use professional help now.

She went into the kitchen and drank a tall glass of water. To keep from drowning in her sorrows, she snuggled into her bed to sleep the day away. She hadn't voiced her concerns to Stella, but she feared Chance wouldn't call at all. Indeed, she knew he wouldn't. After examining the photos, Kat didn't much care.

Drifting into the space between wakefulness and sleep, she caught a glimpse of Brianna's face. But the doorbell jarred her into consciousness, scattering the image. She staggered into the living room, groggy.

Maggie marched in from the opened door in her signature attire: skirt, jacket, and hat. "Let me look at you." She lifted Kat's chin. "I thought as much. You've been crying. You're eyes are puffy. Your face is a mess."

"What are you doing here?"

"You couldn't expect me to sit around and wait for you to call after you hung up so abruptly, and in that shaky tone of voice. I knew something was wrong. So, are you going to tell me, or do I have to drag you in to see Dr. Rosen myself?" When Kat didn't answer, Maggie said, "I'm not leaving here until you tell me what got you so upset."

Hiding anything from Maggie would have taken a miracle. Kat found the envelope where she'd left it and handed it over.

In her usual calm, detached manner, Maggie studied each photo as if she were viewing homes for sale. "So, this is what's got you all tied up in knots."

Kat expected sympathy, not matter-of-fact bluntness. "Wouldn't you be unnerved if you saw your lover in bed with another woman?"

"Who sent you these pictures?"

"Isn't it obvious?"

"Kat, come on. I know these upset you."

"Damn right they do."

"How could Chance have taken them?"

"He could have set up a camera."

"And why would he want to go to all that trouble?"

"To get back at me because I kicked him out."

Maggie put her hand on her hip and gave Kat an impatient look. "Kat Summers, you're not thinking with your head. Where's the logical businesswoman I trained, for god's sake? You know for a fact the man worships the ground you walk on. He's not the vindictive type. The Chance Eliason I know would never stoop so low. Someone else took these pictures."

Maggie shuffled through the photos until she found the one where Monique was allegedly curled up asleep with Chance. "Look here. He looks like he's passed out. Look how slack his face is. And look at the others. You can't even see his face. Her head is in the way."

"That's because she's…"

"She may be kissing him, but is he kissing her? Did you ask yourself that? And look at his arms in this photo. They're lying limp across her back, not clasped in an embrace. And look at this." Maggie held the photo in front of Kat and pointed to the watch on Chance's wrist. "No man I know would wear a cold, abrasive object on his wrist when having sex. If you ask me, whoever took these pictures wants to rattle your cage for some reason, scare you into thinking he's left you. Can you think of any reason why? What is it you're not telling me?"

"You've missed your calling. You should have been a detective. I guess I need to explain something more about my trip to Boston."

"That would be good for a start."

"I need to give you some background," Kat said. "Before Chance moved to Rosswood, he was involved with a consulting firm in Boston that does business...let's just say, in an unconventional manner. That's as detailed as I can get without breaking confidences. What I can say is the firm has been quite adamant about wanting Chance back. He's been putting them off, until now."

Kat took a breath, then continued, "As you know, I went to their offices in Boston to see if I could find out where he is, and that's when I met up with Monique, the woman in the pictures. She said he had a job to do and told me to go home. Trying to get any information out of them was like talking to a brick wall. At first, they said they didn't even know Chance. They're secretive and cagey. Are you shocked?"

"I've heard of outfits like that. I just never knew anyone personally involved. Who would have thought Chance was one of them. He's certainly not the same man now."

"She said he would call me here this afternoon. That's why I came home."

Maggie slid the photos in the envelope and set it on the coffee table. "From all you've told me, do you know what I think?"

"They want me to back off."

"Now you're using your head. They were counting on your feelings for Chance and the gut reaction you'd have. Boy, are they stinkers."

"I feel like an idiot, falling into their trap." Kat started pacing.

"What are you doing?"

"I'm thinking about what to do next."

"Now, wait a minute." Maggie approached Kat. "You need to take a breath here. These people sound ruthless. I think you should let things be. There's nothing you can do. You don't even know where he is." She caught Kat's arm, stopping her movements. "I want you to promise me you'll heed their warning and leave things alone. Get a good night's rest and clear your head."

Kat nodded, but her mind was elsewhere, sifting through the memory of her time in Boston, scanning for any clues to Chance's whereabouts.

"I'd say give Chance my regards, but we both know he's not going to call today. Am I right?"

"I'm sure you're right."

"I had to say it, Kat. I didn't want to leave here with your hopes unreasonably raised."

"Don't worry. I know he's not going to call now. They just wanted me out of Boston. I was getting too close to the truth. God, I feel so stupid."

"Not stupid. You just care about the man." Maggie gave her a warm hug. "I'm sorry you have to go through this. Do you think you should go to the police?"

The answer Monique had given Kat echoed in her mind: you have no proof of anything. "I'll just wait it out."

"Then you have to trust Chance that he's smart enough to extricate himself from the situation. There's nothing more you can do." Maggie opened the door and stepped outside. "I'll check on you tomorrow. Oh, by the way, Jim is handling that open house in the Valley for your client, Ellen Davis."

"I forgot that was scheduled for this weekend. I haven't even touched bases with my clients."

"Don't concern yourself. We're taking care of your list, and Jim is happy to do the open house. Maybe you should stop in at Ellen's. It might take your mind off all this turmoil. And maybe you should see about an appointment with Dr. Rosen. He's a good one to talk to."

"Goodbye, Maggie."

Maggie meant well, but right now Kat couldn't focus on selling property, and seeing Rosen was the last thing she wanted to do. He'd helped her deal with Brianna's death, but talking about her feelings was never comfortable for Kat. The way she handled her problems by stuffing her feelings until they exploded into anger or some other destructive emotion was unhealthy, but being with Chance had softened her, at least she thought it had.

She reflected on their argument. Maybe Chance was right. She hadn't truly dealt with the horrible incident in Rosswood. But there was no time for that now. She had a more pressing problem to think about: how to find Chance.

CHAPTER 8

In the full-length mirror behind her bathroom door, Monique sized up her body. At fifty-two years old, one year older than Chance, she was pleased with her looks. Her hips were girlishly narrow, her stomach stylishly flat. Eating small portions, as the French were prone to do, came naturally to her, so she never starved herself to stay thin. Her breasts worried her though. No one could deny they were round and firm, but they were not set as high as they had been in her thirties and forties.

She looked closely at her face. Tiny lines had crept in around her eyes. Her hair was dark, but stray silver strands were beginning to show some. Soon she'd have to dye it.

How much longer did she have in this business of seducing men for a living? Some of them only wanted companionship—an evening of wine and conversation. Most of the time, they were too plied with alcohol to take advantage of the sex. For her, that was a welcome relief. But then there were others who held their liquor like bawdy sailors out for an all-night romp. Those were the times she hated the job. Those were the times she'd sedate them with drugs.

Maybe if her looks started to fade, Philip would ask her to leave. Before now, before Chance came into the picture again, she'd never thought about it. Chance was the only man she'd given herself to body and soul.

The first time she'd seen him at the London hotel, she'd felt an instant connection. From the start they were good together, in bed and out. She could recall their initial sexual encounter as if it were yesterday. Even at her young age then, he was the gentlest man she'd ever been with, too gentle in fact because having been in the firm two years before he'd joined it, she was used to more aggressive types. She mistook his tenderness for a weakness. She didn't treat him all that well. He'd begged her to leave the firm and run away with him. Too late, she came to love him. Looking back on it now, she wished she'd chosen the path he'd wanted. They might have married, had a child together.

She turned away from her mirrored reflection to avoid seeing the tears form.

For business reasons Philip wanted her to seduce Chance and force him to forget Kat Summers. Little did Philip know, Monique had her own secrets for wanting Chance to forget that woman. So just in case Chance was receptive to her advances, she slipped on a short silk robe and dabbed Chanel along her neckline and bodice.

Peering down the hallway, she noticed a sliver of light on the floor. His door was ajar and his lamp switched on. With caution, she tiptoed to the entrance of his room and peeked in.

With a pillow propped behind his head, he lay on the bed, reading. He was still in the jeans and T-shirt he had on earlier. He'd barely said two words to her since she'd returned from seeing Philip in Boston.

She tapped on the doorjamb. "May I come in? I cannot sleep. I saw that your door was open." Though he didn't acknowledge her and kept his eyes on the papers, she climbed on the bed anyway and propped up the other pillow. As she settled next to him, she adjusted her robe that had slid open. "I see that you are going over the dossier. Do you wish to ask me any questions?"

***

Monique's perfume overpowered his concentration, and he had no choice but to set the papers aside and pay attention to her. If it weren't for Kat, he'd have the woman in his arms. "Answer me this. Philip doesn't trust me, period, so why would he assign me something this sensitive? It doesn't make sense."

"I have told you. These younger men he has working for him, they are, as you say, hotshots with much testosterone and no brains. They are not as intelligent as someone as seasoned as you. Philip is desperate to win this contract for RBK. The political climate is changing. He cannot afford to lose this business."

"I don't buy it, Monique. Philip's never been desperate for anything. I'm beginning to think something else is going on here."

"And what is it that you have decided?"

Chance glanced at her, his gaze centering on the curve of her lapel that had shifted and exposed her breasts. He watched the rise and fall of her chest. The perfume scent unsettled him. He questioned his resolve to steer clear of her and wondered whether or not he was beginning to cave, to give in to their plans for him.

He rose from the bed and walked to the window. A bat swooped by, barely missing the glass. The trees were shadows in the darkness, lit by the moon.

Monique had moved off the bed and was hugging him from behind with no resistance on his part. "Tell me what is on your mind, Chance."

"I don't believe for a minute Philip is sending me on any assignment. I think he's planning to keep me here until he decides what to do with me."

"Oh no, that is not true. I have heard nothing of that." She held him tighter.

Her breasts molded against his back. He was encased in a cloud of Chanel. Closing his eyes, he took a deep breath in. He was so close to giving her what she wanted. He faced her and lifted her chin. Her robe had worked its way open, and the moonlight glistened on her body. "And would you tell me if you *had* heard such a thing?"

"Oh yes, you know I would not let anything happen to you. You have to believe that."

He hoisted her into his arms, her legs clasped around his waist, her arms around his neck, a childlike embrace she'd always shared with him. He laid her on the bed, his eyes drinking in the sight of her naked body framed by her electric blue robe.

He'd loved this woman once more than life itself, and here she was, offering herself to him at a time his mood had shifted from anger to loneliness, to sadness, to hopelessness, at a time he needed the comfort of a woman more than any time he could remember.

"Come to me, darling. Come to me." Her arms opened to him.

With an impulsive desire, he lay with her and held her close. He kissed her neck and shoulder. She responded with a shuddering sigh.

The temptation was unbearably real, and his senses were on overload, but for some strange reason his ex-wife's words resounded in his mind: You'll never change, Chance. Sex is too important to you. You'll always need a woman, any woman.

He rolled away from Monique. "I can't."

"What is it, Chance?"

"I can't do this." His tone was soft yet stern.

"But why?" She lay alongside him and nestled his arm between her breasts.

He ran his finger across her cheek. "You're still as beautiful as the day we met."

She held and kissed his hand. "Do you remember the time we were together before you left the firm? You had come back from your assignment in Brazil, and I returned from Indonesia. It was one of those times we traveled apart." Her voice had taken on a desperate tone. "Do you remember the love we made that day? We could not keep our hands from each other. You loved me that day. You said as much."

Chance freed his hand from her grasp.

"You hated being apart from me. You said that also."

"Monique, that was before..."

"Before you got the call from your daughter about Meredith and the cancer. And you left the firm. I know that. But can you not remember that day we were together and how much our lovemaking meant to us? If Meredith hadn't been sick, perhaps things would have been different between us."

"The past, Monique. That was the past."

"Yes, but here we are together again. It is fate, no? You can see, can you not, that we have a second chance at recapturing the past, perhaps to be together forever?"

"That can't happen."

"For you, I will leave the firm."

"Philip won't let you. You're too valuable an asset to him."

"But one day he will cast me aside. I plan to go before he will do that."

"I don't think you can. You know too much. He'll never let you go."

"I do not care. I will go as you did." She pressed her palm to his face and forced him to look at her. "Give me a reason to leave. You loved me once, Chance. Can you not love me again, as before?"

The woman was asking him to abandon his feelings for Kat. Even faced with the possibility of never seeing Kat again, he wasn't prepared to let her go. "No, Monique, I can't love you the way you want me to." He got up from the bed. "I think you should go back to your room."

"But Chance, I want you to make love to me."

"Please, Monique, just go."

She scooted off on his side of the bed and crisscrossed the flaps of her robe. She stared into his eyes. "You are in love with that woman. I can see it. But if you remember nothing else, Chance, remember this. We made real love the day before you left, a love, I can assure you, that lives on." She kissed him lightly on the lips, then hurried from the room.

Chance wandered to the window and looked out into the void. Monique had enchanted him once and maybe in a way she still did. But not like Kat. He had to find a way to get back to Kat.

CHAPTER 9

Kat made a bed for herself on the living room couch, consisting of a cotton blanket thrown over a single folded sheet. Most summers were comfortable enough with no need for air conditioning, and Kat hadn't found it necessary to incur the cost of having it installed, not even a window unit. After so many cold, damp winters, she craved the heat of summer. However, this week had been exceptionally hot, so she chose to sleep in the coolest room in the house.

After Maggie left, she'd phoned Stella and relayed Maggie's impressions of the photos and also told her Chance hadn't called. She had to assure Stella she would continue on her quest to find him. When Stella begged to spend the night with her, Kat encouraged her to stay put, get a good night's rest, and go to work in the morning, that it was best for her to keep a normal schedule. This seemed to appease her, and they agreed to talk the next day. Taking on Stella's emotions was too much of a burden. At the moment, Kat could barely hold it together herself.

The house creaked as the outside air cooled. The upper floor trapped much of the day's heat. Kat used the upstairs rooms for storage and had closed the area off for everyday living.

As she snuggled for the night in her makeshift bed, recollections of sleeping on the couch after Brianna's death began to surface. She hadn't slept here since those terrifying visions of Brianna had driven her from her bedroom. She shook off other unpleasant memories and thought of Chance.

While she drifted in and out of consciousness, the vague sound of chirping crickets echoed in the background. The *tick tock* of her mother's clock on the wall above the fireplace was exceptionally loud. A car sped through the neighborhood, revving up its engine. Soon the weariness of thinking about Chance's predicament lulled her into a light sleep.

She woke in the middle of the night to use the bathroom, and she was surprised to see that the kitchen was lit up. She could have sworn she'd turned the light off. But faced with a multitude of distractions this week, she wasn't overly concerned that she may have forgotten.

The house hadn't cooled down much, and the wooden floors held the warmth. As soon as she entered the kitchen, the light flickered off and on, off and on. Too weary to give it much thought, she ignored the oddity and continued across the room until suddenly the phone rang. There was no ignoring that. Thinking it might be Chance, she rushed to answer it. A crackling noise came over the line.

Then her attention was drawn to the dark cave of the living room, to the sight of Brianna's shimmering form. A tangerine scent wafted in the air. Kat fled to her bedroom, not out of fear, but out of concern that the visitations were starting up again. The dreams. The visions. Why now?

All her life Kat had tried to suppress her uncanny ability to see the unseen. This facility had emerged full-on after Brianna's death, but had calmed back down. Now, it was active again.

Kat climbed into bed, pulled the sheet over her head, and willed herself to sleep, tuning Brianna out. But she met Brianna in a dream. As before, Brianna led Kat to the same scene in her previous dream: Chance was standing in a room with walls of dark rounded logs, a woman's arms encircling him. This time the picture sharpened to where Kat was able to recognize the petite woman with the shaggy hair, the woman Kat had recently sat next to in Boston. Suddenly the scene changed to the outside of the building. On the front door was the letter M. The picture faded to black. Upon waking, Kat fought for the details: the cabin, Chance and Monique, the letter M.

Waiting for sunrise, she tried to make sense of it all: the blinking lights, the ringing phone, Brianna's ghost, the dream, and especially the letter M, plus Maggie's conclusions about the photos. What did it all mean?

Maggie's interpretation was that Chance had been forced into a compromising position, but if Kat's dreams were correct, Monique was embracing him, and he wasn't exactly fighting her off. The letter M had to mean Monique, or was it Maggie? But why was it on the door? And why was Brianna involved in all of this? She seemed to be urging Kat to do something. But what?

Kat threw off the sheet and headed for the bathroom. The best place to clear her head was in the shower. To her, water was a purifying force.

In the steaming spray she blanked her mind of all thought. Even when snippets of the dream blinked in, she shooed them away. Still, Brianna's face flashed in and out. There was no denying the pixie-like features, opposite of Kat's. As much as Kat tried clearing her mind's eye, Brianna's image wouldn't go away. Kat cried out, "Brianna, what do you want me to do?"

More confused than ever, Kat hastily turned off the water and dried herself off. While she dressed, she grumbled under her breath, "What's the use of having an intuitive gift if you can't get any answers?"

She left the bed unmade. After all, Chance wasn't here to harp at her about it. Besides, after seeing him and Monique together, twice now, Kat wasn't so sure she cared what he thought about anything.

Still mumbling to herself, she rounded the bed and stubbed her big toe on the metal bed frame. "Damn it." As she sat and held her foot, the name "Ellen" popped into her head. What did her client have to do with this?

Kat needed help sorting it all out. Frustrated, she went through the motions of making a pot of coffee and allowing the nutty aroma to sweep her into a better mood. While sitting at the dining room table, she thought of Ellen again.

Ellen's name kept needling her until she remembered a smattering of what Ellen had told her once, that she had a friend, a professional psychic, who used her talents to find missing children. This psychic, who used to work with the police, lived in Harbordale.

Kat gripped her mug to control her shaking hands. That had to be the link she was looking for. Perhaps the woman could help her.

From the corner of the dining room near her rolltop desk, Kat retrieved her laptop, powered it on, and found Ellen Davis's personal information. Too anxious to wait, Kat grabbed her cell phone, punched in Ellen's number, and hoped 8:30 in the morning wasn't too early to call.

After four rings she was about to hang up when Ellen came on the line. "Couldn't wait to hear my dreamy voice again, you sweet thing?"

"Ellen, this is Kat, your realtor."

"Oh my, I thought you were Charlie. Hey, are you all right? Jim said you were taking some time off."

"Sorry to bother you so early. Yes, I am taking some time off, and I'm sorry I had to hand you off to Jim."

"Oh, that's all right. He's a cutie. I know I'm in good hands, but I'll miss seeing you. Are you coming back soon? I hope it's not an emergency of some sort."

"It could be. Right now I'm in need of some extra-ordinary help. You told me once you had a psychic friend."

"I sure do. Libby's the best. Would you like to get in touch with her?"

"I really do need to talk to her. Do you have her number?"

"Listen. I'm just about ready to leave for Harbordale. I'm staying with Charlie until Monday, so I won't be here during the open house. I know for a fact she has a lot of phone readings today. She and her honey are getting married soon, and she's trying to squeeze in as many clients as she can before she takes the next couple of weeks off."

"Oh, shoot. Not good timing then. I was hoping I might consult with her as soon as possible."

"Hey, it's okay. When I get to Harbordale, I'll catch her between clients. I'll ask her if she could see you tomorrow. I'm sure she'll do this favor for me."

"I wouldn't want to impose on her time, especially with her wedding coming up, but the situation I'm dealing with is rather urgent."

"Being as psychic as Libby is, she probably already knows you're coming."

"I'd really appreciate the help."

"I know she has one reading tomorrow. I'll see what I can do and call you as soon as I find out."

"Wonderful. I'll wait for your call."

"Okay, then. I've got to get going. My lover boy beckons."

Kat had to chuckle at Ellen's final comment. Ellen was one of those people who could lighten anyone's mood. She was always so cheerful and upbeat, especially since she'd divorced her two-timing husband and taken up with a high school admirer. When Ellen engaged Kat to sell her house, Kat heard all about her unhealthy marriage because Ellen loved to tell all.

Kat despised waiting for anything, least of all a phone call, but she had no choice. To put her time to good use, she placed a load of whites in the washing machine and went into the living room to fold the bedding that was strewn on the couch. She'd just finished doubling the blanket when the phone rang.

Before she had time to say hello, Stella blurted, "Did Dad call?"

During a long pause, Kat could feel her heartache. "No, honey. I'm sorry."

"Do you have any more ideas about finding him?"

Kat couldn't confide in Stella about the visions or the dreams she was having, at least not yet. Stella had enough to think about. "I might go to Harbordale this weekend to talk with someone who might be able to help us."

"Who is it? Do I know the person? Does Dad know him?"

"No. Neither of you knows her. She's actually a friend of one of my clients."

"Is she a detective or something?"

"I'll tell you about it when I get back."

"When are you going?"

"I'm waiting for a phone call, but hopefully tomorrow morning."

"I want to go with you," Stella said. "I had this camping trip planned with my roommates this weekend, and we were going to be gone till late Sunday night, but I don't think I should go anywhere until I know if Dad's okay."

"Stella, I really don't think you should change your plans. We don't have a clue where your dad is, and until we know something more, all we can do is wait. Tell me where you'll be, and if anything comes up or I hear from your father, I'll contact you. My friend knows a policeman in Harbordale, and if need be he'll help me get a message to you. And if you can, call me anytime on your cell. Okay? And when you get back, I'll tell you what I find out."

"All right, but we won't be very far away, only about thirty miles at a state park. We were going to go up near Mount Rainier, but I'd rather stay closer just in case."

"That might be wise."

Stella gave Kat the location of the campground. "Promise you'll call if you hear from him."

"You'll be the first to know. Now go have fun. Take your mind off this."

After reassuring Stella one last time, Kat spent the next hour reading emails from clients. It would have been so easy to answer the questions posed to her, but Maggie had insisted Kat stay completely detached from work. Maggie had access to her account, and Kat trusted her to take care of things. Even Kat's phone messages were being forwarded to Maggie.

Kat was having a difficult time concentrating anyway, so she grabbed her gardening gloves from the mudroom and continued out to the front yard. She left the door ajar and laid the cell phone she used for personal calls on the porch step. Her garden fork lay in the dirt where she'd left it a few weeks ago.

The neglected flower beds were in desperate need of weeding. Methodically, she moved down the row of geraniums, loosening the dirt and pulling out the grass and weeds that threatened to take over.

Except for the freeway drone and her neighbor's sprinkler swishing next door, the neighborhood was unusually quiet. Every once in a while Kat stopped to check the time. Chance never left her thoughts. Waiting for yet another call was agonizing. When she was nearly done with the first bed, she tore off her gloves to answer the ringing phone.

"Kat, it's me, Ellen. I've got good news for you. Libby agreed to meet with you tomorrow morning around elevenish. The thing is, she's doing a phone reading before she sees you and can't say how long it will last, for reasons she couldn't tell me, so maybe you could meet me at the Starbucks downtown around 10:30. She'll call when she's done, and I can take you out to her house. She wants me to be there to answer the door. You see, Kipp and Kelly are coming down from Port Anderson, and we're all going on a picnic."

"It sounds very complicated. Maybe it's not a good time."

"Oh no, she wants to see you. She *needs* to see you. She's so good. She can sense a problem a mile off. Just meet me at Starbucks. It'll all work out. Do you know where the downtown Starbucks is?"

"I'll figure it out."

After Kat hung up, she went back to her gardening project in hopes of hurrying the day and wearing herself out, but once she was in bed Friday night she couldn't sleep well. She kept waking and glancing at the clock, waiting for Saturday to arrive.

CHAPTER 10

From Seattle, the town of Harbordale was a straight shot south on the freeway. On a warm, sunny Saturday, traffic through the city could be as busy as a weekday morning, and on this Saturday that was exactly how Kat found it.

To gain momentum she moved into the passing lane but couldn't break out of the pack until after she'd passed the old Rainier Brewery. It didn't help that her nerves were already on edge not only because of Chance but also because of her pending meeting with Libby.

Though Kat had certainly had her own experience with the paranormal, she'd never been to a psychic. And from what Ellen had told her, Libby had quite a reputation for zeroing in to the heart of the matter. She was also extremely accurate in extracting the details of a situation and providing answers. On numerous occasions the police had used her services to find missing children. With a psychic of Libby's caliber, Kat had high hopes of finding Chance.

In Harbordale, the town at the end of the inlet, Kat took the parking spot of a Prius that was pulling out in front of Starbucks. As she walked up to the corner shop, a truck stopped at the light, and Ellen leaned over, gave the driver a kiss, and got out to meet Kat. Ellen was casually dressed in shorts and a tank top in contrast to Kat's more conservative slacks and blouse.

"Hey, Kat. Let's go down the block to a local coffee shop. It's bigger and not so crowded."

Upon entering the B & B Coffee Shop, Kat was hit with a blast of rich coffee aroma. The shop was twice as big as Starbucks, had an eclectic mix of funky furniture, and its walls were decorated with artwork by local artists.

After they'd ordered and were seated at a tiny table for two, Kat said, "You're really getting to know this town, aren't you?"

"I love it. It's so much more relaxing than the city, plus my hunk of burning love is here." With a palm patting her chest, Ellen sighed.

"So things are going okay for you two."

"You better believe it. And as soon as the house sells, I'm heading straight here. Besides, Libby, my very best friend in the world, lives here."

"Are you sure she's okay with seeing me today?"

"Oh sure. She's pretty straightforward about these things. If it were a problem, she'd tell me." Ellen bit into the croissant she'd purchased. "Mmm...I shouldn't be eating this. I need to lose weight in the worst way, but it's so hard when you're in love, don't you think? Oh, don't answer that. You're just like Libby. You're both enviously thin."

Kat found Ellen's upbeat nature and funny comments engaging. She certainly had a way of lightening up Kat's day. "From what you've told me about Charlie, he likes you just the way you are."

"Yeah, he sure does." Ellen took another bite. "Do you think the house will sell? I can't wait to move."

"I can't predict how soon, but you're in a good neighborhood, near good schools."

"I'm wondering if I should rent. I know there are a lot of good people who have to leave their homes because they can't afford the payments and they have to rent."

"That's true, but don't give up too soon. We just sold a house not too far from yours on Wilson Street. You've been in your house a long time and don't have much of a house payment, so you can afford to wait a while. Hopefully, the open house will spark some interest."

"You sound like Libby. When I asked her about it, she said to be patient."

"I think that's wise advice." Kat sat back, sipped her coffee, and let the clatter of dishes, the hiss of the coffee machines, and the rise and fall of the voices around her enter her awareness. Customers were entering and exiting the shop or were crowding around the counter.

"So, what brings you down here to see Libby? I know you can't tell me the details. That's a rule Libby has, but is there anything you can share in a general sort of way? You said it was urgent."

"Because of the circumstances I probably shouldn't discuss it. But I don't mean to be rude."

"No big deal," Ellen said. "And you don't have to worry about Libby telling me anything about your situation after you leave. She never talks about her clients' problems. She has oodles of integrity."

The ring of Ellen's cell phone was barely audible over the din of the coffee shop. For a minute or so, she carried on a conversation, then chucked the phone into her purse. "Libby said we can come now. She finished early. That's what she said might happen. She's so good."

With Ellen in the passenger seat rattling off directions to Libby's house, Kat drove the five miles through the countryside via the back roads. At the end of a gravel driveway was a modest rambler, nestled in the woods.

Kat couldn't imagine living secluded this way, but once she was outside, she realized just how peaceful the surroundings were: no highway noise; birds twittering in the fir trees; the air with a fresh, renewing quality about it.

Libby was on the porch, dressed in cotton slacks and a magenta blouse. Ellen said she was enviously thin, but Kat had no idea how different yet remarkable this woman was, though not a beauty in the classic sense. Her overall appearance, her chin-swept dark hair, and her shapely figure were pretty, but were secondary to her unusual blue eyes. They had a transparency about them that held one captive.

Then Libby's body shimmered in colorful lights, catching Kat by surprise. She glanced away, and when she looked at Libby again, Libby's form appeared normal, solid.

Libby smiled. "You must be Kat. I've been expecting you."

Kat felt an immediate connection to this woman, though she hardly knew why.

Ellen nudged her forward. "Go ahead. She won't bite."

"I'm sorry. I thought I saw...Oh, never mind. I guess I'm just a little anxious."

"Have you ever been to an intuitive counselor before?"

"Not really."

"Please, come in. Like Ellen said, I won't bite. Once we get started, you'll relax. I'll get you a glass of water before we go down to my office. Ellen, will you answer the phone if it rings? It might be Kipp."

"Sure thing, sweetie."

While Libby was in the kitchen, Kat spotted the signs of a child's presence: on a rocking chair, a Barbie doll; on the window seat, a little girl's sweater; near the leg of the soft beige sofa, a pair of tiny sandals. "Does Libby have a little girl?"

"She might as well have," Ellen said as she closed the front door. "Actually, it's Kipp who has a daughter. In fact they'll probably be here before you leave."

Libby handed Kat a glass of ice water. "Shall we go?"

Kat followed her down the hallway to a room that had been converted into an office, its walls painted in warm pink. Libby asked Kat to sit in a baby blue recliner while she took her place near her desk in a straight back chair. She left the lights off. "Are you comfortable? Do you want me to turn the air-conditioning down?"

"No, I'm fine," Kat said, but inwardly she found this situation as awkward as a first date.

"I'll be honest with you," Libby said. "Most of the time I'm able to keep from keying in to a client's issues until they get here, but ever since I knew you were coming, I've been bombarded with information. It's as if your guides were already preparing me for this visit. So, after I say a little prayer, I want to convey what I've been sensing. Is that all right with you?"

"Whatever you want to do, but I do have some questions."

"Yes, I know, but maybe all your questions will be answered. Let me say a prayer first." Libby closed her eyes and asked the Light that already surrounded them to offer added protection.

With her luminous eyes opened again, she gazed at Kat. "I have to say, there's something critical about this issue not only because you told Ellen it was urgent but the energy surrounding it is strong, powerful." She paused, letting her gaze drift to a spot near Kat's shoulder. "Is there someone in your life who has passed on relatively recently?"

"Well, yes."

"A sister. She's standing next to you. She has a really cute hairstyle. Like this." Libby pretended to rake her hair forward around her face. "She says you've seen her many times. Is that right?"

A prickly sensation edged up the back of Kat's neck, spurring a shiver. She nodded at Libby.

"She wants you to know how much she loves you. She wants you to stop blaming yourself for everything. Nothing was your fault. Does this make sense?"

From the box near her chair, Kat reached for a tissue. Surprised at what was happening, she hadn't expected Brianna to come through like this. "I was such a bad sister. When we were young, I left her alone with an uncle, a terrible man. And later I couldn't help her."

"She wants you to let that go. She's happy now. Blaming yourself doesn't serve you."

Kat fought for control but couldn't stop sniffling. "She's been coming to me in dreams."

"Yes, and she'll be with you always. She's trying to help you with your current problem, but she also wants to help you accept your intuitive abilities." Libby zeroed in on Kat. "When I look at you, I see you with a heavy cloak wrapped around you with a hood no less, as if you're trying to keep from experiencing the rain or the cold or the wind. To me, this is symbolic of your trying to keep what's natural from touching you. And there's nothing more natural than the energy that surrounds you. You have a psychic gift. I suspect you've had it since you were a little girl, but to keep it at bay, you've wrapped yourself in a protective cocoon. I'm here to tell you, it's as natural as breathing, if you'll allow it."

"It started up after Brianna's death. It went away for a while, but now it's coming back again. When I first saw you outside, I saw lights all around you. It was beautiful, but what I see is not always so pleasant."

"Sometimes it isn't," Libby said. "Your sister's transition wasn't easy because of the trauma. Because of your connection to her and your sensitivities, you probably picked up on that. She's at peace now. And what I want to reiterate is that your sister is here to help you. When you need her, talk to her as if she's standing next to you, because she is."

"I saw her last night, and as I said she's come to me in my dreams."

"Let's talk about those dreams."

"That's why I came here, but I can't recall the details, maybe a couple of things."

"What I've been sensing about your situation since you arrived is that there is someone in trouble. Brianna's hand is over her heart, and she tells me it's someone you care about deeply. Is this person dear to you?"

"Yes. His name is Chance."

"And I'm also sensing there's some kind of secrecy attached to this person. I feel there's a veil over the situation. I'm not sure what it is. Does this make sense?"

"Very much so. He used to work for..."

Libby touched her finger to her lips, stopping Kat from completing her sentence. "That isn't important now. They're telling me the reason he's there is not as vital as finding him. There's an urgency about it. So, talk about the dream."

"There was this room."

"Tell me about the room."

"I don't remember much. It was just a room in a house of some sort."

"Kat, I think I can help you remember more. If it's all right with you, I'd like to bring you into more of a relaxed state of mind and then prompt you with questions."

Kat hesitated. "Okay, I guess."

"Don't worry. It's just easier to remember when your mind is calm and clear. So, sit back and make yourself comfortable. Close your eyes."

Kat complied with Libby's request but fought the urge to argue about the purpose of doing this when the situation warranted immediate attention. Why didn't Libby just tell her what she wanted to know?

"Take a deep breath in and exhale completely. Now concentrate on your breathing until you feel calm and relaxed."

For several minutes Kat focused on her breath, breathing in and out, in and out, waiting for the sound of Libby's voice.

After what for Kat seemed like hours, Libby finally said, "I'm going to ask you questions, and we'll see where this goes. Now go back into the scene with the room and tell me what you see."

As Libby talked in a whispered tone, Kat's muscles softened, and an ease spread through her. It was as if she were being gently rocked into relaxation. "There was a room. But it was different than any room in my house."

"In what way?"

"It was kind of dark inside."

"Were there any colors or shapes you remember? Anything unusual about the room?"

"It just seemed dark, like maybe the lighting was dim."

"Anything else?"

"Yes. Now I see something. There were these round, dark-looking shapes, like logs. That's right. At the time, I remember thinking it might have been a log cabin."

"What else do you see?"

"The windows were covered with wooden slats or something, not curtains, and there was a sofa in the room. Yes, and Chance was standing near the sofa, looking out the window. It's coming back to me." Kat's stomach knotted. "There was a woman with him. She was standing behind him, hugging him at the waist. I know that woman, and I couldn't believe she was there with him. I've seen pictures, too." She fidgeted with a tissue.

"Kat, take a deep breath and listen to me. It's just a dream. It's symbolic. Notice he has his back to her. That indicates to me she means nothing to him. You are still uppermost in his thoughts. Now let's concentrate on how we can help him. Take another breath and go deeper into the scene. What else do you see?"

Kat dried the corners of her eyes and took another cleansing breath. "All I remember is the front of the cabin and the letter M. I don't know what that means."

"What else do you see?"

"Just the door and the letter."

"Look around you, observe where you are."

Kat grasped for details in a long, drawn-out pause. "Nothing comes to me."

"What color is the door?"

"I'm not sure. Maybe a dark color, like the walls inside."

"Do you notice anything else? Any sounds?"

Another minute elapsed before Kat responded. "Birds. I can hear birds."

"What does the air smell like?"

"I don't know."

"What do you sense? Is it pleasing or are there city smells?"

"It's definitely not in the city. It feels more like a fresh, woodsy smell. There are trees close by, like it's in a forest."

"Okay. Tell me about the letter M. What is your impression?"

"All I know is the name of the woman in the dream is Monique. My best friend's name is Maggie. It's all very confusing."

"Is there anything unusual about the letter M on the door? Look closely."

Kat scanned the image in her mind's eye. "I can't see anything different about it."

"Why would Brianna be helping you? What is it you want to know?"

"I want to know where he is."

"Then don't you think Brianna would give you clues to finding him? Look closely at the letter M. Look at the contours."

Kat scrutinized the scene again and followed the outline of the letter M until she reached the end of the last vertical line. "There's a small 'e' tacked onto it. I don't understand. I didn't see it before."

"If Brianna's trying to tell you where he is, what do those letters mean to you?"

"M-e means me, I guess."

"Think location, Kat."

Kat thought a moment. "The only thing I can come up with is Maine. M-e is what the post office uses for that state's abbreviation."

"Take a deep breath, then slowly open your eyes and come back into the room."

Kat felt like napping, not opening her eyes. When she finally did, Libby was smiling at her. "Could Chance be in Maine? That's so far away," Kat said.

"I feel that he is."

"If you knew that all along, why did you make me go through this long, drawn-out exercise? Why couldn't you just tell me?"

"Take a drink of water. You've done some outstanding work."

"You haven't answered my question."

"The reason Brianna didn't make it clear to you was because you needed to come here."

"But why?"

"Because I needed to show you how easy it is for you to get your own answers," Libby said. "You are very intuitive, and you have great visualization abilities. The key is to relax and ask for the answers. They'll come to you. My sense is that you are always running from morning till night, not just literally. Your mind is always ticking away. The key to getting in touch with your intuitive side is to learn to quiet yourself so you can tune in. Brianna and your other spirit helpers will talk to you if you'll listen."

Libby was spot-on with her observations. Kat did have a hard time slowing down; she was always on the go, both physically and mentally.

"Now, we know your man is in the state of Maine," Libby said. "This is what I got while I was working with you. I felt my body lean forward, and that indicates north, so he's somewhere in the northern section of Maine. The letters P and I came to me. The town has two names to it, and I feel he is near this town."

Libby paused a moment. "I see the number 20 on a fence post. Look twenty miles from the town, somewhere in the woods in a log cabin. You must travel there as soon as possible. I sense he won't be there much longer. It's important you look for him now because I sense danger."

"But this is all so vague, Libby. I don't even know where to start."

"Get a map of Maine and follow the interstate north. The town will jump out at you. You'll know when you see it. The cabin is good-sized. I saw many windows in it. And when you get to the town, ask around. You'll be led. If things get confusing, take the time to get quiet and ask for your answers. They'll come to you."

"Will I find him?"

"When I tune in to the overall picture, there's a fog around it, meaning it's not crystal clear to me. For reasons unknown, I'm not being given all the answers. What I will say is there will be obstacles and false starts, but you have to try."

Libby looked off into the distance, then back to Kat. "What I'm getting is your trying will bring him hope and a will to break the hold. And that will be the purpose of your going." She closed her eyes and said a thank-you prayer, then rose from her chair.

Kat took out her checkbook and paid Libby her hourly fee. "I think you have more faith in me than I do."

"You'll get through this." Libby opened the door to the hallway, and a child's laughter drifted in from the outer room. Libby's face radiated love. "Kipp and Kelly are here. You can meet my sweethearts." She stopped Kat before Kat left the room. "If you ever have questions about how to deal with your intuitive gift, call me anytime."

"You may just hear from me."

Libby led the way into the living room where an adorable blond-haired girl raced into Libby's opened arms. When the girl saw Kat, she hid behind Libby. "This nice lady's name is Kat. Tell Kat your name."

Kelly peeked around Libby, then inched forward. "My name's Kelly, and I'm seven years old."

"You're a very pretty seven-year-old," Kat said.

Kelly pulled at the hem of her shorts. "I have new pants, and we're going on a picnic."

"That sounds like fun."

"We're going to a park downtown near the lake," Libby said. "I'd invite you to join us, but I know you need to take care of business."

"I wish you could come," Ellen said. "It would be just super having you along."

Male voices sounded from outside. A tall, burly gentleman came through the doorway, carrying a medium-sized box with a bag of tortilla chips on top. "Should I bring this in?"

"Uncle Charlie!" Kelly dashed to Charlie's side.

"Hi, Kelly."

"Move out of his way, honey, so he can put the box down," Libby said.

"Hey, big boy." After Charlie deposited the box in the foyer, Ellen gave him a peck on the cheek.

A man of medium height with blondish-red hair came in after Charlie, and Kelly took him by the hand. "This is my daddy. His name is Kipp and he's forty-something."

"Hey, don't tell all your daddy's secrets."

"Out of the mouth of babes," Ellen said. "This is my realtor, Kat Summers. I was hoping you'd all get to meet her."

Charlie wiped a hand on his Hawaiian shirt and extended it to Kat. "I've heard a lot about you. If you can't sell Ellen's house, nobody can."

"We're trying our best."

Kipp shook hands with Kat, then slipped an arm around Libby. "I see you've already met my beautiful bride-to-be."

"Yes, and she's quite amazing. You're very lucky."

"She gave me my life back. I owe her everything."

"That's for sure," Ellen said. "But living with a woman like Libby, he's going to have to mind his p's and q's. He won't be able to get away with anything."

"She's got that right," Charlie said.

Libby's face reddened. "Oh, you two."

"That's a chance I'm more than willing to take," Kipp said.

Kelly tugged on Kipp's hand. "Can we go now?"

"Kelly, you have to be patient," Kipp said.

"I won't hold up your picnic any longer," Kat said. "I really need to get going myself. It was nice meeting you all."

"My daddy and Libby are getting married. Can you come to the wedding?"

"That's an excellent idea," Libby said. "We'll see about that later. Now let's let Kat be on her way. She's got important things to do."

Kat followed Libby out on the porch. "Kelly's quite a talker, but I'm certainly not expecting a wedding invitation."

"I feel a real kinship with you, Kat, and I'd love for you to come," Libby said. "And listen. Remember what I said. Don't hesitate to contact me. I'm here to help." She latched on to Kat's arm. "Make your airline reservations as soon as possible. More than anything right now, he needs to feel your presence around him. It will give him hope."

Kat gave Libby an affirmative nod, though at this point Kat wasn't quite sure what Libby meant. There seemed to be no guarantee how this would all play out. It was as if she were leaving Libby's with more questions than answers. Nevertheless, on the way home, Kat labored to put together a plan.

CHAPTER 11

On Sunday Monique rose early. There were no signs that Chance was up and around: no coffee aroma permeating the hallway, no dishes rattling, only birdsong and the murmur of voices from outside. She glanced out the window. The two men assigned to guard the cabin were talking and having a morning cigarette near the adjoining bunkhouse.

She slipped on her robe, wandered down the hall to Chance's room, and tapped on the door before pushing it open. As far as she could tell, by the steady, rhythmic rise and fall of his chest, he was still asleep. Even in slumber, he excited her.

Love was too weak a word to describe her feelings for this man. If only Philip hadn't sent her overseas so many times while Chance was in Rosswood and she'd had more opportunities to meet with him, she could have convinced him how much she cared for him and wanted him back in her life.

Philip knew what he was doing by keeping them apart. He knew she'd leave the firm in a second if Chance had wanted her to. But the firm wasn't her only obstacle. It was another woman. She couldn't lose him to another woman. She had to keep trying to win his affections. Failure meant answering to Philip, but it also meant answering to her heart.

As she tiptoed across the room, he turned over, and she stopped and waited for him to settle down. She removed her robe and slipped into the bed, hoping she could coax him into having sex.

With a sleepy sigh, he cuddled close, then planted his lips on hers. He nuzzled her neck and whispered Kat's name.

Monique drew back. "Oh no, darling, it is your lover of many years. I want to be with you." To keep him from moving away, she placed his hand on her breast. "You cannot stop once you feel the pleasure of touching me. You will remember the love we had together."

"Is this what you want?" He began caressing her, spurring those familiar tingly sensations.

"Oh, yes. Make love to me as you have done in the past, Chance, over and over again." When he leaned down, and she felt his lips on her breast, she gasped. "Oh, Chance, keep going. I have waited so long to have you."

He slid his hand down her backside, pressing her closer. "Do you want me even if I don't love you?"

What he said hurt, but if they continued down this path she was certain she could change his mind. "I know you will remember how it was between us."

"You're willing to take that chance?"

"Oh yes." The feel of his touch was too much to bear. She grasped his shoulders and pulled him upward, but instead of holding her he swiftly took hold of her arms and braced them over her head. She sucked in a breath. "I know you can love me. I know it. Please, come to me, my sweet. I beg you."

He whispered in her ear, "If I make love to you, will you promise to get me out of here?"

Her body went limp. In her profession this type of ploy had been used countless times: special favors for sex. Only, she'd been the one doing the asking. This wasn't something she would ever have expected from Chance. "You know I cannot do what you ask. I would be jeopardizing my own life."

"I thought you loved me."

"But you love another."

He rolled off of her. "It was worth a try. I should have known where your allegiance lies."

She scrambled from the bed. She wrapped up in her robe, head lowered, avoiding eye contact. "It does not have to be this way, Chance. It is your call. You know my feelings. I will be downstairs making our breakfast." She fled to the hallway and leaned against the wall. The tears flowed easily. Chance was the only man who could spur this reaction in her.

In the kitchen she took out a carton of eggs and poured water in the coffee maker, but serving a meal was the furthest thing from her mind. She felt torn between her love for Chance and the only job she'd ever known. Leaving the firm would be suicide, but giving up Chance was as lethal as driving a stake through her heart. Not much of a choice. Not much of a life.

There was a knocking against the window. One of the guards held up a cell phone and motioned for her to come outside. He unlocked and opened the door for her. She tightened the ties on her robe and stepped onto the porch. The sun was peeking through the trees, promising to warm the crisp morning air.

"I think you'll want to take this."

"Is it Philip? Who else would call here?"

"It's your sister."

Monique grabbed the phone. "Who is this?"

The voice on the line replied, "It is Paulette."

For privacy Monique walked to the end of the porch. "Why do you call me here?"

"I talked to Philip. I had to tell you. Michel is ill."

"What is wrong, Paulette? Hurry. Tell me."

"I could not reach you before. I took him to emergency. I thought he had a touch of pneumonia. He could not breathe right. I was so frightened. You must come home."

"Yes, of course. I will see what I can do. We will talk soon." She ended the call.

The guard took the phone from her. "Clean up and pack an overnight bag. Philip told me he'll have the plane ready for you. You're to meet with him Monday morning." He let her back into the cabin.

She rushed upstairs and ran into Chance in the hallway. "I must hurry."

"You don't look well. What is it?"

"I must dress. Soon I am leaving for Boston. I will return in a day or two."

Chance followed her to her room where, without bothering to conceal herself, she shed her robe and picked out underwear and a pair of cotton pants and a T-shirt. She dressed and ran a brush through her thick, shaggy hair. All she could think about was Michel's welfare.

"I'm not used to seeing you in clothes like this. Everything you wear is always so provocative."

"You do not know everything about me, Chance."

While she packed her suitcase, he leaned against the doorjamb. "So, Philip snaps his fingers, and you snap to attention like a trained animal. Aren't you sick of it?"

She zipped up her bag and stared at Chance, her eyes searing into his. "You know nothing of what I do. And what do you care anyway? My sister, Paulette, has a child to care for. He is very ill, and I must go to them. I am their only support."

Chance stepped aside to let her pass through the doorway. He trailed her downstairs. "Monique, I had no idea."

She set her bag by the door. "I will forgive you that, but I cannot forgive how you treat me. I have loved you many years."

"I'm sorry, Monique. I loved you once, but I've moved on."

"I see that is so."

"I hope the child gets better."

"Between Paulette and me he will be cared for." She picked up her bag and rapped on the door. She was let outside.

Over gravel roads through thickly forested land past the entry gate and onto the asphalt arterial, Monique's thoughts rocketed between Michel and Chance. First and foremost was Michel's wellbeing, but her feelings for Chance wormed their way in, and she mourned the loss of their loving familiarity. Yet she would still have more time with him on their overseas assignment. The longer he was away from Kat Summers, the greater the chance she would win him back.

The men guarding Chance were privy to Monique's assignment, and at one point when she and the driver slowed through the town of Ashford, he asked if she was having any luck with Chance. She kept that information private.

***

After Monique left, Chance went back to his room and paced. On a whim, he slid his hand behind the headboard and felt a rise in the wood. He yanked out a listening device. Just as he thought; they were capturing his and Monique's conversations and intimate moments. Perverted bastards. He crushed the device with his boot. He made a sweep of the room but found nothing else.

If Monique wouldn't help him escape this prison, he'd do it himself. They hadn't barred the upstairs windows, and the window frames were just wide enough to squeeze through.

Looking out, he calculated the roof's pitch. It was too far of a jump from a second story window, but directly below him was the porch. If he could somehow make it to the overhang, he could crawl to the eaves and lower himself down. All he had to do now was find a way to ferry himself from the upstairs window to the overhang.

CHAPTER 12

Kat had taken a nonstop red-eye to Boston on Saturday night. During the flight, besides capturing a few hours of sleep, she'd studied the highway map of Maine and found her destination: Post Island, the only town with two names beginning with the letters P and I. Though the town wasn't surrounded by water, as its name suggested, it *was* in the middle of nowhere.

About twenty miles to the west of Post Island was a spec on the map called Ashford. Kat couldn't fathom why Libby was sending her to this obscure, out-of-the-way town, but Kat sensed an authenticity about Libby and had faith in Libby's impressions. By seeking Libby's counsel, Kat was beginning to trust her own instincts.

On the flight north from Boston to Post Island, she dozed and was jerked awake when the plane's only flight attendant announced their imminent arrival. The land encircling the town consisted of rolling hills and clumps of trees, both deciduous and evergreen. To the west, as far as the eye could see, was a heavily forested area, a beautiful but desolate landscape.

Kat took her turn, along with twenty other passengers, down the plank of stairs onto the tarmac. The morning air was nippier than in Boston or Seattle, the breeze brisk and held a chill. The terminal, a building the size of a large post office, was a short distance away. Kat felt the isolation settling in. Before she went inside, the squeal of a jet engine caught her attention. Taxiing on the runway in preparation for take-off was a private Learjet. She couldn't help wondering how many high-rollers flew into this remote region and for what possible reason.

In the musty-smelling terminal, a few people were waiting to board the plane back to Boston. She noticed a young mother and her temperamental toddler, both battling for the upper hand. These were the times Kat was thankful she wasn't a parent.

She stepped up to the Avis rental car counter, produced her credit card, and asked for a compact car. The attendant, a man of slight build with coarse, untamed hair and a congenial smile took his time punching in the required information. His mug steamed with coffee, and Kat longed for a cup but saw nothing but a nearby vending machine.

When the attendant finished, he handed her the paperwork and the keys. "Are you headed into town, miss?"

"Actually, no. I'm on my way to Ashford. Could you tell me which road to get on?"

"Yep." He pointed the way from the terminal. "If you turn right, then left, you'll be going the right way. You got family in these parts?"

"No."

"You must be visiting a private party off in the woods."

"I'm not really familiar with this area, but I *am* looking for someone who may be at a cabin in the woods around here."

He grinned. "You *don't* know much about this area. You see, the forest around here is all privately owned, either by the timber industry or private parties. Most of those people have cabins, so you might be looking for a needle in a haystack. When you get to Ashford, go see the old gatekeeper. He might be able to help you."

"And who's that?"

"There's an association that keeps a kind of order up here. There are various checkpoints. You have to pay to use the roads. Keeps the riffraff out. It's kind of a protection for the owners. You talk to the old gatekeeper. He can help you. Oh, and you might want to think about staying the night in Post Island. There's not much in Ashford." He held out a business card. "Nice motel."

Kat took the card, though she hoped later she and Chance would be on a plane back to Boston. She found the rental Ford and set her bag in the backseat.

Heading toward Ashford, she was surprised that in this part of the country the narrow roads were even paved. The roadways dipped and turned over rolling hills, which were sparsely populated with clumps of evergreens, ash, and maple. Only two cars passed from the opposite direction.

To Kat, the dinky town of Ashford represented the end of the world not only because of its location but also because from here she had no real plan. Libby said to ask around about a cabin in the woods. Could that description be any more general? And where would Kat find this gatekeeper? The rental car attendant hadn't even given her his name. Subtle doubts about Libby's judgment were beginning to creep in, and Kat longed to turn around and go home.

Ashford consisted of two blocks of weathered wooden structures. On her first pass through, she spotted a store, a cafe, and hole-in-the-wall bank. On her second trip through, she slowed in front a building housing The Woods Association. On the door hung a CLOSED sign. Now what? She motored on and parked in front of Al's General Store, the only business around with a congregation of trucks, all heavily coated with dust.

Inside, the store was larger than it appeared from the street and had numerous well-stocked shelves. On the far wall were dry goods and hunting supplies, such as fishing tackle and hunting vests. Above the proprietor, a paunchy gentleman with a white crew cut and beard and a snake tattoo on his bicep, was a trophy head of a black bear. A woman wearing overalls and a ball cap had just finished at the counter. She hefted a large grocery bag in her arms and passed by Kat on her way out.

"What can I do for ya?" the proprietor asked Kat as she lingered nearby.

"I'm looking for someone who may have come this way recently." From her purse she produced a picture of Chance in his cowboy hat, taken in front of her house. "His name is Chance Eliason."

The man studied the photo. "Can't say that I've seen him. Of course, a lot of folks come through these parts on their way to hunting camps. Some stop, some don't."

"Actually, I heard he was at a private cabin. All I know is it's a fairly large building, has lots of windows."

"A lot of places fit that description. Whereabouts is this cabin supposed to be?"

"I don't know for sure. Maybe I could have a look around."

The man chuckled. "Miss, these cabins aren't in any one place, like in some cul-de-sac in the city. They're scattered all through these woods. You have to know where you're going."

Kat's patience was wearing thin, along with her resolve to locate the cabin. "Someone told me to talk to the gatekeeper. Where can I find him?"

"Oh well, it's Sunday. He's probably off fishing somewhere." He stroked his beard and thought a moment. "On the other hand he could walk right in here."

The image of a hamster running in a wheel flashed in Kat's mind. She took a calming breath.

A younger man came into the store, picked up a newspaper, and laid it on the counter. "Hey, Ted."

Kat left them talking and slipped outside to regroup. She sat in her car, parked next to a mud-caked 4 x 4. She was getting nowhere fast and beginning to get an unsettled feeling. If Brianna wanted to help, where was she now?

Libby had told Kat to get quiet and ask for answers. Easy for her to say. Nevertheless, Kat adjusted the seat, laid her head back, and closed her eyes. The sunlight, filtering through the windows, warmed her body, and she drifted near the edge of sleep. She heard a vehicle drive by, a mosquito's high-pitched hum somewhere in the car, and the faint sound of voices that faded into the void. But in Kat's mind nothing was happening, not even an image of Brianna's face. Kat pleaded, "What am I supposed to do now?"

In the space of a minute, the name Topping popped into her head. Kat's eyes shot open. "Topping. What about Topping?" Then she heard the word *ask*.

She hurried into the store where the two men were still gabbing. Their conversation centered on hunting.

The proprietor turned to Kat. "Thought you'd left."

"Do you know anyone by the name of Philip Topping?"

"Sure. He's a regular up here. Likes a good bear hunt."

"Does he have a cabin around here? I'm sure that's where my friend is."

"He might, but I don't know exactly. If your friend's there, you can call and get directions. A cell tower was put up a while back for all these big time hunters. Can't seem to get away from technology, even in the woods. Sorry I can't help you." He and the younger man exchanged looks that had Kat wondering if she were the brunt of some inside joke.

She picked up a local area map of the roads leading into the woods. Without skipping a beat, the clerk took her money and continued talking to the younger man, even as she walked away.

She sat in her car and examined the map. From Ashford two arterials led into the forest with several roads branching off each one. Which road then? Libby's method of getting information had worked before, so Kat closed her eyes and tried silencing her mind, but a loud tap startled her out of her quiet space.

The younger man from inside was cranking his hand, gesturing for her to roll down her window. He had a heavy beard and dark glasses. "I heard you ask about Philip Topping's place. Don't mind Ted. He's pretty leery of people he doesn't know, but he warms up after a while. He's protective of the landowners. Now, don't get me wrong. He likes us regular folks, but we call him the gatekeeper. He's the head of an association trying to protect the woods, but if you ask me, all it's doing is catering to the rich guys. Maybe I can help you."

"Do you know where Topping's cabin is?"

"I'm fairly new up here, so I'm not exactly sure of the location, but I've heard talk about what road it's on. Let me see your map." While he held it in place, he traced the direction along one of the main roads. "There's a checkpoint you'll stop at to pay a day fee. And that's another thing's stuck in my craw. These woods should be open to everyone, not only to the people who can pay." He shrugged. "Ah...never mind. Keep going down this street and turn right at the sign. That will get you on the right road."

"Thanks." Kat laid the map on the adjoining seat while the man climbed into the filthy 4 x 4 and pulled out.

So, the storekeeper was also the gatekeeper. She should have known. Philip Topping probably paid him to keep quiet about his property. In spite of them, she was determined to find Chance.

After leaving Ashford and stopping to pay the ten-dollar-a-day fee, she continued deeper into the forested land. She'd wanted to talk to the man at the checkpoint, but he was already listening to a pair of campers relate a story about the moose they'd seen. She didn't have the patience to wait.

Traveling farther into the woods amidst the spruce and balsam fir, she found herself wondering what she was doing in the middle of nowhere and what would she do if she encountered a moose, or worse yet a bear. Her thoughts were on the probability of seeing a bear when rounding a corner she had to swerve to the side of the road to avoid an oncoming timber truck, enough of a scare to cause an adrenalin rush.

She stopped to compose herself and spotted a narrow gravel road. Following it, she realized she'd made an error in judgment. No cabins were anywhere in the vicinity. On her way back to the main road, a white-tailed deer darted across her path, and she had to slam on her brakes. What next?

At the intersection she checked the map. Her sense of direction was usually quite keen, but not in these woods where everything looked the same, where everything was hidden. It was as if she were in a maze of trees, meadows, and roads to nowhere. Still, if she had to go down every last one of these dirt byways, she'd do it. She drank the last of her bottled water and continued on under blue skies scattered with billowy clouds.

It seemed as if she'd been on these desolate roads for hours, and still no trace of Philip Topping's cabin, or any cabin for that matter. She'd driven up and down every gravel and dirt road she'd come across. Some were dead-ends. Some led to camping sites. All she could think of was she'd picked the wrong arterial. Perhaps the younger man at the general store had purposely steered her wrong. Perhaps Topping had paid him off, too.

She was about to circle back to Ashford when up ahead she saw a wooden sign painted with pictures of fish, bear, and deer surrounding the words "Porter Lake Camp." At the sign she turned right and followed the treed road that led to a large lake and a chalet-style cabin. Three 4 x 4s were parked out front.

She parked alongside a GMC pickup and got out to stretch her legs. The air was as pristine as pure oxygen. The sunlight shimmered off the water, and the gentle wind cascading across the lake was as chilly as an autumn breeze. Kat gathered her sweater and slipped it on.

Before she ventured inside, a gentleman, thickset and solid as an old stump, gingerly walked up to her, carrying a tackle box and a fishing pole. His white hair stuck out from under a ball cap. "Who are you looking for?"

Kat shielded her eyes from the sun's glare. "How did you know I was looking for anyone?"

"This is a private camp, and you have to have reservations to come here. I didn't see a woman's name on the books. I'm Walt, by the way. I own this place, along with my brother, Fred."

She moved sideways to the sun and introduced herself. "I'm trying to find a private cabin owned by Philip Topping. Do you know him?"

"Sure, I know Phil. He used to stay at this camp during bear hunting season. Owns his own property now, not too far from here."

"Can you give me directions to his place?"

His brows narrowed. "Haven't seen ol' Phil lately. Usually he stops by when he's around. Don't think he's here, though. You probably wasted a trip."

Kat could feel the man withdrawing. She had to think fast. "Look, I happened to come up here to visit an old friend in Post Island, and Philip told me I should check out this area and swing by to have a look at the cabin. I was just out for a drive."

Walt looked at her hard and long. "We all look after each other up in these parts. But if Phil said it was all right, then turn right at the main road and follow it about, oh, I'd say a couple of miles as the crow flies. It's on the other side of the lake but in the woods, oh, I'd say about three or four roads down that way, maybe five."

"Is there a sign with his name or a mailbox to look for?"

He smiled, shook his head. "Private owners don't advertise up here, miss. You'll just have to have a look. Never been there myself."

Since Kat had arrived here, she couldn't help feeling as if she'd been struck by the ol' boys' club and given the royal runaround. She thanked the man and drove back toward the Porter Lake Camp sign in search of Philip Topping's cabin.

***

Ever since Monique left for Boston earlier in the day, Chance had been racking his brain to find a way to escape. Instinct told him Philip had other plans for him—sinister plans. Even if he *did* find a way out, how would he get back to civilization? His only option, if he was lucky, was to flag down a passing logging truck barreling its way to town.

He paced the bedroom floor. Being confined like this was as stifling as the desert in summer. Back at the window he peered out at the forest. In every tree he saw Kat's face. In every bird's chirp he heard Kat's voice. He pictured her sitting beside him in his truck, his hand resting on her thigh. A comforting feeling coursed through his body. He could almost sense her presence. In the worst way, he want-

ed to be near her. He ran his hands through his hair. He couldn't live
without Kat. He had to find a way out.

He ball-parked the distance of the porch overhang and looked
around the room for an answer. His gaze lit on the bed. He lifted
the covers off the floor and examined the metal frame. He pulled
on one leg, testing its strength, then threw the bedspread back and
pulled off the top sheet. Every foot or so, he fashioned knots, making
the sheet rope-like, and tied the end securely around the leg. After
opening the window, he pushed the bed closer and tossed out the
makeshift rope. It fell halfway to the overhang.

He strode to Monique's room. When he tugged off the sheet
from her bed, the scent of Chanel, the scent of the woman he'd almost made love to, stabbed him with a sense of guilt. If he ever made
it out of here, he'd make it up to Kat.

He stormed from Monique's room, but her scent followed him
back to his room. Not only was it on the sheet but also on his hands
as well. He couldn't get away from her scent, or the guilt.

Focusing his attention again, he tied several knots on the second sheet, fastened the two sheets together, and yanked them hard,
tightening them. He cast the rope out the window. It tumbled down-
ward and reached just above the overhang.

Back in Monique's room he looked out the front window for
the guards. Earlier in the day the man who'd taken Monique to the
airport had returned, and now both men were nowhere in sight.
Chance rushed downstairs to see if they were on the porch and saw
them disappear into the bunkhouse. Now was the moment to act.

He raced upstairs. He grabbed the rope and climbed onto
the window ledge, turned, facing the building, and began to rappel
down. With no rubber-soled shoes provided, his boots slipped and
slid on the metal. He lost traction, fell forward, and the front of his
body banged flat against the hard surface of the roof. Attempting to
get a foothold, he lost his balance, let go of the rope, and slid, flattened to the metal toward the edge of the roof. He couldn't stop the
inevitable. To slow his descent, he grasped the gutter. As the gutter

broke loose with a cracking sound, he plummeted to the ground and rolled onto his back. The grass softened his landing.

Groaning, he pushed himself upright. Nothing seemed broken, but his body ached from the strain of the fall. He fisted his left hand and rolled his wrist. It felt weak and achy. His hands and arms were scraped and burned. Dirt clung to his shirt and jeans. But he had no time to dwell on his physical condition.

He surveyed the area, getting his bearings. The air was fresh and alive. A gray jay squawked in a nearby cedar. Just this little bit of freedom revitalized him.

His plan was to follow along the private drive in the shadow of the trees. He listened for any movement from the front of the cabin, but heard nothing. Satisfied, he set off across the yard and aimed for the woods behind the bunkhouse.

He tromped around fir, cedar, and spruce, swishing through a thick growth of bunchberry and wintergreen. A red squirrel scurried into the underbrush. The forest floor was swampy in places. He swatted the mosquitoes that hounded him. Once, he stopped to listen for the sound of voices. Satisfied no one was close by, he gauged the gate to be about a half mile from the cabin and kept on, though wading through these woods in cowboy boots was tough going. He didn't dare step out into plain sight. Finally, the gate became visible. It was camouflaged with large fir branches.

As he neared the end of the driveway, still shadowing it in the trees, a car slowly drove by. At the wheel was a woman with shoulder-length hair. Her profile bore a striking resemblance to Kat's. He could have sworn the woman was Kat. But that was impossible. Or was it? His heart pounded with expectation. In his fervent need for the driver to be Kat, he couldn't hear or see anything else. Letting his guard down, he shouted Kat's name and lurched into the open. In the middle of his shoulder blades, he felt the hard, cold barrel of a gun.

"Slowly turn around, and let's go," the man with the gun commanded, and his partner shoved Chance in the direction of the cabin.

Chance's first reaction was to push back, fight them both if he had to, or break for the woods. He wasn't about to give up his newly gained freedom, not when he'd just seen Kat. But another jab with the gun brought him back to reality. If he made either of those choices, he was as good as dead. He knew these thugs had their orders.

Mumbling between them, the men, one on either side of Chance, marched him down the gravelly path and up the porch steps. The burly man opened the door and gave him a healthy shove inside. Chance stopped the forward momentum of his fall by grasping the arm of the sofa. They urged him upstairs where the bald man held the gun on Chance and the other man took out a pocket knife and cut the sheet tied to the bed frame. He wadded up the rope and tossed it out the window.

The bald man nudged Chance with the gun. "Don't bother trying that stunt again."

"When is Monique due back?"

The burly man looked at Chance, a sly grin forming. "If you were smart, dude, you'd make it easy on yourself. Go along with the program and give her what she wants, a good fuck."

"Watch your filthy mouth."

"Hey, just giving you some advice. Come on, Terry." He and the other guard filed from the room and clomped downstairs. The door below banged shut.

Chance wandered to the window. Soon the men came around from the front and gathered the knotted sheet. The foul-mouthed one looked up at Chance and gave him the finger. Chance turned away, glad to be rid of them.

It was late afternoon, but deep in the forest it seemed darker and later than it really was. Chance went into the bathroom to wash the dirt from his superficial wounds. He splashed cool water on his face, slicked back his hair.

In the bedroom he changed into cleaner clothes. He lay on the bed, his hands clasped behind his head, and stared at the shadows on the wall. Kat inhabited his thoughts.

Had he imagined her in that car? No, it had to be her. He could feel it. She was capable and resourceful. If anyone could find him, she could. For the first time all day, he relaxed in the comfort of knowing she was out there looking for him. But at what cost?

***

After turning at the Porter Lake Camp sign, Kat had explored every offshoot of the main road but only came upon camping sites or dead-ends, same as before, except a while back she'd passed something strange-looking: branches blocking an entrance of sorts. She glimpsed what appeared to be a gravel driveway.

At this point in her journey, she was about ready to give up when out of nowhere a moose lumbered onto her path. She hit the brakes just in time. The magnificent creature, uninterested in the car, stayed centered in the road and turned his head to look at her. Suddenly, Chance's face flashed before her. She felt a flutter in the gut. Was this a sign she was close to him?

The moose seemed perfectly happy, blocking her way forward. He wasn't budging an inch. She backed the car around. Just as she stepped on the gas and accelerated, a timber truck bullied its way toward her, the driver laying on the horn. She swerved to the shoulder and stopped the car. The moose could never get out of the way in time. Kat's horror at the inevitable erupted into a scream. Fearing for the animal, she twisted around to see what was happening, but there was nothing to see, just the tail end of the truck speeding in the opposite direction. It was as if the moose had never existed.

She leaned her head against the headrest. In her mind, Brianna's voice, as clear as chimes, told her to follow her instincts. To Kat, that definitely meant examining the camouflaged road she'd seen.

Her cell phone rang, startling her. She thought it might be Chance. With hands shaking, she rummaged through her purse and salvaged her phone. On the line was an unfamiliar deep voice, asking if she was Kat Summers.

"Yes, and who's this?"

"If you don't go back to Seattle now," he said, "you'll never see Chance's daughter again."

Chance's daughter. "Who *is* this?"

"Don't bother getting the police involved, or she's as good as gone." Abruptly, the call ended.

Kat's heart locked in her chest, and she suddenly felt weak and nauseated. She punched in the number of the caller. No answer. No voice mail. She rifled through her purse for her address book and called Stella's number. It went to voice mail. She tossed her phone into her purse. They knew she was in Maine. At any moment they could abduct Stella, if they hadn't already.

Kat was torn. How could she leave now without finding Chance? On the other hand, how could she risk staying and calling their bluff when Stella's life was at stake. From what she'd already learned about the firm and from her own visit to Topping Ventures, she knew these people meant business; they didn't play games.

She had no choice. She jammed the gear in drive and pressed on the gas. As she sped past the odd-looking entrance, she gave it a passing glance, then raced toward Post Island in hopes of catching a plane back to Boston and on to Seattle. On the way, not one timber truck passed her. Not one animal blocked her path.

An hour later, after she'd left the deep woods behind, she arrived at the Post Island airport. The parking lot was empty. She charged inside only to discover the last plane to Boston had taken off two hours before. She drove into the town of two thousand and got a room for the night in the motel suggested by the rental car attendant.

As soon as she was in her room, she called Stella's number. No one answered.

She looked out the window at the rolling hillside. The sun was setting in the shadow of the trees. By leaving, was she doing the right thing? In that deep center of knowing, she was certain Chance was here. Hadn't she heard Brianna's voice?

She sat in a chair, leaned her head back, and closed her eyes. What had Libby told her? That there would be obstacles, false starts, yet no assurance Kat would find him. She felt a hollowing. She had no patience to meditate and ask for answers, though when she relaxed into herself from sheer exhaustion and quieted her thoughts, Libby's face appeared in her mind's eye, and Kat remembered another thing she'd told her: that Kat's presence in Maine would somehow bring Chance hope.

CHAPTER 13

The condo where Monique's sister Paulette resided was located in Boston's Beacon Hill District, not far from the city center. Monique also stayed there when she was in town. It belonged to Philip Topping.

Every time Monique entered the brick row house, she was reminded that she and Philip had been close once, close enough for his wife, an attorney living part-time in New York City, to threaten divorce and take him to court for everything he was worth. When he cooled the relationship, he professed guilt, but the real reason was worry over his money. For Monique, their involvement was nothing more than a diversion, a rebound affair.

The third-floor condo was modest compared to others in the upscale neighborhood. It was less than 1000 square feet with two bedrooms and one bath. It had a bright interior and was professionally decorated with furnishings in neutral tones of black, beige, and white with touches of color scattered about in glass vases and modernistic paintings. It was quite adequate for two people and one visiting from time to time.

Monique tiptoed from Michel's room, closed the door softly, and joined Paulette in the living room. It was 8:00 in the evening, sunset. The sky was a violet blue. She pulled the shades and switched on a lamp.

Paulette was on the sofa with legs curled, thumbing through a *Vogue* magazine. She was four years younger and four inches taller than Monique, and had a mane of dark hair halfway down her back. She carried more weight.

Monique sat in a neighboring chair and propped her feet on the ottoman. "He hates taking the medicine, but he is sleeping, finally. I had to read him a story."

"He loves you, too," Paulette said. "You should come more often."

"I feel guilty when I cannot be here."

"You should, you know," Paulette said in her usual haughty manner. "Do you want tea?"

"No, thank you." Monique yawned. "It has been a long day." She turned down the sounds of a jazz quartet playing on the radio next to her. "Do you have everything you need, Paulette?"

Paulette uncurled her legs, sitting up in the process, her facial expression somber. "I want to talk to you about something. I want to return to France. I have been here longer than I promised. There is nothing here for me."

Surprised, Monique had never heard her sister so serious or forceful. For as long as she could remember, Paulette was the happy one, always adjusting to any situation, but this wasn't the first time she'd voiced her displeasure. "You know I want you to stay."

"Yes, but Michel is getting older now, almost six. This place is not good to live in for a boy. He needs a big yard to play in. Plus, I only promised you two years. It has turned into five. I want a life of my own."

"You have to stay, Paulette. I need you here."

"Why? You are hardly ever in this condo. And when I talked to Philip, he hinted that he wanted it back."

"Did he say that?"

"Not in those words, but I could tell the impatience in his voice."

"You are reading too much into it. He would never ask us to leave."

Paulette shrugged a shoulder. "I am only telling you what I feel from him."

Monique picked up a newspaper nearby and passively turned a page, pondering her sister's comments. When she and Philip were together, he knew her heart was spoken for. His wife's objections aside, Monique and Philip's relationship had been withering on its own.

Deep down, he resented her feelings for Chance, out of competition if nothing else. But still, Philip would never be so cold as to throw them out, especially Michel. He'd grown very fond of Michel. She set the paper on the ottoman. "I will talk to Philip."

"I still want to go back to France. This is not home to me."

Monique picked up the paper again, hoping by ignoring Paulette's plea, Paulette would let the subject go. Monique's feelings for France were not as strong as her sister's.

Their father, a United States citizen, had journeyed to France as a young man and had met their mother, a French woman. Upon marrying, they made their home in the French countryside where their children were born. The family had visited the East Coast, particularly New York City and Boston, on several occasions. After high school, Paulette had chosen to stay in France while Monique attended college in the States and afterward joined the firm.

"You do not listen to me." Paulette slammed her magazine on the couch. "I have met someone on the Internet, a woman in Paris."

"Oh, Paulette, you cannot be serious. You would leave for some woman you do not even know? Please, Paulette, just a while longer. Give me time to figure this out."

"Why do you not quit this job that takes you away? It is not right what you do."

"I have no choice."

"Huh! I cannot talk to you." She wandered off toward the bedroom.

"I will come to bed soon," Monique called after her.

With a shrug Paulette disappeared from sight.

Left alone with her thoughts, Monique wondered what she would do if indeed Paulette escaped to France. Paulette did have more of a pull toward her birthplace. Despite Monique's desire to live in the States, their mother had been adamant about the girls retaining their French cultural identity.

Paulette had threatened to leave before, but never followed through. Hopefully, this was one of those times. But then there was

Michel's welfare to consider. It would break Monique's heart if, with no other choice, she had to let them go. She loved Michel too much. Though Paulette loved him, too, most of the time she was absorbed in her magazines or on the computer and stayed aloof. She and Michel were Monique's family now. Taking all of this into consideration was when Monique longed to make a life with Chance.

She yawned again. It had indeed been a long day, a long day away from her lover of many years. She turned off the lamp. The evening waned, its last whisper of light filtering through the shades, enough light for her to find her way to Michel's room.

She twisted the doorknob ever so slightly and looked in at this angel of a boy. The night-light revealed his black hair, matted from sweat, and his olive complexion, deepened from the white of the pillowcase. He slept soundly. His breathing was clear and even, not raspy anymore. Monique blew him an airy kiss. "Sweet dreams, little one."

She meandered toward the bedroom she shared with Paulette, then stopped in mid-step and turned an ear toward the living room. She thought she heard a rustling outside the door, then the click of a key in the lock. By the time she reached the living room and fumbled with the lamp, a man dressed in casual pants and polo shirt was coming through the doorway.

"You frightened me, Philip. What are you doing here this late?"

He grabbed her arm and pulled her into an embrace. His shirt smelled of cigar smoke, his breath of whiskey.

She shoved him away. "You have been drinking. Go home to Charlotte." He reached for her again, but she recoiled and clasped her arms to her chest.

"I haven't had that much to drink. I came here to check on Michel."

"He is much better. Paulette handled it well."

"Where *is* Paulette? Maybe she'll give me a hug if you won't."

"Leave her be, Philip. She is sleeping."

"Then I want to see Michel." He started toward the boy's room and bumped into the end table, wobbling the lamp.

Monique rushed to steady it. "Sit down, Philip, and let the boy sleep. He does not need to be upset right now. I will make you coffee."

He waved her offer away. "Charlotte went back to New York."

"So soon? I thought she was staying in Boston this week."

"We argued. About you and Paulette and Michel."

"Still? After all these years? And you came here."

"I wanted to see the boy." He paused. "And you."

Monique eyed him suspiciously. "And why me, Philip? I am to see you tomorrow. What could not wait?" Observing the expectant look on his face, she nodded. "I see. You cannot wait to find out about Chance, if I am seducing him. The answer is no, not yet."

Philip's face relaxed, as if her reply were what he'd wished to hear all along. "Come away with me tonight. We'll fly wherever you want to go."

He attempted to hold her, but the smell of alcohol disgusted her. She pushed him away. "You are drunk, Philip. You know I will soon be on an assignment with Chance."

His eyes narrowed with contempt. He reached for her again and grasped her arm.

"It was your doing to put us together, Philip. What did you expect?"

He backed off, as if she'd doused him with a sobering glass of ice water. "Come to the office in the morning. I have papers to send back with you. Be in the office at nine sharp."

"Shall I call you a cab?"

"My driver is waiting." On his way out, he stopped in the doorway. "Give Michel a hug for me."

Monique locked the door behind him, a large breath escaping her lungs. Looking back on it now, she knew her biggest regret was ever having involved Philip in Michel's life.

***

In the morning Monique was in the bedroom, packing her suitcase with a fresh supply of clothes for the rest of her stay at the cabin. Philip had told her they'd be there for a couple of weeks, but the timeframe could alter. Into the bag she tucked another sexy silk nightgown in case a new opportunity arose with Chance.

Cupboard doors opened and closed. Pans clanked on the counter. Paulette was in the kitchen, preparing breakfast for Michel. On waking, she'd greeted Monique with a smile, her mood seemingly shifting from the sulk of the night before.

Monique zipped up the suitcase and slid it off the bed. Michel stood in the doorway in the pajamas she'd bought him: sky blue cottons, laced with pictures of multicolored trucks. His hair was matted. His face was drawn and pale.

"What are you doing up? Go back to bed."

"Are you going away again, Aunt Monique?" His voice was soft and squeaky.

She lifted him into her arms. "You are such a big boy, and soon I will not be able to hold you like this." She kissed both his cheeks. "You are warm still, and oh, you need a bath. You smell like a little stinkbug." She carried him into the kitchen where Paulette was putting bread in the toaster. "I will give him a sponge bath before I go and also change his bed."

Paulette stood barefoot in a loose-fitting robe. "You said you had to be at work by nine. You will be late."

"This is more important than that." She took Michel into the bathroom and stripped him down on the plush white rug.

He held his fists under his chin, his elbows to his chest. His knees were knocked together. "I don't want you to go, Aunt Monique. I cry when you are gone."

His words hurt. She lifted him into the bathtub she'd filled with warm water that hit above his ankles. She soaped a washcloth and sudsed the front of his body. "I do not like to be away from you, darling, but I must work, you know. Turn around so I can finish in a hurry."

He slowly swiveled, facing away from her. His body shivered a little. She ran the cloth over his shoulders. "Ah, Michel…you will be strong like your father."

He turned back around, causing her to drop the cloth with a splash. "I don't like my father."

"Why do you say that, Michel?" She picked up the wet cloth and squeezed water down his chest and over his shoulders.

"He is never here to take me anywhere."

"He is a very busy man, you know. But he loves you very much. I can assure you of that. But you have me and Paulette and this beautiful house to live in and friends at school."

"But they have fathers."

"Yes, I know." She drained the water, wrapped him in a towel, and lifted him onto the rug. "Wait here, my pet."

She hurried to his bedroom and returned with a clean pair of pajamas, patterned like the others only with a red background. After dressing him, she herded him into his room and sat him in a chair while she made up his bed with clean linens. The morning sun brightened the room and shined on a trunk stacked with stuffed animals.

She patted the mattress. "Come to bed now."

"I feel better. Can I stay up and watch TV?"

"No, no, no. Paulette will bring you your breakfast and your medicine. Maybe later after you rest in bed a little longer." He climbed in, and she tucked the covers around him. She kissed his forehead and brushed his hair to the side. "Now you smell like flowers."

"I don't want to smell like flowers."

"Then you smell like…cinnamon."

"I don't want to smell like cinnamon."

"Then you smell like…monkeys."

He giggled. "I like monkeys."

She tousled his hair, messing it, and smoothed it back. "Promise me you will be a big, brave boy while I am away."

He nodded, though his lips were turned down. She gave him a tickle under his chin, and he grinned. He looked so much like his father. From the doorway she blew him a kiss.

In her room she changed into her customary low-cut dress and slipped a sweater over her shoulders. She pulled the suitcase into the front room. Paulette tightened her robe over her nude body and accompanied her to the door. The haughty look, along with no well-wishes, left Monique feeling as though she'd misjudged Paulette's mood after all. But she had no time to smooth things over or think of how to resolve the issue of Paulette's yearning to leave Boston. She was already late for the office and would have to face Philip's unpredictable disposition.

***

All the way up to Floor 14, Monique thought about Chance. By now he would be prowling the cabin like a madman. He was not the type to easily suffer confinement.

When the elevator bounced to a stop and the doors slid open, she held her head high and breezed past the reception area. She never had to show her badge. She could feel the men shifting their attention just to catch a glimpse of her. She had a mesmerizing effect on them.

Striding down the corridor, she smelled the aroma of freshly brewed coffee and the faint odor of cigar smoke. Philip was in. As she rounded the corner, male voices filtered out from his office. The sound of Chance's name caused her to slow her pace. Outside the door, she stopped to listen.

"I guess he knotted some sheets and used them as ropes," said a man with a Southern drawl.

"The sonovabitch. And did you take care of the Summers woman?"

"We scared her into going home. Told her if she didn't, she'd never see Chance's daughter again. We'll keep tabs on her every step of the way."

"Good. And keep an eye on the girl, too. She might be of use to us."

"Anything else?"

"Has Monique had any luck with him?" Philip asked, as if he hadn't been to her house, as if he hadn't a clue.

"They said she wouldn't talk about it."

During a long pause, Monique worried she'd be found out. She prepared to move away from the entrance. She heard papers rustling.

"The sonovabitch isn't going to cooperate," Philip continued.

"Do you want them to get physical with him?"

"It might come to that, but don't do anything until I give the word."

"And what about the girl? Do you want us to take her now?"

"Hmm...not quite yet. Soon though."

Horrified at what she'd been privy to, Monique strode into the room as if she'd been hurrying to get there. "*Excusez-moi.* I know I am late, Philip."

Carl Banks, the man who had interviewed Kat, glanced at Monique, then said to Philip, "Is that all?"

"Remember what I said. Don't do anything else until I tell you to." After Carl left the room, Philip motioned for Monique to sit, but she remained standing. "So, how much of our conversation did you hear?"

"I did not hear anything," she said. "I was late and speeding down the hallway to get here."

For a moment he eyed her, as though he didn't quite believe her. "How is Michel?"

"He is much better, but he needs to have his strength back."

Philip wandered to the window, his hands clasped behind his back, the morning sun flooding the room around him. Whenever he maintained this stance, she knew something weighed heavy on him.

"What is it, Philip?"

"This isn't working."

"What? Tell me." She had a sinking feeling.

"Chance. He tried to escape yesterday." Philip turned around. "I'm giving him an opportunity to redeem himself, but he's not taking it. And you haven't succeeded in bringing him around like I'd hoped you would."

"But it is too soon to judge."

Philip walked to her side and raised her hand to his lips. "He's a lost cause."

"What are you saying?"

"I can't trust him."

Monique's whole body deadened. "This is not true. He will come around in time."

"I can't wait that long. This deal with RBK is too important."

"Let me handle him," she said. "I will impress upon him the gravity of the situation, and I am sure he will cooperate. He has a daughter. I will remind him of your threat. You warned him. I know he will turn in his thinking. I know it. You would do the same for Michel. Please, Philip. Do this for me. Let me try to convince him before you do anything reckless."

"I can't trust Chance with the responsibility of this job. I thought I could break up his relationship with this woman, Kat Summers, but he's not falling for it. He's changed. He's a stubborn S.O.B. Something's got to be done."

"Please, Philip, do not rush into it. I will do anything."

He picked up a cigar he'd laid in an ashtray, put it to his lips, then set it down again, all the while studying her.

"I beg you, Philip."

"Begging doesn't become you." He touched her cheek and ran his finger down her chin. "I want you to promise when this is over you'll go away with me. I want you back in my life."

Monique's heart raced. Under his sly, steady gaze, she had no time to question his motives or appease him in any other way. For Chance's sake, she said, "Yes, Philip, I will go away with you. Whatever you ask of me. Just let Chance be."

Philip took his customary stance, looking out the window, hands clasped behind his back. "Carl will drive you to the airport. Go back to the cabin and keep Chance occupied. I need to think about what I'm going to do."

"Philip, please."

He turned around with a look that frightened her, and she felt the sting of his gaze. "Everything depends on you, Monique. It always has."

CHAPTER 14

From the time Monique was escorted to the airport until her arrival in Post Island, all she could think about was how to extricate Chance from the situation. Because of the way the firm did business under Philip's tutelage, coupled with his increasingly erratic moods, things didn't bode well for Chance. Gerald Morningstar was a prime example. But all Gerald had done to betray Philip was talk too much to a few people. Chance, on the other hand, had written an exposé that could possibly be read by millions. She was sure he had copies of the manuscript stashed away somewhere, and Philip was astute enough to know that, too. It sickened her to think of the consequences of Chance's actions.

Philip's words haunted her: Everything depends on you, Monique. It always has.

At first she didn't understand why, with the disclosure that he wanted her back in his life, he would throw her and Chance together with the likelihood of their becoming intimate. Then it dawned on her. By bringing them together, Philip was accomplishing two things. He was punishing Chance by disrupting his life and wrecking his relationship with Kat Summers. But Philip was also testing Monique's love for Chance.

By now Philip was perceptive enough to realize her feelings for Chance would never go away. So, what would be her punishment? She shivered at the thought. The only way he could make her life miserable was to take Michel or to eliminate Chance. Either way she would suffer terribly. She wouldn't let that happen. Somewhere on the road leading to the lodge, with the bald man in the driver's seat, she'd hatched a plan for Chance's freedom.

At the cabin the burly man, decked in military khakis, his revolver holstered, opened the car door for her. She stretched her sweater over her chest. Though still sunny with billowy clouds forming overhead, the air was at least ten degrees cooler than in Boston.

"He's safely inside." The man in khakis carried her suitcase up the porch steps, then drew his gun. "You heard what happened." When she nodded, he said, "One of us will be outside, checking the perimeter at all times. Make sure he understands that. If necessary, we have our orders to shoot."

She relinquished her cell phone, and he let her inside. The room seemed cold and uninviting, but a hint of fried egg odor gave the house a lived-in feel. On the stove was a frying pan.

Chance came down from upstairs, carrying a dinner plate. He walked into the kitchen smiling and laid the dish in the sink.

Monique set her bag by the couch. "Did you think you could get away with it? Now, Philip has ordered them to shoot if you try again."

"How is the child?"

"He is much better, thank you, but please do not change the subject. This is serious."

"Listen to me, Monique."

After what he'd been through, she expected to find him to be depressed with no appetite or will to talk to her, but instead he'd come down the stairs with a bouncy step, and his tone was oddly cheerful.

"When I was out, I made it as far as the end of the drive where the gate is, and I saw her. I swear I did. Kat's out there looking for me, and it's only a matter of time."

As much as his enthusiasm for another woman stung, Monique couldn't delude him into thinking there was any hope. "Chance, you must hear me. You did see her, yes, it is true. But she is no longer here. She is on her way back to Seattle. I know this because I overheard Philip say that they..." Telling Chance they had their sights on his daughter would infuriate him to the point he might do something rash and place himself in more danger than he was now. Monique thought it better to follow her plan.

"What did Philip say?"

"That they warned her somehow and made her go back. They watched her get on the plane, and they are watching her every move until they see her off the plane in Seattle. She is gone, Chance." Monique reached for his hand, but he clenched his fists, drawing them inward, and wandered toward the stairwell.

"Chance, wait." She ran after him as he ascended the steps. "We can fix this. I promise you." But he continued to his room and closed the door, shutting her out. "Chance, let me in, please. I want to help you," she said, knocking. When he didn't answer, she entered anyway and found him staring out the window. Fearing he might lash out at her in angry bursts, she cautiously approached him. "I have been thinking of what to do to help you. Will you listen to me?"

He answered by keeping his back to her, but she could feel his anguish and frustration as if it were her own. He finally sat on the edge of the bed with his elbows resting on his thighs and his head lowered in his hands.

She sat beside him and rubbed his back. "You were right. Philip has an ulterior motive for bringing you here. He does not trust you, and I think he will not let you leave. This is not about the job. Carl could very well handle that. This is about destroying you for what you have done." She purposely left out how she believed Philip was testing her. Speaking of her and Philip's relationship in front of Chance was too painful. "I have a plan, darling. I will help you escape. I cannot let Philip have his way. I will not let him do anything to harm you. I love you too much."

He remained silent, ignoring her.

"I know you do not love me. You have made that perfectly clear. Your heart belongs to another, but still I cannot let them hurt you. You have a child to think of." She pressed her lips together to stop the tide of emotion, but being this close to Chance and knowing he was lost to her forever was too much to take in. She broke down and wept.

At the sound of her weeping, he turned to her. For several minutes he held her and let her cry. "I'm sorry I don't feel the same as I once did, Monique. I truly am." He reached for a box of tissues.

She dabbed her eyes and nose, and after finally regaining her composure, she ran her palm over his cheek. "Will you have sex with me one last time? I know it will not be out of love, but I want to be with you once more, just to remember the smell of you and the texture of your skin against mine, just to remember you when I am alone in my bed."

He kissed her hand and laid it in her lap. "I'm sorry, Monique. I can't."

She stared at the floor and let the waves of sadness subside until she felt sufficiently in control again. She stood and adjusted her dress, grabbed another tissue. "Forgive me, Chance." She lifted her chin high to collapse the embarrassment she felt. "I am too emotional. I do not think clearly this way." Her voice commanded strength again.

"It's all right, Monique. This has been a difficult time for both of us."

"Yes, for both of us."

"I have to find a way to get out of here."

She sat with him again. "I think I can help you."

***

The sun was slipping behind the trees as Chance and Monique finalized their scheme to release him from the fate Philip had planned for him. He waited upstairs while she prepared the drinks she would offer the guards, drinks laced with the drug she used in her profession to sedate unmanageable men. In her purse, she always kept a ready supply.

According to the plan, Chance would remain in his room until she called him to help, but he was too anxious to stay put. He walked to the top of the staircase. The house smelled like chocolate. Monique had sliced and baked a batch of frozen chocolate chip cookies to give to the men, hoping they would welcome a drink to wash them down.

Chance heard the sound of silverware clinking a glass and Monique humming a French lullaby. She seemed more relaxed than he was. He could remember times in the past they had to lie and deceive their way out of precarious situations. But he had been away from the business way too long.

Monique stopped singing. There was tap on the window. The door opened and closed.

Ever since his failed escape, he knew Philip had ordered the men to remain outside and keep the door locked at all times. Monique had told him so. He hurried into her bedroom and looked out from there. They were out of view. He edged the window open, and the conversation drifted upward.

She was saying Chance was asleep in his room, he wasn't cooperating. She was too bored to sit around. She wanted some fresh air and someone to talk to. Only one male voice answered back.

The burly man came out of the bunkhouse, buttoning up his trousers. He slid his holster off his shoulder and positioned it around his waist. Chance lost sight of him, then heard him remark about the cookies.

There was easy chatter about the relentless mosquitoes and the mice in the bunkhouse. The exchange turned serious when one of the men spoke about the length of their stay and how they were anxiously waiting for the green light from Philip. They talked as if doing away with Chance would be as satisfying as bagging a deer.

Monique was humoring them, going along with everything they said. Chance could hear her laughter. If nothing else, she was good at deception. She'd had years of experience. It sickened him to think he'd been a part of it all—the lies, the debauchery, living as if nothing mattered but money, power, and sex. If he could only turn back the clock, he would never have gone down that path.

Monique insisted they finish the lemonade and continued to chat until Chance heard a loud thud. One of the men yelled, "You stupid bitch." Monique let out a painful wail.

Chance flew downstairs. The burly man had her backed against the window with his hands around her neck. Chance pounded the glass. The man glanced up once, then fell against Monique and slumped to the ground.

Monique bent over, coughing and hacking. Chance hammered the window again. She knelt by the man, pulled the keys from his pocket, and unlocked the door.

Chance pulled her close and held her until her breathing evened out. "You could have been killed. I shouldn't have let you risk it."

She coughed and massaged her neck. "It is done now."

"Are you sure you're all right?"

"Yes, but we must hurry. We must finish with them and be on our way. I gave them a larger dose than usual, and they should be out all night, but who knows for sure." She went inside and came out with a roll of duct tape.

Chance unbuckled the burly man's holster and rolled him onto his stomach. With Monique's help, he wound the tape around the wrist and ankles. Monique emptied the man's pockets of a cell phone and wallet and laid them on the porch. Chance slapped tape over his mouth.

When Monique started to roll the bald man over, Chance stopped her. "I'll put him in the backyard. That way they can't try to communicate with each other." He removed the man's gun and grabbed his wrists. Working hard at gripping the ground with his boot heels, Chance dragged him around the corner. Halfway there, Chance stopped to catch his breath, then continued to the back of the house and laid him in the middle of the yard. He tied him up identically to the other with duct tape around his wrists and ankles and a swatch of tape over his mouth. Monique confiscated the man's phone and wallet, along with a pocket knife, plus her own cell phone he'd taken from her earlier.

They tromped over the grass together and stood on the front porch. The sunlight was fading, and the mosquitoes were swarming.

Monique removed bills from the men's wallets and counted out $417. She handed the money to Chance. "Take this. You will need it. This way they will not have a cent to their names. Their credit cards will be of no use to you. You do not want to leave a money trail. And I suggest you do not use your own cards. I will also give you some cash. Buy everything with cash. And same with the phones. I would not use them. They could track you that way, or I would give you mine."

Chance stuffed the phones in his pockets and gathered the guns. "Take the wallets and follow me." He stomped through the tall grass behind the bunkhouse, stirring up the bugs. He emptied the guns and hurled the bullets like confetti, scattering them into the woods. He tossed the guns as far as he could. Monique handed him the wallets, and he threw them in a different direction and did the same with the phones. "That should slow them down."

"Quick. We must go back to the cabin. You can change while I call around to see what airlines have space available. Remember your bag. You'll need it to satisfy airport security."

"What about you, Monique? Have you thought about the consequences?"

"There is no time to discuss this. We must hurry." She rushed ahead.

On the porch, Chance gave the drugged man a passing glance. The man lay motionless.

Chance dashed upstairs. From the wardrobe they'd provided him, he'd already laid out a pair of casual slacks, a shirt, and a pair of loafers. He dressed quickly. In the canvas bag he'd packed earlier, he buried his cowboy boots under the clothes he'd had on when they'd abducted him. He rummaged through the closet and found an oversized windbreaker with a good-sized collar.

Downstairs, Monique was waiting for him. "Come, we must go. We have a long drive ahead of us. There were no spaces out of Bangor or Portland on the early flights, so we must take our chances and drive to Boston. We must hurry to get you there before dawn.

Many early flights have seats available. You can pay for your ticket
before you board."

  "Boston. That's like walking into the lion's den."

  "We have no choice."

CHAPTER 15

After spending a restless Sunday night at the hotel in Post Island, Kat had caught the morning flight out, but the day had proven to be one of the most frustrating and tiring days of her life. Because she'd wanted to leave as early as possible, she had to work her way across country by taking any flight available and had spent the last eleven hours zigzagging across the States like someone trying to connect the dots: from Post Island to Boston to Atlanta to Dallas and on to Seattle. Sleep had eluded her. She was too worried and agitated, not only about Chance but also about Stella.

It was now 8:00 in the evening. Dusk had settled in, the sky a shadowy blue. Kat's house was dark inside. From being cooped up inside multiple aircraft, her lower back ached, her ankles were swollen, and her clothes and hair smelled like a locker room. All she wanted to do was take a calming bath and go to bed, but how could she sleep, knowing Stella could possibly be out there somewhere scared to death, and Kat had no way to reach Chance.

She unlocked the back door and set her bag in the mudroom. When she snapped on the kitchen light, she drew in a quick breath. All the drawers and cupboards hung opened. She told herself to get out, but her feet were anchored to the floor.

She listened for any unusual sounds coming from inside, but not even the floorboards groaned upstairs, so she ventured farther into the house and switched on the overhead light that lit up the dining and living areas. The couch was pulled away from the wall and the chairs had been moved. The desk drawers jutted out with the contents askew. Checking the bedroom, she discovered the same disturbing scene: dresser drawers opened and the insides a jumble, the clothes in her closet piled on the floor, her mattress jockeyed off center.

She gave the downstairs a thorough examination. As far as she could tell, nothing was missing. Her spare checks were accounted for. Even the sapphire ring she wore on certain occasions sat untouched on a bathroom shelf.

The light on her answering machine was as fixed as the overhead light. Her heart sank. She'd hoped for a message from Chance or Stella, assuring her everything was all right.

She strode to the foyer and tested the front door. It was locked. Then she noticed the door to the second floor. She always kept it latched, but now it was ajar. Her body tensed with panic.

From the fireplace hearth she grabbed the iron poker and took it with her to the stairwell. She flicked on the light and slowly crept up the stairs, the wood creaking with each footstep. On the top stair she could hear the thrumming sound of the freeway, matching the pulse in her ears. Turning the corner, she was shocked to find storage boxes flipped and emptied of their contents. Christmas decorations were strewn on the floor, along with the clothing items she'd planned to give to charity. Cautiously, she walked from room to room, checking for anything missing.

She thought of her laptop, which she hadn't recalled seeing. She hurried downstairs, dropped the fire poker on the hearth, and aimed for her desk. Just as she'd feared, the laptop was gone. Her limbs felt heavy, almost paralyzed. She forced herself to think. With both doors having been locked and only her laptop stolen, she knew who the perpetrator was: Chance's former employer. The firm was looking for copies of Chance's manuscript and in the process warning her to stay out of their business.

In utter shock, she wandered back to the living room and pushed one of the chairs in place. She picked up the magazines that were spilled on the floor and set them in a tidy stack. Her mind was on overload with all that had happened. As much as she craved a bath and a good night's sleep, she had to do something besides putting her house in order and worrying all night. She longed to call

Maggie, but Maggie would only encourage her to call the police. She'd already been warned against that.

As Kat remembered, Stella had been on a camping trip, and Kat wondered how the firm knew her whereabouts. Silly question. The firm knew everything. She tried Stella's cell phone. No one answered. Kat found her purse on the kitchen counter, left a light on inside, and locked up. She didn't care about the time. She had to find out for sure if Stella was home.

It took Kat fifteen minutes to drive over the freeway and into the Fremont District. It was getting darker now. With the help of the streetlights, she slowed to read the signs, which were cloaked in an amber glow, and turned off the main thoroughfare.

She found a parking spot one block away from the downstairs apartment Stella shared with two other young women. To save money they'd managed to squeeze their belongings into the one-bedroom space. Kat hiked up the sidewalk and approached the house divided in two, wedged between two older single-family homes. The living room light was on. After knocking and stating her identity, she was allowed in.

Nona, the gangly roommate with sallow complexion, fine straight hair, and timid eyes, offered Kat a chair, but rushed to clear off a backpack and pushed a rolled-up sleeping bag out of the way. The coffee table was cluttered with water bottles and camping dishes. Kat could see through to the kitchen where a tent was laid flat across the floor. Nona apologized for the mess.

"I don't want to sit," Kat said. "I want to know about Stella. Where's Teresa, by the way?"

"She's out with her boyfriend. She should be back soon. Would you like a Pepsi?"

Kat found herself becoming irritated with Nona's casual attitude and Teresa's obvious lack of concern. "I don't want anything to drink. I want to know where Stella is. Did she go camping with you?"

"Yeah, but we came back early this morning so she could go to work."

"Do you know where she is now?"

Nona lifted a shoulder. "Not really."

"Aren't you worried about her?"

"No, because she went to see her dad."

"Her dad…" Kat stared at Nona, confused.

"Yeah. About an hour ago these two guys came to the door. They were like older, like around forty. They told Stella if she went with them, she could see her dad."

Kat was stunned. "I find it highly unlikely she'd just go off with two men she didn't know."

"They were really nice, and they gave her a note and told her it was from her dad. I don't know what it said, but as soon as she read it, she grabbed her backpack and took off with them."

"Do you have the note?"

"Stella does. She said she'd call, but she hasn't yet. Is there something wrong?"

Yes, something was wrong, something was *very* wrong, but Kat didn't want to worry the girls. "I hope not, but call me if you hear from her." Kat edged toward the door.

"Sure, but is she in trouble?"

"I think I know what's going on, but you and Teresa will have to trust me. If Stella doesn't call or come home tonight, don't get scared or call the police. Just let me handle this. I'll check with you later."

On the drive home she thought how Stella must be terrified, alone with two strange men. It sickened her to think the firm had lured her away with a trumped-up note. Stella was so vulnerable and anxious about her father she would have believed anything.

Kat could barely keep her eyes open. She'd been up the night before, had traveled all day, and was sapped of energy. The light, shining from her house, was a welcome sight, though she didn't relish facing the mess inside.

She unlocked the door and paused, listening for any unusual sounds. Satisfied, she checked her answering machine. No new messages were waiting for her. She poured a glass of water and drank it in one long gulp, then retreated to the bedroom.

Given the shape she was in, bordering on total exhaustion, she shut the dresser drawers, straightened the mattress, and lay on top of the covers, promising only a catnap before getting up and tackling each room, deciding what to do next. Only a short doze, she reminded herself. Staying guarded and alert was essential. But one yawn followed another. As soon as she closed her eyes, she fell asleep.

Later in the night, a siren-like yowl scared her awake. She shot up out of bed and had to sit down again, the blood pooling in her legs. The neighborhood tomcats were riled up about something.

The clock read 1:00 a.m. In the dark with a slit of moonlight sifting through the curtains, she remembered she'd woken from a dream, a dream about Chance. She was cocooned in his arms. Though the dream didn't match her reality, the feeling it evoked was one of safety and well-being. She fought to stay awake, but succumbed to this sense of all-encompassing warmth.

CHAPTER 16

Traveling south on I-95, Chance and Monique had taken turns at the wheel. Monique relished this time with him, their last hours together before he flew west to join the woman he loved and she drove into Boston to face Philip. Life as she knew it was about to change. No longer could she caress the dream of being with Chance in whatever capacity he allowed, and who knew what Philip had in store for her, especially now after what she'd done.

She swallowed hard to keep the rush of emotion from bubbling up and overtaking her in front of Chance. She'd already broken down once, and once was enough. She needed to stay strong and resolved on executing her plan. Otherwise, on top of everything else, she'd lose her pride, and she couldn't let that happen.

On the first leg of their journey, the trees on both sides of the interstate had been dense and dark as night, shadows upon shadows, and the moon lit their way. They stopped at rest areas and ate the snacks Monique had hastily tossed into a bag—apples, oranges, crackers—and bought coffee to stay alert. Farther south the twinkling of lights ushered in civilization.

When Chance drove, Monique attempted to lighten the situation by talking about old times and bringing up some of their exploits, such as the time they swam naked in the Mediterranean Sea. He wouldn't crack a smile or show a glimmer of interest, and her attempts fell flat. His eyes stayed steady on the road.

When he was focused like this, she knew he was intent on the mission. Whenever this intensity had spilled over into their lovemaking, Monique had found it thrilling, at least in the past when he cared about her. These hours of quiet reminiscing were agonizing. She had no choice but to honor his wishes and let him be with his own thoughts. When she drove, he would sometimes doze.

Once they reached the outskirts of Boston, Chance took the wheel. By 4:00 a.m. they were parked in the Central Parking Garage at Logan International Airport. The first thing Monique did was use her cell phone to call the airlines to book him on the first flight out. As a precaution, she'd waited until the last minute in case Philip caught wind that Chance had escaped and was checking flights looking for him. She'd made arrangements for Chance to leave on a 6:00 a.m. flight, giving them only a short time together. Soon he would leave her to go inside the terminal. In her heart of hearts, she knew this would be the last time she'd ever be this close to him.

In the dark of the car's interior, she strained to see the outline of his profile: the curve of his chin, the slant of his nose, the lips she'd never again feel against hers. She memorized every feature so in her mind she could picture his face in the coming days when she was alone with her thoughts, her regrets, her sorrows. She placed her hand on his thigh to feel the give of the body she would miss most of all.

He made a move to grasp the door handle, and she squeezed tighter. "Will you kiss me once, Chance, to say goodbye, for old time's sake?"

He shifted to look at her. "Why are you risking your life for me, Monique? When Philip finds out what you've done, there will be hell to pay."

"You know why," she said. "I know you do not love me as you once did, but I had to be sure. I have reasons beyond your imaginings, things I cannot tell you now."

"What things?"

"There is no time to explain. You must go soon. Just promise me one thing."

"Monique, I can't."

"No, it is not what you think," she said. "Promise me you will give to Philip any copies of your manuscript you have locked away. I know you have them, and Philip knows that, too. He will hound you. You will never be free. It is not worth it to expose him. He will come after you until he gets what he wants."

"I can't promise that."

"Be reasonable, darling, be reasonable," she said, "and if you hear that anything has happened to me, anything at all, promise me you will contact my sister, Paulette. I will always worry about her and the child she cares for. She may need assistance."

"Your sister doesn't know me."

"Oh, but you are wrong. She knows you very well, as I have talked about you many times. She must hear from you. Promise me, Chance, please."

"I have to go."

Monique held his face in the palms of her hands, memorizing the texture of his skin, the scratch of his morning stubble. She kissed him, and he didn't resist. She felt him lean into her. She moaned contentment. Satisfied he'd offered her this one last crumb of affection to remember him by, she lifted her hands and whispered, "Please, Chance, if anything happens to me, promise you will contact Paulette."

"Yes, I promise. I owe you my life." He exited the car and bent down in order to see her. He reached in and clasped her hand. "Thank you, Monique." He started to close the door.

"Wait." She handed him a card she'd pulled from her purse. "Paulette's number. Be careful, Chance."

After he'd walked away, she got in the driver's seat. His smell and the heat from his body clung to the fabric, and with her eyes closed it felt as if he had his arms around her. She basked in the warmth. She turned the key to accessories and sat very still as she watched the clock's numbers change until it was after seven and his plane was well out of Boston.

The emptiness nagged at her, clawed at her insides, until she felt as though she were going to go mad. She'd lost him, this time for good. A car's horn blasted, echoing through the garage, and snapped her out of her reverie. She thought of Paulette and Michel. She desperately wanted to see them before she had to face Philip. In a blur of tears, she drove straight to the condo, dodging the morning traffic. She pulled up to the curb. Parked ahead of her was Philip's Mercedes.

She checked in the mirror for any lingering traces of mascara from tears shed, and blotted her face with a tissue. She fastened the top button of her shirt that had come undone when she was kissing Chance. Lastly, she took the perfume spritzer from her purse and misted around her neck and down her chest, washing away any hint of his scent.

Philip strode toward her. His appearance reflected less than his immaculately dressed and manicured self; it looked as if he'd thrown on yesterday's slacks and shirt, and his hair was uncombed. His expression was as dour as she'd ever seen it. She looked away, unable to meet his gaze.

He opened the car door, grabbed her by the arm, and yanked her out of the SUV, causing her to gasp in alarm. A door from a nearby house closed, and a vehicle started up. A middle-aged woman, walking her poodle up the sidewalk, eyed them suspiciously.

"Philip, not out here," Monique cautioned.

"Get in my car then." He held on to her arm until he'd pushed her into the passenger seat of the Mercedes and slammed the door.

She placed a hand over the skin he'd easily bruised. When he got in, the smell of cigar smoke mixed with bourbon masked the odor of the new leather seats. Bracing against his rage, she reminded herself she'd risked it all for Chance.

For the first minute, Philip remained silent, allowing her to become even more anxious than she already was. She tried focusing on her plan to avoid being sucked into the fear. The firm had taught her to stay strong under pressure, stay focused on the goal. "Philip, I want to explain."

"Don't worry about your lover. Or maybe you should." He studied her face for a reaction, but she stayed composed. "I have men stationed in front of Kat Summers's house. As soon as he tries to connect with her, they'll have him. I'm thinking about what to do with

you." He'd spoken as if he hadn't heard her. His tone was low and
steady, but he was not spewing outrage.

She felt the prickles on the back of her neck. "Listen to me,
Philip. I know what you were doing, throwing us together. You were
testing us to see if we still cared for each other. Your experiment
worked. He would not take my advances. He does not love me anymore. Of that I am sure." She choked back the sadness.

"But you still love him. Why else would you do what you did?"

"I did that, yes, but because I could not let you hurt him. He
has a child. It would be heartless. But it is over between Chance and
me. He does not love me, and now I can go forward with my life,
with you."

The sun peeked over the buildings, shining in the passenger
window. Monique turned her back against the warmth and took
Philip's hand. "We can have time together now just as I promised
you."

His expression softened a bit as he brought her hand to his lips.
Slowly, he kissed each finger, then threw her hand aside and sank into
a pout.

She waited for him to pull out of his funk, a mood he so often
dipped into whenever situations hadn't gone exactly as he'd planned.
The excitement of being with Chance, if only superficially, was more
bearable than these moments with Philip.

When she and Philip were together, he always fell into depres-
sion. Objectively, he knew she was the best woman in her line of
business, that of seducing men and having the intelligence to see a
job through. She was a great asset to the firm. Yet, ever since their intimate involvement, fits of jealousy plagued him. In numerous ways
he'd take it out on her: bouts of silence, endless phone calls to check
on her whereabouts, dropping in at unexpected times, having the
power to send her anywhere in the world, knowing if she dared quit
the firm, her safety was in jeopardy. After Chance left Topping Ventures, she should never have given herself to Philip.

He slipped the key into the ignition.

"What are you doing?"

"My plane is being prepared, and we're leaving town. We're going to hash this out."

Monique reached over and pulled the key out. "First, you must promise me. I want to go inside to pack some extra things and to see Paulette and Michel before I go. And..."

"And what?"

"If I go with you," she said, knowing she had no real choice in the matter, "promise me you will leave Chance alone."

Scarlet seeped into Philip's cheeks.

"For the child's sake, Philip. That is all."

"I'll let you see Paulette and Michel." But that was all he would agree to.

She dared not argue with him and opened the car door. He met her on her side and walked with her up the sidewalk and into the building. Without speaking, they took the elevator to the third floor. Philip unlocked the door and let Monique inside.

Michel, barefoot and in his pajamas, came from the bedroom. "Monique...Philip."

"What are you doing out of bed, my little man?" She scooped him into her arms.

Paulette rushed in from the kitchen in her bathrobe, her wet hair wrapped in a towel. "I heard the door opening." She stopped when she saw Philip.

"Why is Michel not in bed?"

"He is doing much better. Tell them, Michel."

Michel hugged Monique's neck. "Yes, yes, I am better. Put me down, please." He ran to Philip, who knelt to give him a hug. "You smell bad, Philip."

"Let me talk to Paulette while I pack. Come with me, Paulette. Michel, stay with Philip and show him your new truck." In the hallway closet, Monique found a small suitcase and took it into the bedroom.

Paulette sat on the bed. "Why is Philip here so early?"

"Never mind that now. I want you to open the safe and get me the manila envelope on top. Hurry."

"What is happening, Monique?"

"My plans have changed. I will be with Philip this week. Now please do what I say."

They both entered the walk-in closet, and Paulette worked the dial on the safe while Monique absentmindedly picked out sundresses and sandals, unsure where Philip intended to take her, nor did she care.

Paulette handed her the envelope. "What is in here?"

"When I reach my destination, I will write to you with a sealed letter to be given to Chance Eliason. If I do not return in a week's time, I want you to get it to him per my instructions. He is the only person to see it. Not even you are to read it. Do you understand? I will tell you everything in the letter I will send to you and how to reach Chance. Promise you will do this for me."

Paulette stared at her, hesitating. "Is this one of your dangerous assignments? Is that why you are being so secretive?"

"Yes." Monique hid the envelope under her clothes and zipped up the suitcase. "Michel is all right, is he not?"

"He is much better, yes. The medicine is working. But I will take him back to the doctor to be sure."

"I hate to leave him."

"Yes, yes, I know. You must work."

Monique picked up her bag and walked down the hall. When she neared the living room she held back. Philip was lying on the floor and letting Michel wheel a toy truck over his chest. Philip was making growling sounds, and Michel was giggling.

Oddly, this scene sent shivers up Monique's spine and tears down her cheeks. She turned and said to Paulette, "Take good care of Michel, and do not let him out of your sight. Do not let anyone in this house unless you know them, not even if they say they are friends of Philip. Do you understand?"

"Yes, but why are you crying, sister?"

Monique shook her head. "Just sad to leave."

Michel let go of his toy and ran up to Monique. "Are you going away again?"

"Yes, my little tomato." She gave him a long hug.

He tried pushing away from her. "I am not a tomato."

She squeezed him to her and breathed in the scent of his child-like sweetness. "You are my juicy little tomato, and I will miss you until I see you again."

Philip looked at his watch. "We have a plane to catch."

"Yes, Philip, I know."

Philip tousled Michel's hair. "See you later, alligator."

"See you, 'gator."

Monique hugged Michel again.

"Come on, Monique. It's getting late."

At the door she nodded to Paulette and blew Michel a kiss. Once she and Philip were in the car and Philip had slowly pulled away from the curb, she glanced back at the building. The pain in her heart was so strong she thought she would faint. The day was full of unbearable leavings: first, Chance, then Paulette and Michel. She grasped the seat cushion for support and stared ahead, prepared to accept her unpredictable fate.

CHAPTER 17

Kat moaned in her sleep. She heard a ringing sound and man's voice in the distance. It was all in her dream. She sleepily opened her eyes to a room filled with bright summer light. Her hair smelled like the inside of an airplane. The cotton pants and shirt she'd worn yesterday were still on her body, wrinkled and damp from sweat.

She stretched and yawned. Groggy, she tried to recapture the events of the last twenty-four hours, but as soon as she rolled over and looked at the clock, she abruptly sat up. It was 11:00 a.m. She'd wanted to stay awake and alert but instead had slept the morning away.

The faint drone of the freeway and the clank of metal on metal from nearby hammering were the only noises she could make out. Nothing stirred from inside the house.

The sight of her trashed room brought back the reality of her homecoming. She wiped the drool from the side of her mouth and picked up some underwear that had been cast on the floor. Rearranging the contents of her dresser drawers, she considered washing everything, but not now.

In the bathroom she straightened everything in the cabinet under the sink, righting the cleanser container and stacking rolls of toilet paper that had tumbled out. Too numbed to face cleaning up the rest of the house, she went into the kitchen to get a glass for water and noticed the light blinking on her answering machine.

She hit the play button. Over the speaker a man's voice said, "We have Stella. If you call the authorities, you'll never see her again. You will be contacted later." The time of the recording was shortly before eleven, right before she'd woken completely.

She leaned against the counter, her heart bucking against her chest. They had Chance, and now she knew for sure they had his daughter. But Kat couldn't understand why, after she'd returned home as she'd been warned to do, they would take Stella? Kat couldn't understand any of it. She had no choice but to wait for their call.

The doorbell rang. Through the kitchen and the living room, she dodged scattered papers and dining room chairs flipped on their sides. Before reaching the foyer, she snatched a decorator pillow from the floor and tossed it on the couch. Wary, she asked her visitor's name, and when she heard Maggie's familiar nasal tone, she opened the door.

"This is the first chance I've had to connect with you. I had to go out of town unexpectedly and just got back. I was..." Maggie's voice trailed off as she looked Kat over. "You look like you slept in those clothes. Your hair's a mess. You've got a wild look in your eyes. What's the matter?" She looked past Kat, then stepped into the living room. "What's going on here?" She surveyed the area. "Obviously, you aren't rearranging the furniture. This looks like you've been burgled. Am I right? Did someone break in? Have you called the police?"

"It's nothing like that." Kat pushed the couch back into its normal spot and set the pillows in place.

"Is anything missing?"

"Just my laptop."

Maggie hesitated, focusing intently on Kat. "This is about Chance, isn't it? What haven't you told me?"

"They have Stella, Chance's daughter."

"Chance's daughter? Who are *they*?"

"I was in Maine, looking for Chance, and came home last night to this, and then Stella was gone," Kat blurted in one long breath.

"Wait, wait, wait. Back up a minute. You were in Maine, as in the state of Maine. Why in the world would you go there to look for him?"

"Let's just say I had a reliable tip," Kat said, knowing if she told Maggie the truth about her visit to a psychic, Maggie wouldn't be open to listening to anything else.

"Obviously, that didn't pan out, or did it? Honestly, Kat, I don't understand why you can't just call the police and let them handle this."

"I can't do that. I didn't have enough time to look for him because—and this is what I'm trying to tell you—the people he used to work for called me while I was in Maine and warned me to come home or there would be consequences."

"For his daughter? You're frigging kidding. What the hell have you gotten yourself into, Kat?"

"When I got home, my house was like this. Chance has something they want, and I guess they think he might have hidden it here."

"What is it?"

"A memory stick with a manuscript on it."

"Do you have it?"

"No."

"Have you heard from the kidnappers?"

"No, and I don't know what to do. I'm worried sick."

"I think you should go to the police."

"They warned me not to do that. I might put her life in danger. They said they'd contact me later. I'll just have to wait."

"Listen to me, Kat. You have to get the police involved. They know how to handle these kinds of things. The longer you wait, the longer they'll have the girl, and then who knows what will happen?" She checked her watch. "I'll call Jim and tell him where I am. I'll stay here and help you handle this. We should definitely call the police."

"No, Maggie, please," Kat said. "You don't understand who I'm dealing with. I know a lot more about these people than I've told you. They're like dealing with the Mafia. You can't handle this the normal way. I have to wait for their call. Otherwise, they'll do something to Chance, and I'll never see him again."

"All right, dear. We'll do it your way. But I'll wait with you. They have to call back soon."

"You go back to work. I know you have a lot to do, especially with me gone from the office."

"I can't leave you like this. At least let me stay and help you clean up this mess."

"No, no. I can do that. It will give me something to do. I'll take a shower, then start upstairs."

"They were up there, too? You better let me help."

"Please, Maggie, just go. I need to do this alone."

"Alone." Maggie shook her head. "Now, see? This is what you always do. You go it alone and close everyone out. You did that with Chance."

"Don't remind me. I feel terrible about that now."

Maggie squeezed Kat's hand. "Sorry, dear, I shouldn't have said that." She ambled toward the door. "If I hadn't been away from the office yesterday, I'd insist upon staying, but I'll call you. No, you better call me. I don't want to tie up your phones. Promise me, though, if nothing happens today, you'll call the police."

"Maybe tomorrow."

"Kat...?" Maggie gave Kat a hug. "Not maybe, dear. If they haven't contacted you by tonight, promise you'll call me and we'll get the police involved. They'll know what to do."

Kat nodded, knowing full well she had to take care of this her own way and let the firm call the shots. She watched Maggie walk down the sidewalk and get into her car.

As Maggie drove away, Kat noticed an unfamiliar white van with a man in the driver's seat, parked across the street. From this angle, with sunlight glinting off metal, she couldn't make out if there was another occupant inside. Just to be safe, she bolted the door and slipped the chain lock in place.

***

To avoid suspicion, Chance had paid for a round-trip ticket and had boarded the jet with no hassles. Since no one had cornered him in the airport, he felt confident the two men at the cabin hadn't found a way out of their predicament to signal Philip. He was less sure of who might greet him at his destination. So, in mid-flight he befriended a young woman traveling with a toddler and offered to help with her carry-on luggage as far as the baggage area where her parents were supposed to be waiting. There, he could slip outside and grab a taxi.

Before he deplaned, he pushed his hair back inside a ball cap and put on sunglasses, both of which he'd purchased at Logan, and pulled the collar of his jacket up around his neck. The woman with the little boy gave him a quizzical look but didn't question him and seemed grateful for the help.

Through the airport, amidst the summer travelers, Chance, juggling two carry-on bags and a diaper bag slung over his shoulder, accompanied the woman and the child. He scanned the crowds, keeping a watchful eye on anyone who looked as though they were trying to keep pace with him. At one point he placed a hand on the stroller, making it appear as if he were guiding it along, as if he belonged in this woman's life. Most of the time she was preoccupied with the cranky, whiny child, giving Chance the freedom to stay alert to his surroundings.

Once they'd reached the baggage claim, the woman pointed to where her parents were standing, not far from the escalator. Abruptly, Chance dropped her bags by the stroller and darted around other travelers and out the door without a word of goodbye. He hailed a cab.

Inside the taxi, he removed his ball cap and glasses, smoothed his hair, and relaxed back, at least for a while. The baby powder scent from the diaper bag he'd carried was still on his clothing. He instructed the driver to take him to the University District.

The Indian gentleman wanted to chat about the weather. It had been hot all week with no relief in sight. But Chance preferred to stare at the brilliant blue skies and to be cloistered with his thoughts. In twenty minutes he'd be with Kat. He'd only been gone days, but to him, it had been a lifetime.

He could only imagine what she'd been through, not knowing if he'd ever come back. He wondered if she'd given up on him.
He thought back to his failed attempt to escape the cabin when he
thought he'd seen her in a passing car, how he'd sensed Kat's presence even before Monique had told him she was there. He and Kat
had a special connection.

When the taxi exited off the freeway and turned down Kat's
street, Chance donned the ball cap and sunglasses. He cautioned the
driver to continue to the end of the block while he scanned the neighborhood. A white van was stationed across from Kat's house, and a
man stood next to it, smoking a cigarette. Chance scrunched down
out of sight and instructed the driver to keep going. Just as he'd
suspected, they had Kat's house under surveillance, and they were
waiting for him to show up.

Well past the Catholic church down the block from where Kat
lived, Chance removed her business card from his wallet and gave
the driver the address of Loggins Realty. Three miles up the road in
the Green Lake area, the cabbie dropped Chance off in front of Kat's
workplace. Even on a weekday the path around the lake teemed with
walkers and joggers, some with dogs or strollers in tow. But Chance
had no interest in gawking at the lazy summer scene.

He took off his cap and barged in without a thought as to his
appearance—his matted hair; his scruffy beard; his clothes, dirty
and wrinkled from two days' wear. When the receptionist glanced
up to greet him, her smile faded and her eyes widened. She looked as
if she were about to be robbed.

"Is Maggie Loggins in? Tell her Chance Eliason wants to see
her."

Jim, Maggie's coworker, strode into the reception area, which
was bright and cheery with a philodendron hanging in the corner.
One look at Chance and he gasped. "What in the world happened
to you?"

"Where's Maggie?"

"She's with a client. She should be back soon."

"Then I'm going to need your help." He hesitated, wondering how much to explain without going too far. The fewer people involved the better.

The decision was made for him because Maggie walked in, followed by a smartly dressed middle-aged couple. She glanced at Chance, then without missing a beat said to Jim, "Take Mr. and Mrs. Bradley to the conference room and show them some listings in the Wallingford area. I'll be there shortly." After the conference door closed, she turned to Chance and, keeping her voice low, said, "What are you doing here, and where in the hell have you been?"

"There's no time for that now. Can we talk privately? I'm sorry to interrupt like this, but it's important."

With Chance following, Maggie set off down the hallway. She left him in her stylish office that had dark oak flooring and a matching oak desk, plush leather chairs, and in the corner a stand-alone fountain with water trickling over polished rocks.

He'd barely had time to look out the window when she stepped in and closed the door. "Has something happened to Kat?"

"I haven't seen her yet," he said. "I just got into town."

"Then I take it you haven't heard the news."

"What? Is Kat all right?"

"Oh lordy, you don't know."

"Know what?"

"Look, Kat told me everything. I know about the people you worked for. They trashed her house, looking for the memory stick."

"Is she all right? Did they do anything to her?"

"She's fine. Just tired as far as I can see after traipsing all over Maine looking for you."

He started for the door. He had to be with Kat. Nothing else mattered.

"Hold on, Chance. That's not all. She's worried sick about your daughter."

"What's happened to Stella?"

"Oh, god, you don't know that either. Those creeps you worked for have her. Kat's waiting for their call."

His knees buckled at the news, and he grasped the back of a nearby chair. This turn of events changed everything. "I didn't think Philip would stoop that low."

"Philip. Who is Philip?"

"I have to go."

"What are you going to do?"

"What choice do I have? I'm going to Kat's."

"What if someone's watching the house?"

"They *are* watching it. That's why I came here first."

"Then maybe you're letting your emotions cloud your thinking. Won't you be falling into their hands?"

Chance considered his options. "If I can get into the house undetected, I could be there when the call comes in. I want to talk to the bastard who's responsible for this. Of course, with all their spying capabilities, it might be a moot point. But I have to try."

"Then that's probably what you should do, see if there's some way you can gain entrance to the house without their knowing, but I don't know how you're going to accomplish that."

"If they've been inside, the house is bugged. I know how they operate," he said. "Do you think you could drive over there and deliver a written message? Then I'll need Jim to drop me off where I tell him to. They won't know his car."

"What about meeting her at my house?"

"They'll follow her there. I can't risk that. Plus, we need to be there when the phone call comes in."

Maggie handed him a pen and tablet that were lying next to her computer. "You write your note, and I'll get with Jim to coordinate our time. And you know, if Kat didn't love you so much, I'd give you a piece of my mind for ever involving her in this insanity. She's barely over the Rosswood incident. I hope you're aware of that."

"I know, and when this is over, I'll see to it she gets the help she needs."

"You better, or you'll have me to answer to."

"One more thing, Maggie. On your way back from Kat's would you stop at a drugstore and buy me one of those disposable phones? If I need to use it, they can't trace that number back to me."

"I'll have Jim do that. There's a store around the corner."

Left alone, with the pen poised to write, Chance thought of his daughter and felt the bitterness rise. The bastards would pay for this. Philip would pay. Maybe he should forget all this stealing around and walk right up to the house in broad daylight. Let them come for him. He'd take them on.

But if he tried to bully his way through this, they'd have him in their custody, and he'd be no good to Stella, or Kat. Besides, it was Philip he wanted to deal with, not his guard dogs. He had to stay calm and gain control of the situation. They'd threatened the two people he loved most in this world. He'd have to give Philip what he wanted, but on his *own* terms.

Maggie popped her head in the doorway. "As soon as the Bradleys leave, which will be in about ten minutes, we can put your plan into motion."

***

Kat was upstairs, sweltering in the afternoon heat, picking up the last of the Christmas ornaments that had been dumped on the floor, when the doorbell rang. She dodged boxes and checked out the window of the gabled bedroom facing the street. At the curb was Maggie's car. The van was still parked out front. She rushed downstairs and opened the door.

Maggie, exhibiting a peculiar strain on her face, much more than normal concern, charged through the doorway. "I came to see how you're doing and if you need help cleaning this place up." She'd belted out her words in an uncharacteristic manner.

"I've got it under control."

"Oh yes, I can see that." Maggie examined the rooms where the chairs and couch were set right again and the floors cleared of papers. "Have you heard anything yet?"

"Not a thing, and I'm just so worried about her."

"I know, dear, but another reason I came, and I hate to bother you with this, but since your laptop is missing I had to bring this document to you in person. I want you to check the figures on this Harrison deal before we move forward on it. I need you to read it now so I can take it back with me." She whispered in Kat's ear. "Don't say a word until you've read this." She handed over a manila envelope.

Maggie's behavior was odd at best. Kat wasn't aware of any "Harrison deal," but she went along with it and pulled out a sheet of legal paper. She recognized the broad, heavy strokes as Chance's handwriting. She cocked her head at Maggie, who answered her with an affirming nod.

In the letter, Chance warned Kat that the house was bugged and cautioned her not to mention his name after reading the letter. He also cautioned her about using her cell phone because they could possibly hack into it. He knew about Stella's kidnapping. He was at Maggie's office and would be with her soon. After he arrived, it was imperative she remain calm and not say one word. There were no terms of endearment, but Kat wasn't hurt or offended. When dealing with serious matters, Chance was all business.

Despite the gravity of the note's contents, Kat could hardly contain her excitement at the prospect of his homecoming, that he was only a few miles away. Her eyes filled with tears while Maggie kept nodding and smiling. "I think this is a very sweet deal indeed," Kat said out loud.

"I thought you'd like it. And since you have everything under control here, I'll go back to the office and get the ball rolling."

Kat walked her to the door. "Thanks for everything."

"Be sure to keep me informed. If they call, let me know." Maggie hugged Kat and whispered, "Be careful, my darling."

After seeing Maggie off, Kat started upstairs to finish sweeping up some of the ornaments that had broken, but changed her mind and turned around in mid stairwell. All she cared about now was waiting downstairs for Chance. When she reached the bottom step, she glimpsed a man striding past the front window, breaking toward the right side of the house, and continuing past the dining room window.

She looked out front. The van was still there, but the driver was absent. She hurried through the kitchen to the mudroom, peeled back the door's curtain a notch. The dark-haired man was rifling through the recycle barrel and examining her discarded papers. He glanced toward the house, and she backed against the wall, hoping he hadn't seen her shadow.

A minute later she peeked out to check his whereabouts. He was standing in the middle of the alley, lighting a cigarette, as if he planned to station himself there for the duration.

Kat had to warn Chance before he walked into an ambush, but how could she make a call if the house was bugged? She'd have to code her message.

She took her cell phone from her purse and punched in Maggie's number. When Maggie answered, Kat said, "Are you still in your car?"

"Let me pull over." After a long pause, Maggie came back on the line. "What's up?"

"I was thinking about that deal we just went over," Kat said, "and I'm not sure it would be wise to get it in the works right now. There are some obstacles around the property. It might be better to wait a while until things settle down. At least warn the buyer before he goes through with the deal. Do you understand?"

There was another long pause before Maggie spoke up. "Gotcha. Still, I'm sure the deal will go through despite the obstacles."

"I'm counting on it."

It was edging toward suppertime, and no calls had come in about Stella. Chance hadn't arrived yet. Too nervous to concentrate on anything of substance or something as trivial as thumbing through a magazine, Kat divided her time scurrying from the front of the house to the rear, watching out the windows, trying to discern what might be going on outside. On one of her last passes through, she looked out back and noticed two of her car's tires had been flattened.

Earlier, her neighbor Mr. Singleton, who always kept an eye out for anything strange in the neighborhood, actually walked over to the van and conversed with the driver. Whatever lie the driver had told him seemed to satisfy him because he went back to his house and never approached the van again.

At one point the man who'd been rummaging through her garbage made a call on his cell phone. Kat opened the kitchen window but could only hear the drone of his voice, nothing distinct or easily understood. He hurried across the yard. Soon a sedan pulled up next to the van, and the two men changed places.

Kat was too tense to eat, and her back ached from standing most of the day. She lay on her bed for moment's rest, hoping to calm down enough to tune in, perhaps to get answers to the questions that were haunting her: How would this all end? Would Chance come through this safely? Would Stella make it through unharmed? These were questions even Libby hadn't addressed. She'd said the ending was hazy. Why wouldn't she know for sure? Or was the outcome too horrible to say?

To settle her nerves, Kat took a long, even breath. But the harder she tried to focus, the more distracted she became. It was no use. She couldn't even tune in to get her own answers. She thought of calling Libby for help, but remembered Libby was taking time away from work. Bothering her now before her wedding was utterly unthinkable.

Kat's bedroom had warmed from the afternoon sun. She was hot and sweaty. She fled to the bathroom and splashed her face with cold water. There was nothing to do but wait.

CHAPTER 18

While waiting for Maggie's return, Chance wandered across the hall into Kat's office, which consisted of a desk, chairs, a small bookshelf, but no plants. Kat had a brown thumb when it came to indoor plants. Her desk was relatively neat: a computer, a pen lying on a stack of folders, a mug half-filled with coffee. He smiled just thinking about the woman he loved and how she had to work at keeping things tidy.

He picked up the black cardigan that rested on her chair. It carried the scent so familiar to him. On the desk was a photo of the two of them that Stella had taken in front of Kat's house. "We'll be together soon, Kat. I promise you."

Maggie's voice sounded in the hallway. He laid the sweater down and joined her in her office. She was setting her hat and purse on the desk and removing her jacket and slipping it over the back of her chair.

He gave her an expectant look. "How is she?"

"Under the circumstances she's fine. She's anxious to see you, I might add."

"Any word about Stella?"

"Not yet. What do you think they're waiting for?"

"For me to show up, no doubt."

"You'll most definitely walk into a trap if you go there now. On my way back here, Kat called my cell and in a round about way implied that they have the whole house covered, front and back. You'll be caught for sure."

The phone rang, and after listening a moment to the caller, Maggie replied into the receiver, "Tell him I'll be out in a minute." She said to Chance, "I have to take care of business. You know, you could come to my house."

"Let me make a call before I decide that." After Maggie left, Chance took out his wallet and fished out a well-worn business card, then grabbed the disposable phone Jim had bought him. It was early evening on the East Coast, but the firm never slept. Someone was always working, and if he remembered correctly Philip was available by phone anywhere, anytime. He had his finger on the pulse of the organization; he maintained tight control.

Chance had the distinct feeling they were waiting for his call, and his hunch was right. Whoever answered put him on hold for a short time, and the next voice he heard was Philip's. "What took you so long?" Philip asked.

"Where's my daughter?"

"If you care about her, you'll listen to what I have to say."

"Where is she?"

"You won't see her until I get what I want."

Chance was so angry he felt the veins in his temples throb. The room seemed unbearably hot. "So help me, Philip, if your men lay a hand on her—"

"I'm calling the shots now, Eliason, so listen up. I want you to go to the Summers's house and wait for further instruction."

"Why? So your men can nab me?"

"I want to know where you are."

"How do I know you'll call off the dogs?"

"You'll just have to trust me."

"When pigs fly."

The line went dead.

Maggie walked in and stared at Chance. "You're as red as a beet. Who were you talking to?"

"The cause of all this misery. I won't know anything about Stella until I go back to Kat's. They knew I'd show up. They've been waiting for me to call."

"What if you go there and it's some kind of trick?"

"Is Jim available?"

"If I catch him before he leaves, but I can take you if you're sure you want to go there."

"They know your car."

"So, how are you going to get into the house without being spotted?"

Chance was already at the door. "Can we find Jim?"

Maggie pushed ahead of Chance and stalked down the hallway, mumbling, "You and Kat are just alike, both headstrong as hell." She looked in on Jim, along with Chance. "If you're close to finishing for the day, Chance needs a lift to Kat's house."

Jim raised his eyebrows, giving Chance the once over. "You might want to consider taking a shower and cleaning up before she sees you."

"There's no time for that. This is an emergency."

"Oh." Jim shoved away from his desk and followed them out to the reception area. "Is Kat ill?"

"Good luck, Chance," Maggie said. "And please call me as soon as you can. I'll be on pins and needles."

"Thanks for your help."

"Isn't anyone going to tell me what the emergency is?" Jim asked.

"We need to hurry." Chance walked out into the sunshine. A steady stream of walkers circled the lake.

With Chance in tow, Jim strode around the corner of the building and unlocked the car door. His Prius was immaculate inside and out as if it had been recently polished and vacuumed. A pineapple scent permeated the interior.

On the drive over, traffic inched along. During a lengthy wait at the first stoplight, Jim glanced in the rear view mirror at Chance, who had taken his place in the backseat. "Now, will you tell me why you're riding in the back? If I didn't know you better, I'd take offense. What's going on, anyway?"

"Did Kat or Maggie tell you anything?"

"All I know is you and Kat had a monster of an argument, and you left town. She was worried sick about you. And now you're back. But I haven't the foggiest idea why you couldn't just show up at her house."

"It's a long story, which I don't want to go into. For now, the thing you need to know is there are people watching Kat's house, people who are looking for me, and I need to get inside."

"Oh my gosh, this is like one of those crime dramas on TV. Wait until I tell Rick. He'll just die. Are we in any danger?"

"You'll be fine," Chance said. "Here's what I want you to do. When we reach Kat's street, I'm going to duck down so I won't be seen. Park a couple of cars down from her house. I want you to knock on her door and talk to her in the doorway. Don't mention my name. Just small talk and don't go inside. I'll make a run for it, and once I'm on the porch, you can go back to your car and drive off."

"What if they follow me?"

"They won't, trust me. I'm the one they're interested in."

"Won't they just break into Kat's house and come after you?"

"It's not supposed to go down that way. I'm just taking precautions."

"What in the world did you do? Why are you running from these people?"

"It's a very complicated matter. That's all I can say."

As the enormity of the situation sunk in, Jim lapsed into silence, and Chance left him alone with his thoughts. When they reached the end of Kat's block, Chance hid behind the front seat while Jim sought out a parking spot. As he backed in, the rear tire hit the curb, and it took him two tries to parallel-park. He turned off the engine. "I'm nervous as hell."

"Just walk up to the house as if you were coming for a visit," Chance said. "Don't look back at the car."

"Are you sure I'll be able to get away from them?"

"As soon as they see me, you'll be as invisible as the night air. I can guarantee you'll be in no danger."

"Okay, then, here goes." Jim opened and shut the door.

Chance raised his head a notch, far enough so he could see Jim progressing across the yard, up the porch steps, then ringing the doorbell. As soon as Chance saw Kat in the doorway, he snuck out of the car and barreled across the neighbor's lawn. The van's doors opened, but by then he was already on the porch and Jim was jetting back to the Prius. The two men stood beside the van, watching the spectacle. Jim sped down the street and swerved around the corner. The men didn't make a move to go after Chance.

Chance closed and locked the door. Kat stood, solid to the spot, with questioning eyes, as if wondering what to do next, until he took her into his arms. She squeezed him tight, her body shaken with emotion. "Darling, it's all right," he said. "I'm here now." The caring look on her face told him more than she could have ever said. She put a finger to his lips, and he grasped and kissed her hand. "I'm sure the house is bugged," he whispered, "so we'll keep our conversation neutral for now. I've missed you so much."

"Oh, Chance. If we'd never had that argument, none of this would have happened. It's all my fault."

He wiped the moisture from her cheeks. "That had nothing to do with this. It was only a matter of time before they came after me."

"What about Stella?"

With Kat close by, Chance glanced out the living room window. One of the men stood outside the van with a cell phone slapped to his ear. "They're probably talking to Philip, letting him know I'm here." He strode into the kitchen with Kat behind him and checked the back door to make sure it was secured, then went into the bedroom closet, reached into the far corner of the upper shelf, and retrieved the pistol she concealed there. He found the box of bullets, hidden in the back of a dresser drawer behind her sweaters, and loaded the chamber.

Kat watched him, alarmed. She grasped his shoulder and whispered, "What are you going to do with it?

He whispered back, "Insurance purposes. All we can do now is to wait for the call. If I know Philip, he'll make me sweat it out all night long."

Chance set the pistol on the dresser and embraced Kat. Her hair's lemony scent momentarily swept him into the times they'd been together. He ran a hand up and down her spine in reassuring strokes. If circumstances had been different, he wouldn't waste another moment to make love to her. He wanted to so badly, but holding her would have to do. Right now, he was primed to react to any situation cast his way. It wasn't that he was afraid of Philip. Far from it. But he had to stay focused, for Stella's sake.

He broke away from Kat, switched on the clock radio, and turned it up loud. The DJ was rattling on about the next tune he intended to play.

Chance combed the bedroom for listening devices. He checked behind the dresser, swept his fingers along the tops of the doors, felt behind the headboard and all around the bed frame. Near the nightstand on Kat's side, he found a small, inconspicuous device. He crushed it with the heel of his shoe and disposed of it in the waste can. He turned the radio off and shook his head in disgust. "Sick bastards."

In the bedroom closet he searched the corners and crevices and came up empty handed. "I'm sure there are others around the house, but if I destroy them and they can't hear anything at all, they'll get curious. Until I hear from Philip, I don't want to arouse their suspicions. At least we can talk in the bedroom."

"I can't believe this is happening."

"Philip's a sociopath. He'll do anything to protect himself and his precious possessions. I'm just sorry you've had to endure this."

"Don't worry about me," Kat said. "Stella is the one you need to be concerned about."

"If I give them what they want, they'll let her go." He looked out the bedroom window at the ivy climbing up the exterior of the house next door, a strangled sensation gripping him. To have Stella back, he'd have to cave in to Philip's demands, which went against everything he believed in, the values he'd set for himself since leaving the firm. Perhaps he could find another way to get back at them.

"Chance." Kat hugged him from behind. "You're more than concerned, aren't you?" In response he turned and held her close. "Why don't you take a shower? I'll listen for the phone. Or I could fix you something to eat."

"Not until I know more. Why don't you fix yourself something?"

"I'll make us both a snack. You need to eat."

As soon as she'd disappeared around the corner, he wandered into the bathroom. His hair was greasy and slicked back from wearing a ball cap, his beard was bristly from day-old growth, and he smelled like airplane interior and sweat. He washed his hands and splashed water on his face. He owed Kat everything just for sticking with him through this nightmare.

He was drying off when Kat returned with a plate stacked with two peanut butter sandwiches. She went back for napkins and glasses of water. On the bed she set the plate between them. He wolfed down his share before Kat had finished a half. She gave him her second portion.

"I guess I was hungrier than I thought," he said.

Kat eyed his scraped arms and hands. "How did you get those cuts?"

Chance gave her an account of his incarceration and how he'd spent his time thinking about a way to escape so he could get back to her. He described his attempt to rappel from the upstairs window and his eventual capture. He purposely left out the intimate moments with Monique since they meant nothing to him, hardly worth mentioning. "I thought I saw you drive past the entrance to the cabin, and later Maggie told me you'd flown to Maine to look for me. I shouted your name, but by then they had me."

"I drove by what looked like a gate covered with limbs. Up the road a ways, a moose blocked my path. Your face flashed before me, and I knew it was a sign that I should go back to investigate, but then they called me about Stella and warned me to go home. I wanted to stay and look for you, but I didn't know what to do."

"I knew you were there, Kat. I knew it. I was so depressed without you, but just the thought of your being that close lifted my spirits."

"That's what Libby said."

"Who's Libby?"

"One of my client's friends is a psychic. I was so frightened, Chance, I went to see her, and she gave me the clues I needed to look for you; but as it turned out I couldn't get to you. The psychic couldn't see the outcome. I don't know why."

"Maybe there were multiple ways this thing could have played out. At least we're together now. We just need to get Stella back."

"But how did you finally get away?"

How indeed? His mind drifted back to the scene in the Boston airport and the final kiss he'd shared with Monique. The last thing he wanted to do was to upset Kat. He thought it best to downplay that part of his escape. "It's a long story I don't want to go into now. Suffice it to say, I was able to get the keys to a vehicle and get to an airport."

"Are you prepared to let go of this one-man crusade to bring down Topping Ventures?"

He hesitated. "To get what I want, I'll do what I have to do… for now."

"Chance, you don't have to compete with Philip anymore. You can let him win. You can't change the world."

He took the empty plate into the kitchen and deposited it in the sink. Someday he'd settle the score with Philip. He didn't know when or how, but someday the man would pay.

***

Kat stood in the dining room and watched Chance pace from one window to another. He was back, but not the way she wanted him. When she'd held him, despite his soothing words and actions, his muscles were taut. He was like a watch spring wound tight. She wasn't sure if he'd ever relax. Maggie had questioned Kat about what she'd gotten herself into. With everything that had happened so far, plus observing Chance's behavior now, she wondered that, too. Still, their relationship had progressed to the point she couldn't back out. She loved him too much.

She was about to encourage him to sit and rest when the land-line rang. Before she could make a move, Chance pounced on it. Soon his face darkened with contempt.

He nodded at her and drew his attention back to the one-sided conversation. Finally, he said, "How did you know about the memory stick?" Pause. "Did you threaten her?" Pause. "I want to talk to her." A longer interval ensued, then his expression softened to concern. "Stella, honey, have they hurt you in any way?" He listened for a moment. "Calm down. You don't have to apologize. It won't be long now." Another pause. "So help me, Philip, I want my daughter back. You can have the damn memory stick, you sonovabitch. Just leave her alone."

"How is she?" Kat asked after he'd hung up the phone. "She must be terrified."

He took Kat into the bedroom where they could talk freely. "She was anxious, of course, but she said they were treating her all right. A car will pick me up tomorrow morning and take me to the bank for the memory stick. I don't know why he wants it. I could have a number of them hidden away, but I have to play his game. Stella was upset because she told them about it and she had to give them the key to the safety deposit box. They threatened to harm me if she didn't."

"Why wouldn't they just take her to the bank to get it?"

"Philip wants to see me in person, probably for the satisfaction of seeing me defeated. He always has to have the upper hand. But I'm not done with him."

"What if they won't let you go?" Kat was conjuring up any number of horrific scenarios. "What if they do to you what they did to the last man that defied them?"

"*Disappear me* like they did to Gerald Morningstar?"

"You have to be done with this once and for all, Chance. No more books. No more revenge. You have to let it go."

"Someone has to stop all the corruption and the killing."

"Does it have to be you? How can you go against a powerful organization like Topping Ventures? These companies are like poisonous mushrooms. If you stomp on one, there will always be others to take its place. Isn't that what you told me once? You're just one man, Chance. You can't fight the system."

He sat on the bed and pulled Kat onto his lap. "After I get Stella back, I'll think of something."

"I don't like it when you talk like this. I'd die if I lost you," she said, and he hugged her close. She ran her fingers through his hair. "Why don't you take a shower and clean up. It will do you good. It might clear your thinking. I'll make us some coffee. It's going to be a long night. I know you won't sleep."

"Sweetheart, I'm so glad I have you." He gave her a warm squeeze. "I'll just wash up."

She left him wandering into the bathroom. She hoped he would eventually release his destructive feelings toward the firm and his need to retaliate. Their future depended on it.

In the kitchen, as she filled the coffeemaker with water, her thoughts lit on the woman who had played such a crucial role in taking Chance away. Now that he was back, Kat wanted to know more about Monique's role in all of this. He hadn't mentioned her. But considering his weariness and anxious state of mind, now was an inappropriate time to ask.

CHAPTER 19

A truck's engine revved up, then idled, startling Kat. She opened her eyes to a room brightened with morning light. Hot and sweaty, she lay fully clothed on her bed with a blanket thrown over her. It was 8:00 a.m. In the kitchen, water was running. She thought of Chance, and the events of the night came rushing back to her.

They had stayed up, drinking coffee until after 3:00 a.m. He hadn't been in a talkative mood. He'd paced. He'd checked the security of the doors and windows. How many times, she'd lost count of. Finally, he'd sat near the fireplace, staring at the floor, withdrawn into his private world. She recalled sitting at the table, having rested her head in her arms. The next thing she knew he was guiding her to bed, slipping off her shoes, and after sliding the hair off her face, kissing her cheek. After that, she'd drifted off until morning.

The garbage truck continued down the alley, and Kat went in search of Chance. She found him at the kitchen sink with a mug in his hand. He looked pale, but twenty pounds lighter. He'd shaved and dressed in a clean pair of slacks and shirt he'd kept in her closet. Outwardly, he looked like the man she knew before he'd left her.

Coming closer though, she observed the heavy eyelids, the bloodshot eyes, and the downcast expression on his face. No amount of sprucing up could mask the anguish he was suffering over his daughter's abduction. Until Stella was safely in his care, nothing would ease his weary heart. What struck Kat the most about him was his fierce and abiding devotion to the ones he loved.

Without conscious thought, she squinted while looking at him, and the soft light from the window behind him gave rise to the energy around his body. His energy was constricted, yet sparks of light shot out, razor-sharp. She was taken aback. She'd seen his aura,

and she could tell his nerves were prickly, on edge. She stopped short
of hugging him and poured herself a cup of coffee.

She swayed a little and leaned against the counter for support.
She had an overwhelming sense of dread. She didn't want him to go.
The message was strong. Her intuition told her, if he *did* go after
Stella, something about Kat and Chance's relationship would change
dramatically. Her cup rattled in her hand. She set it down.

He walked toward her, planted a light kiss on her cheek, and
continued into the living room. She watched him from the doorway.
He glanced from the window to his watch and out the window again.
A car honked, and he strode toward the door.

"Chance."

He stopped before he turned the doorknob and hurried back to
hug her. She clung tight. The expression on his face was immovably
pained. He looked as if he'd aged ten years.

"Be careful," she warned as he pulled away from her. "I love
you."

She watched him leave the house, his progress down the sidewalk bold and purposeful. He climbed into a late-model sedan. Then
he was gone. The van pulled away from the curb.

Kat was relieved to have her privacy restored, but an emptiness
so deep and strong sunk into her. It was as if she'd lost Chance all
over again. She roamed from room to room, searching for something
to occupy her time, to keep her mind from blowing the situation out
of proportion and projecting it to a tragic ending. Too antsy to settle
down, she picked up the phone and dialed Maggie's number.

"I've been waiting for this call," Maggie said. "Tell me everything. Is Chance all right? Did he get his daughter back? And how
are you doing?"

"He left with them to make the exchange. The memory stick
for Stella. I have no idea where they took him. I'm just so worried he
won't come back."

"Do you want me to come over and wait with you?"

"I wouldn't be good company."

"Since when do you and I stand on such formality? You could sleep for all I care. Perhaps you should. I could get take-out. I'm sure you haven't eaten a thing."

"I'm not hungry. And I'm sure you have work to do since you're carrying my load, too."

"I must confess I do have work piling up and clients wanting my attention, but if you need me I can make time."

"I'll be fine, Maggie, and I'll call you as soon as I know anything."

"You're sure?"

"I promise."

"I'll wait for your call."

Kat hung up, but after five anxiety-ridden minutes, longed for Maggie's company. To fill her time, she sat at her desk to finish straightening up the contents, starting with the bottom drawer. Lying on top of a stack of papers was the envelope the firm had sent her with the intimate photos of Chance and Monique. She wished she'd thrown them away, out of temptation's reach. As difficult as they were to look at, she found herself drawn to them and slid the pictures out in full view.

***

The two men on either side of Chance were tall, muscular, and dressed in dark suits. They'd driven him to the bank to retrieve the memory stick from the safe deposit box he co-rented with Stella and were now guiding him through the massive lobby of the Seasons Hotel in downtown Seattle. Shades of beige, brown, and cream with splashes of maroon highlighted the rugs and furnishings. They passed a massive stone fireplace before turning left toward the elevators. Up to this point no words had been exchanged.

They exited on the ninth floor, escorted him down the hall, and unlocked the door to Room 926. The men hesitated, waiting for Chance to enter. They left him alone, but he was sure they'd been instructed to wait outside. Confined to the suite, he felt the walls closing in again.

The living room of this thousand-square-foot suite had a sweeping view of the Sound. The walls were painted taupe, and the sofa and chairs were marine blue. The artwork on the walls had an Asian influence.

No one came out of the other rooms. No sounds alerted him to any other occupants, though a newspaper was spread out on the glass coffee table and two coffee cups sat on a table in the dining area.

He glimpsed the bedroom and the king-size bed, its covers in need of straightening. In the air was a hint of Chanel. He thought about investigating further into the area of the bathroom to check the personal items to see if more than one person had slept here, but his thoughts were interrupted when the door opened.

Philip, immaculately dressed in casual attire, entered with a self-assured gait and a relaxed smile, as if he'd just come from playing a round of golf. "Sit down, Chance." He set his briefcase near a chair. "We have some negotiating to do."

"Not until I see my daughter, you sonovabitch." The blood rushed to Chance's face.

"Take it easy," Philip said, "or one of these days you'll have a heart attack."

"Where is she?"

"You'll see her in due time, but only if you'll calm down and cooperate."

"You didn't bring me here for the memory stick. Your men could have taken it from me, so what do you want? I won't work for you."

"Sit down." Philip focused keenly on Chance, who hadn't made a move. "If you don't do as I say, you'll never see her again. Do you understand?"

Chance thought better than to continue down a path that would only push Philip into acting on his threats. He took a seat in one of the lounge chairs. "You must be desperate, Philip. You've never used a child as a bargaining tool."

"I thought after all I'd done for you, taken you under my wing, mentored you, given you everything you ever wanted in life, plus access to women like Monique, you'd never leave the firm. But I was wrong. You not only left, you were working to destroy me and my organization. I'll do whatever it takes to keep that from happening."

"If I give you the memory stick, then you better leave me and my family alone."

"And what guarantee do I have you won't write another book?"

"My word."

Philip eyed Chance with disdain. "Your word means nothing." He fished some papers from his briefcase and set them on the coffee table in front of Chance. "I want you to sign this legal document. If you say or write anything exposing the firm's business practices, or if you express anything of a derogatory nature about me or the firm, you'll be liable for twenty-five million dollars."

"Twenty-five million." Chance huffed. "You've got to be kidding. And if I don't sign? This is a free country. I have a right to free speech. I'm not going to sign anything. Just give me my daughter in exchange for the memory stick as we agreed to on the phone."

"How do I know you won't go to the media, or the FBI, for chrissakes? Your word isn't good enough."

"It'll have to be. A deal's a deal. My daughter for the memory stick." Chance felt as if he were gaining a foothold.

"You might have other copies stashed away. I'm not a fool, Eliason."

Chance pushed the papers toward Philip. "I'm not signing."

"Oh, I think you will," Philip said. "You'll sign this because I have something else you want. In fact, when you discover what it is, you'll beg to put your signature on this document."

"You couldn't have anything more important than my daughter."

Philip laid his briefcase on the tabletop. "What about your son?"

Chance was thrown completely off balance. He stared at Philip while gathering his thoughts. "I can't believe you're resorting to making things up just to get your way. You're more than desperate. You're crazy."

Philip snapped open his briefcase, pulled out a photo, and held it out for Chance to see. The picture was of Monique standing by a little boy with curly black hair and aqua eyes. For Chance, it was as if he were staring at his six-year-old self.

Chance snatched the photo from Philip and tossed it on the table. "This is a lie." But his mind was churning with the possibility he'd fathered a child with Monique. The handful of times they'd been together in recent years, the intimate moments they'd shared, and she'd never even alluded to a child. This had to be a hoax that only Philip could perpetrate.

While Chance was deep in thought, Philip had been on the phone, and within a minute Monique came though the doorway in one of her seductive dresses, her perfume sweetening the room. Philip took her hand, drew her familiarly close, and gave her a hard kiss on the lips. "Don't be long, my dear."

Chance observed this aggressively warm exchange. After Philip left, Monique passed by Chance and sat on the sofa without looking him in the eye. He shoved the photo across the table, as far away from his reach as possible. "There better be an explanation for this. Are you helping Philip with this deception? I saw the kiss he gave you. What's going on, Monique?"

"Please listen to me, Chance." Her voice was soft, shaky. "I have many confessions to tell you. It will not be easy for me to say and for you to hear."

CHAPTER 20

Chance was in no mood to sit and listen to anything Monique had to say, especially if it had to do with this phony story about their having a child together. All he wanted to do was to have his daughter secure in his arms. "Where's Stella?"

"Chance, please be patient and hear what I have to say. You will see her soon enough." She held the photo out to Chance. "This boy is our son, Chance. His name is Michel."

Michel was the French version for Michael, Chance's middle name. Chance pushed Monique's hand aside. "We never had a child."

"Oh, but darling, he is ours. It is true."

"The only child you've ever mentioned was your sister's. You said she had a child."

"No, no, Chance. I said she was caring for a child. You just assumed the child was hers. But I know I have not told you the truth."

Chance studied Monique's expression, trying to discern if he could catch her in a lie, but her eyes were steadfast on his and she neither blinked nor turned away from him. "This boy may be your child, but you've been with other men, probably Philip, too. I saw the way he kissed you when you came into the room. Sex is your job, isn't it?"

"You do not have to hurt me with your words," she said. "You know how I work. I do not have sex with every man I am with. I may seduce them into the bedroom, but that does not mean I give myself to them. You are the only man I have loved, or ever will love. Believe me when I say Michel is yours."

"You still work for Philip and are sleeping with him, no doubt, so how can I believe anything you say. You're as despicable as he is."

Tears flooded her eyes. She unfolded some papers she'd taken from her purse, her hands trembling. "Look at these if you do not believe me."

He hesitated, wondering what lies awaited him. He snatched the papers and skimmed a copy of a Court-Ready Paternity Test Application and a Legally Binding Paternity Test Report, both with his name marked as the father. The DNA analysis showed that the probability of Chance being Michel's father was over 99.9999 percent.

"I don't know how you managed this." He dropped the documents on the table next to Monique and Michel's picture. "But this is a scam. Philip could have had these doctored."

She stood, facing him. "Listen to me. This has nothing to do with anything Philip did. I had the test done a long time ago, a year after Michel was born, just to satisfy myself." She held the photo for him to see. "Look at his picture, Chance. Look at it. Look at his hair and his eyes. Look at his smile. You cannot deny it. Michel is your son."

Chance walked to the window with the photo. Michel was the spitting image of himself at this young age. Thinking back six years, he recalled the one night he'd spent with Monique that could have possibly led to this. They had been so eager to be together, he hadn't used any protection. They very well could have conceived a child.

The sunlight glistened off the Sound. The ferry to Bremerton churned through the water. He let the warmth radiating off the glass seep into his body, let the news about his son seep into the tissues of his brain until he came to grips with the possibility. In the photo, if he substituted his Italian mother for Monique, in looks alone the boy would fit into his family and could indeed be his.

Chance's feelings were all a jumble. The thought of having a son thrilled him, but if it were true, the years they'd been kept apart both saddened and infuriated him. He turned to Monique with a hard, level stare. "Why didn't you tell me when you knew you were pregnant?"

Her cell phone rang. *"Excusez-moi.* I must take this." She shifted the phone to her ear, listened a moment and said, "I need more time, Philip. Please."

After ending the call, she said to Chance, "I did not tell you because by then you had left the firm and had gone back to take care of Meredith. I did not tell you because it would have made no difference. When we were together in Seattle a year later when I knew for sure he was your son, I wanted to tell you, but you said you would never go back to the firm, and you made it clear to me you did not love me. I could not bear to tell you then because I knew if I had, you would have taken him away from me. You would tell me I was an unfit mother because of the work I did. He was a part of you, Chance. He was all I had."

"I had a right to know."

"I wanted to tell you at the cabin, but you were so angry with me. I thought we could have a life together, the three of us, but you are in love with someone else."

"Where is he now?"

"In Boston with Paulette."

"I want to see him."

"That is why I am here. He needs his father." She reached into her purse for a tissue and dabbed her eyes. "I cannot care for him anymore."

"You're willing to give him up that easily? What kind of a mother are you?"

"Paulette and I have cared well for him." Monique sniffled and wiped her eyes. "But Paulette wishes to return to France, and I must work."

"How can you dump him on a man he doesn't even know?"

"It has to be this way, Chance. I would rather Michel be with you than to be around Philip."

"What does Philip have to do with this?"

"Oh, darling, let me explain it to you," she said. "I have made such a mess of things. When you and I returned from our assignments overseas we made such love to each other. Do you not remember that night? That was the day Michel was conceived. We even talked of marriage then, do you not remember?"

"Words spoken in the heat of passion, Monique. We were never serious."

"I know that now, but I can assure you it meant something to me." She swallowed hard, trying to maintain her composure. "Right after you left the firm, I was so distraught I turned to Philip for comfort. I know now it was the wrong thing to do. When I found out I was pregnant, he wanted me to have an abortion. I had second thoughts myself about having the child, because of my age. But in my heart I knew Michel was yours. I could not destroy that part of you, so I gave Philip the impression Michel could possibly be his child. He was not happy about it. He did not want a child, but he stopped pressuring me about the abortion and gave me and Paulette his condo to stay in. He let me take a year's leave."

"Then you came out to Seattle to see me."

"Yes. A year after Michel was born. But you did not want the life we'd shared. You were making a new life for yourself. You were never coming back to the firm, or me. You had changed how you felt about me. Your love had turned to lust. That was all."

She took a moment to wipe the tears and blow her nose before continuing on. "I had taken your hairbrush when we met in Seattle and had a paternity test run just to be sure. In the meantime, Philip's wife found out he was seeing me, and you know how Philip is about his money. He did not want a divorce, so we ended the relationship. But now and then he would come around to visit Michel. Philip was good to him."

"Does Philip know the truth?"

"I just told him recently."

"And you're alive to tell about it? I can't imagine him letting you pull off this charade without dire consequences to your well-being."

"I think he knew deep down Michel was not his son. By the looks of him as he grew older, Philip had to know. But he kept silent about it. That is another reason why you must take Michel."

"Has he threatened to hurt the boy? That would be just like Philip if he knew Michel was *my* son."

"He would never harm Michel," she said, "but now that Philip finally knows the truth, he does not want to raise your son, your flesh and blood, especially now after what you have done. He will not have anything to do with Michel. He told me so. You see, Philip's wife has filed for a divorce, and he and I are getting married." She lowered her head to avoid Chance's piercing stare.

"Have you lost your mind?" Chance couldn't believe this turn of events. The Monique he knew, the woman who claimed to love him, was selling her soul to the devil. "Don't do this, Monique. Don't turn to Philip again. You could have any man you want. You're beautiful and intelligent."

"Yes, but he has made me a promise, so I cannot refuse him."

"What in the world is so important that you would marry this despot?"

She met his gaze straight on. "You and your daughter. I promised to marry Philip in exchange for your lives. He will never bother either of you ever again."

Chance stared at this woman, a tangle of contradictions. A seductress, a mother, one of the most intelligent women he'd ever known, a woman who loved him so much she was willing to protect him and his daughter from an unknown fate. "Your life will be ruined if you marry Philip."

"It does not matter. But the only way you will ever see Michel is if you sign the papers he brought and never speak of him or his firm again."

"And if I don't agree?"

"I do not wish to think about what Philip will do. Please, Chance, Paulette is leaving for France. I have no one to care for Michel. And then there is Philip. Please help me keep our son safe. It is the only way."

Monique was like a mother bear safeguarding her cub. He'd never seen this side of her, except when she'd helped him escape. He hated to feed her to the wolves, but now he had a son to think about. He looked at the picture of the boy and felt a swelling in his heart.

"When I get back to Boston, I will let you know how we will arrange for you to come for Michel." She hesitated. "But I suppose you will need time to talk to your lover."

For a brief moment Chance thought about Kat's reaction and what this would do to their relationship, but if this boy was indeed his son, Chance couldn't turn his back on him, not with Philip in the picture. "You're not opposed to having Michel around another woman?"

"It is not what I would wish, that is true, but the decision has been made for Michel's welfare. That is all that counts."

"It will hurt him to leave you."

"He knows me only as his aunt," she said. "He thinks he is adopted and his real mother lives far away. I planned to tell him the truth when he got older, but I did not want him to think of me as his mother in case something should happen to me. I wasn't prepared for a child. I did not know what else to do. You know how dangerous the work can be. Plus, I was gone much of the time. Philip saw to that. He kept me busy on assignments so I would not be tempted to see you again. He was so jealous."

Her cell phone rang. Her eyes narrowing, she answered, aggravated, "Give me one more minute, Philip," and hung up with a resigned sigh. "Promise me, Chance, you will sign the papers and you will look after Michel. Promise me before Philip returns."

Chance's head reeled with everything Monique was pitching at him. He had no time to think the situation through, no time to consider the consequences, no time to get used to the idea of having a son. "I wish you would have told me before now."

She touched his cheek, encasing him in the sweet cloud of her perfume. She questioned him with her eyes. Though no words were spoken, he knew what she was asking. He held her wrist and moved her hand away from his face.

"Well, then," she said, "there is nothing left to say, except for your promise to sign the papers."

The door burst open, and Philip entered the suite just as Chance dropped Monique's hand. With haste, she gathered her purse from the sofa. "I will be in touch," she told Chance.

As she approached Philip, he slipped his hand in hers, keeping her from leaving the room. "Stay, dear. This will only take a minute," he said, and her face reddened.

"I'm not signing anything until I see my daughter." Chance couldn't even think about the boy, who at this point was no more than an abstraction, until he had Stella by his side.

"You'll see her as soon as you put your signature on that document. That's the deal."

"And how do I know you'll let me see my son?"

"Monique and I have plans for our future that don't include children," Philip said, "especially yours."

"Do not be cruel, Philip," Monique said.

"I swore to Monique I wouldn't stand in the way. You'll have your son. And then I never want to see or hear from you again."

"Then give me five minutes." Chance sat and skimmed the legal document while Philip spoke quietly to Monique. It looked as if Philip had every angle covered, leaving Chance no room to say or do anything to tarnish the firm's reputation. No way would he be allowed to write, speak, or use the Internet to defame his former employer. Philip had won. If Chance ever wanted to see Michel, he had no option but to sign. Though signing the paper went against everything he stood for, he lifted the pen and scribbled his signature. With the document held tight, he rose and shook it at Philip. "Unless I see my daughter in the next few minutes, I'm tearing this up."

Monique broke away from Philip, marched up to Chance, and grasped the document. "Let it go, and you will see your daughter. I swear to you." He loosened his grip, and she replaced Philip's document with the paternity papers. As she and Philip neared the door, she glanced back, her face showing the strain of leaving Chance, her eyes teary and sorrowful.

Once more, Chance found himself in the suite alone. He folded the paternity papers and shoved them into his pant pocket. He raked his fingers through his hair and realized for the first time he'd been perspiring. His shirt had circles of moisture under the arms. Waves of exhaustion poured through him. But he wouldn't let down for a second. When dealing with Philip, Chance had to stay poised for any possibility.

He paced the room for what seemed like an hour. Kat came to mind, along with the reality he had a son, but before he could venture down that line of thinking, he heard a rumbling of voices in the hallway.

Before he'd made it to the door, Stella rushed in and ran into his opened arms. "Daddy." She clung to him, trembling.

He stroked her hair and kissed her forehead. "Baby, I'm here. I'm here. It's over. You're safe now." The prospect of losing her rattled him to the core. After what he'd put her through, he never wanted to let her go.

One of Philip's men held the door open. "I'm supposed to drive you back to the house."

"No! We'll take a cab." Even if it were an innocent offer, he wanted none of Philip's men near his daughter. "You can tell Philip a deal's a deal. Stay away from us, all of you." In a protective manner he held Stella close and guided her past the man.

CHAPTER 21

All the way from the hotel to the University District, Stella nestled against Chance. She was subdued but seemed happy just being close to her father. The slacks and blouse she'd worn to work when she was abducted were wrinkled, and a hint of cigarette smoke lingered in her hair. As far as Chance knew, she wasn't a smoker. The hotel had restrictions, but Philip and his men were never bound to any rules.

Chance felt a surge of loving protectiveness toward his only child, at least the only child he'd known of until today. Monique's confession had shocked him. He tried tucking the revelation away. Still, it nagged at him, but he couldn't cope with it now.

At Kat's house he paid the taxi driver and stepped out into the heat of the day. Upon seeing Kat in the doorway, Stella took off running, and Kat captured her in her arms. Chance hurried to join them, and all three hovered together in a group hug, the women with tears rolling down their cheeks and Chance tearing up, trying to maintain a sense of propriety but doing a poor job of it. Curious, Mr. Singleton was watching them from his porch. For privacy Chance herded them inside.

"They called while you were gone and told me where the listening devices were hidden," Kat said. "I got rid of them."

"That was big of Philip." Chance couldn't hide the sarcasm.

"Are you all right, Stella?" Kat asked.

"I want to go home and take a shower and get out of these clothes." Stella seemed almost frantic, and Kat glanced at Chance for help.

"Honey," he said, "why don't I drive you there, and you can pack a suitcase? I think you should stay here with us tonight."

"But, Dad, I have to go to work."

"I think you need to take the rest of the week off. You've just been through a traumatic experience, and you need time to decompress, take time to relax a little."

"Your dad's right."

"Yeah, but you guys don't need me hanging around. You'll want some time alone, and you don't need me here."

Chance embraced his daughter again, and she started to weep. "You're staying here with us. Kat and I will have plenty of time to be alone."

"That's right, sweetie. We should all be together now. Chance, I called my roadside service, and they came out and pumped up the tires, so the car is ready to go."

"Good, because I have an idea," he said. "Why don't we spend the next few days at the ranch?" He studied Kat's expression to get a read on her feelings about going to Rosswood. She was quiet on the subject, and suddenly the flaming argument they'd had before he'd been taken away came rushing back to him. "I'll have you back by Sunday night, and I promise you, you won't have to go into town. I think it would be good for Stella to have a change of scenery and to be in the outdoors with the horses and burros. I don't want to leave you here, but I do have to check on my property. I've left Rusty there without a word. So, will you please come with us?"

"Please, Kat, I want to go with Dad, but I want you to come, too."

Kat was slow to respond, and Chance could tell this was a difficult decision for her. She finally answered with a half smile. "I guess I'm outnumbered."

"We can be in Rosswood by suppertime," he said.

"Now? I couldn't possibly be ready."

"Please, Kat. You can get ready while Dad and I go get my stuff."

Chance wasn't about to leave without Kat. Their relationship had almost been dealt a fatal blow. More than anything, he wanted her with him. "Please, Kat."

Kat looked from Chance to Stella. "Okay, you two. If it will make you happy."

***

The SUV purred nicely on the other side of the mountains. Kat sat on the passenger side. Stella dozed in the backseat. Chance had insisted on driving. He was still hyped up from all that had happened. He was unusually quiet, as if something else were bothering him, but Kat didn't press him. He'd been under enough stress. Besides, traveling to Rosswood, she had enough of her own issues to think about.

They'd had no opportunity to be alone, and with Stella riding along, Kat couldn't tell Chance how uncomfortable she felt about going back to the house where Monique had been, where those intimate pictures had been taken. The sheets were still on the bed, her perfume scent on the pillow. Chance should have thought of that, but he seemed too preoccupied for her to question him about it. He was intent on his driving, but to her it seemed more than that.

Stella was always more emotive than her father. Now, she was more subdued and she too seemed to be holding a lot inside. Chance hadn't pushed her to talk about her ordeal, and up to this point she hadn't volunteered anything.

Before Kat left Seattle, she'd called Maggie and arranged to be away from work until Monday. Maggie had been beyond patient through Kat's Rosswood experience, and now this. Kat had to get back to the office soon not only for financial reasons but also to repay Maggie for her kind understanding.

Sometime while Chance was at the hotel, Kat's laptop had turned up on the porch. She'd been in the shower and hadn't heard the knocking. Apparently, Philip was satisfied Chance hadn't downloaded any manuscript copies on her computer. Her work files were intact.

The sun baked the windshield, but the air-conditioning kept the car cool and comfortable. Eventually, they rounded the final curve toward their destination. Though she'd recently been in Rosswood, coming here again wasn't any easier. Approaching the Pine Road cutoff, she kept her attention focused ahead, anticipating Chance's private drive. But she couldn't relax fully until he'd pulled up to the ranch house.

Chance got out first, placed his hands on the small of his back, and arched his spine. Zeke came running from the barn, yipping and whining, and practically knocked Chance over. Chance rubbed his neck and ears. Zeke wagged his tail while wiggling and licking Chance's arms.

When Kat and Stella opened their doors, the dog rushed around the front bumper. He circled from one to the other, barking and trying to lick their hands.

Chance slapped his thigh, saying "Here, boy," and Zeke charged back to him.

Rusty waved his hat in recognition and strode toward the SUV, a huge grin on his face. Zeke ran to him and back to Chance. "Hey, boss. I ain't never heard from nobody. Didn't know if you was dead or alive."

"Sorry I didn't call you," Kat said, "but there was too much going on."

"She's right, Rusty. But everything's back to normal now."

"You mean that French lady ain't coming back?"

Kat watched for Chance's reaction, but he never smiled or showed any emotion. If anything, he frowned a little when he replied with a shake of his head.

"We'll be here until Sunday, and then I'm taking Kat and Stella back to Seattle." Chance looked toward the barn. Stella was wandering in the direction of the fence line where the burros were braying. "I thought she might need time with the animals, Rusty. She's been through some trauma, but I don't want you to ask her about it."

"Anything I can do to help?"

"Just let her be. But help her saddle one of the horses if she wants to ride. It might be good for her. Did you have any problems here while I was gone?"

"No, but..." Rusty stuck his hands in his back pockets. "Didn't know if you was gonna be around to pay me."

"I'm late, aren't I? I'll have your check ready tomorrow morning."

"No hurry, boss, now that I know you're home."

Chance draped an arm over Kat's shoulder. "I guess we'll go in and have a look around."

Rusty tipped his hat. "Ma'am."

Chance unlocked the door for Kat, then went back for the suitcases. On the counter were his car keys, his hat, and his cell phone. A coffee cup was on the table. Near the sink were an opened wine bottle and two wine glasses, which she hadn't noticed on her previous visit.

Chance hauled in the bags and disappeared down the hallway. She lagged behind to stick the cork in the wine bottle. When she entered the master bedroom, he'd opened the blinds and was tugging off the bedcovers. She helped him strip off the sheets. He worked in silence. She didn't pry. Peeling away the pillow case, she caught a faint whiff of perfume, which she couldn't ignore. She dropped the pillow and looked at Chance, questioning.

"I'm sorry, Kat."

Setting that painful matter aside, she was just happy Chance was saying anything. "You don't have to apologize. You had no control over what happened to you." She hurried around the bed, but as she approached him, she slowed her pace, wondering if holding him now was the right thing to do.

Instead of recoiling, he accepted her into his arms. "I'm so sorry, Kat." He kissed her forehead, her cheeks, her lips with kisses, forceful and urgent, everything he'd been holding inside.

She wanted more, the sex, the intimacy, everything they'd both held back. Wrapped in his arms, she fell on the bed with him. "Let's never argue."

He quieted her with a vigorous kiss and caressing fingers. She craved his touch, the feel of his powerful yet gentle hands. She grabbed his shirt. It was all she could do to keep from shredding it into a million pieces. He thrust her T-shirt up and seized the top of her shorts. Just as he grasped the zipper, the screen door banged shut. They both froze.

"Dad...Kat...!" Stella's voice rang through to the bedroom.

Kat was the first to plant her feet on the floor. They both tucked in their shirts and ran their fingers through their hair in an attempt to look presentable.

Chance let out a long, frustrated sigh. "Be right there, Stella!" He grabbed Kat's wrist and drew her close. "Later."

Kat hung her arms around his neck and kissed him all the way to the door, then broke away so they could file down the hallway.

Stella was in the kitchen, looking in the refrigerator. When she turned around, she had a distressed look on her face. "I interrupted something, didn't I? See? You probably wish I wasn't here."

"No, honey," Chance said. "Kat and I will have plenty of time to be alone."

"That's right, sweetie. This is where you belong. With us."

Stella smiled, seemed more at ease. "I was going to ride Hazel, but I got hungry."

"Why don't we go to the Grill?" Chance glanced at Kat, and now she was the one who looked distressed. "Not a good idea, huh? Then I'll make something here."

Chance made them toasted cheese sandwiches with bread he'd stored in the freezer. Kat cut up carrots and apple slices.

Before they sat down to eat, Kat removed the coffee cup and noticed a sticky film on the tabletop. She scrubbed it clean with a sponge. They ate in silence, and Chance stared at the table as if he were remembering that dreadful night of deception. It left Kat wondering if coming here had been a mistake. It was as if they were all still in a state of shock from what they'd been through, like from the aftermath of war.

"I think you'll feel better if you go for a nice, long ride, Stella."

"I hope so, Dad, because I can't stop thinking about it."

"Do you want to talk?"

Kat could hear the hesitancy in his voice. He didn't want to push her until she was ready, but Kat knew he had questions about her captivity. Because Stella was withdrawn and not the vivacious young woman Kat was used to, Kat was afraid the unthinkable had happened to her.

"Look, honey, if they did something to you, I want to know."

Stella's face paled. She slouched and stared at her plate.

"You don't have to say anything if you don't want to," Kat said. "It's just that we're concerned about you."

"They didn't do anything!" Stella blurted.

Chance glanced at Kat, then said to Stella, "That's good, honey."

Before Stella spoke again, several minutes of silence had passed. "They didn't do anything, except in the beginning one of the guys seemed pretty nice. He played cards with me, but then he came on to me, but I kicked him in the shins. After that he just left me completely alone. He'd bring me food, but he acted really mean. Whenever he'd come in, I was scared, and I couldn't sleep. I was afraid to get in the shower. I thought I was never going to get out of there. I didn't have anyone to talk to. It was awful." With her hand, she shielded her eyes.

Kat knelt beside Stella and held her hand. "You're here now. It's all over. You're safe with us."

Chance's face turned crimson. "I'll kill Philip for this."

Kat cast him a disapproving look. "Chance, did you hear me?"

He pushed away from the table. "If it's over, then he's won. He's stolen my manuscript, he's slapped a muzzle on me, he's terrorized my daughter, and he's put us all through hell. There's no justice."

"I know that, Chance. But we have to let it go. If we...if Stella's going to heal from this, you have to let it go. Dredging it up will only make matters worse. Help your daughter heal. That's what's important now. Not how you're going to get back at Philip."

"Yeah, Dad," Stella said through her tears. "I just want all of it to go away."

Chance rubbed his daughter's shoulders and kissed the top of her head. "I'm sorry, honey. I won't bring it up again. You're both right. We have to move on. Just promise me, if you ever need to talk about any of this, you'll come to me or Kat."

Stella nodded. "All I want to do is go out and ride Hazel."

"If that will make you feel better. Just don't overdue it. Come in if you get tired. You haven't slept much."

Stella gave Kat a quick smile before she slipped outside where Zeke had been pawing the front door. The clomp of her footsteps sounded down the porch stairs.

Chance turned to Kat. "Thanks for being here. Stella really relates to you."

"She needed to release all that bottled up gunk. She'll be okay."

"And I promise not to fly off the handle and upset her anymore."

"I know how you feel about Philip, but it's not worth hanging on to the anger. No one wins in a case like this."

He walked away, mumbling, "Believe me, I know."

"What did you say, Chance?"

"I said I'm going to take a shower, and then maybe we'll have time to finish what we started." He left the room without a wink or a smile.

While Chance was in the bathroom, Kat cleaned off the table and rinsed the remnants of wine from the wine glasses. Of late, this house held too many unpleasant memories. She kept reminding herself that staying here was for Stella's sake. Nevertheless, she wished she were in her own house, although thoughts of the break-in still troubled her.

Chance's behavior also troubled her. He wasn't quite himself. Since his return, he seemed lost in thought much of the time. Then again, she had to cut him some slack; he'd been through a lot, too.

She wandered into the utility room. A pile of laundry needed washing, but not enough for a full load. She went in search of the clothing he'd taken off, positive he'd want to put on something cooler than the slacks he'd worn. The shower water sounded like rain spattering. She picked up the dirty clothes he'd laid on the bed.

Before placing his slacks in the washing machine, she removed his wallet and checked his other pockets. She fished out some folded pieces of paper. Before tossing them into the recycle bin, she unfolded them to have a look.

On top was a paternity test application. Kat dropped the slacks she was holding and sat on a nearby stool. Monique Bouvier was penned as the mother of a child named Michel, and the father was listed as Chance Eliason. The other paper was a paternity test report, confirming that Chance could not be excluded as the biological father of the child, and the probability he was the father was close to 100 percent.

Kat's chest tightened so much she could barely breathe. She had a second look, but her eyes hadn't deceived her. The results were proof positive. According to this application that had been submitted five years ago, Chance had fathered a child with Monique. How long had he known? And when was he going to tell her?

Her mind was awhirl with questions when Chance called her name and appeared in the doorway, dressed in shorts, a T-shirt, and sandals, rubbing his wet hair with a towel. His gaze fell on the documents.

"Were you ever going to tell me?" Her eyes flooding with tears, she shoved the papers at him and went in search of her purse.

He caught up with her at the door and held it shut. "Believe me, Kat, this is as new to me as it is you. I just found out this morning. It happened a long time ago, long before we ever met."

"That may be true, but you can't dismiss a child like you can one momentary lapse in judgment. He's not going away. Now you'll never be able to put your past behind you. Monique will always be between us."

"Yes and no."

"And what's that supposed to mean?"

"Let's sit down and talk. I can't deal with this without you. We've been through too much."

She let him steer her to the table, but she wouldn't sit. "There's nothing you can say that will make me feel any better about this."

The door swung open. As Stella entered the room, Chance stuffed the papers into his back pocket. He forced a smile. "How was your ride, honey?"

Stella looked at Chance, then Kat. "Are you guys all right? You look like you lost your best friend. If it's about what happened, I don't want you to worry about me."

"We're just worn-out," Kat said. "In fact, I think I'll take a bath and go to bed early." On her way to the bathroom, she wondered how Chance would break the news to Stella. Kat wanted to support him, but right now this bombshell was too much for Kat to handle.

Her skin was chilled from the air-conditioning, and she longed to soak in the hot water, longed to spend time alone to sort things through. Plus, she was dead tired. Forget about driving back to Seattle. But with Stella staying in the guest room, Kat didn't want to upset her any more than she was by taking the couch. Despite Kat's wounded feelings, her only choice was to sleep with Chance.

CHAPTER 22

Chance ached with exhaustion. Though his mind was all fired-up, as if he'd had a caffeine hit, he knew if he lay down he would sleep for hours. Before he let himself relax, he had to think of something to say to Kat about the paternity document.

Stella plopped down on the couch next to him, and he hugged her close. "I wish you'd left me in Seattle, Dad. I can tell you and Kat need to be by yourselves."

"It's just been a hard week. We're both drained. Kat needs a little space to come down from all the stress she's been under. But you belong here." He thought of Michel and felt a surge of longing to also have his son with him, but because of Stella, he felt a twinge of guilt. He gave her a reassuring squeeze. "You're the best, honey. Did I ever tell you that? You'll always be number one in my book." He didn't have the heart to tell her about the boy.

"You're the best, too, Dad. I'm glad it's just you and me and Kat. The three of us make a great family." She untangled herself from his hold. "I'm going back out for a while and talk to the burros. I just love them. Also, I'm going to help Rusty with the horses. I'm glad you brought me here. This was just what I needed."

"Are you hungry? We didn't have much of a dinner."

"I can get a snack for myself when I come back in."

He studied her expression, searching for any signs of distress. "Are you sure you're all right?"

"Yeah, I'm okay."

"The guest room is all made up for you. Come in before it gets dark."

"I will." She grabbed an apple from the refrigerator on her way out.

Chance turned his attention to the sound of water filling the tub in the guest bath, not the master bath. Kat was keeping her distance and most likely wanted to be left alone, but he felt the urge to talk to her. While she was in the bathtub, he would have a captive audience, and perhaps she would listen to his side of the story. He prepared her a cup of lemon ginger tea.

He knocked on the bathroom door, then opened it a crack to the scent of lavender. "Kat, may I come in? I brought you a hot drink."

She didn't answer, but she didn't say no, so he slipped inside, closing the door behind him, and set the cup on the tub's edge. She was lost in a sea of bubbles, except for her breasts and an upper thigh. He yearned to touch her. "Scrub your back?" He smiled, but she shook her head.

He sat on the toilet seat cover and rested his arms on his thighs. "Will you listen to what I have to say?" When she wouldn't reply, he decided to launch into the subject anyway. "I was as shocked as you were when I found out, and I'm still trying to come to grips with it. I must have been an idiot back then to have let it happen."

"You can't go back and undo it, Chance. This isn't going away. So, why didn't she tell you before now? Why did she keep this from you?"

"I'd left the firm by then, and when she saw me a year after he was born, I'd changed my life and moved on. I didn't want to see her again. I wanted her out of my life. In fact, I was downright cruel. After the way I'd treated her, she thought I would try to gain full custody."

"Why did she decide to tell you now? Does she want you back in her life? And I suppose you'll be flying to Boston every month just to be near him, and then you'll see her again, and she'll work her sexual magic on you."

"Oh, Kat, that's not how it's going to be."

"How can you be so sure?"

"She's marrying Philip, and he doesn't want to raise my son, so she insists I take care of him."

Kat stared at him, stunned. "You mean she wants you to raise him after all this time?"

"She's giving me custody."

"Why would she do that? She's his mother. I don't trust her. What else does she want?"

He couldn't tell Kat that Monique's decision was partially based on her love for him. "She works too much, and she doesn't want him to be around Philip. He doesn't want to raise the boy either."

"Why would she marry that horrible man?"

"She owes him, I guess. Besides, they'd been lovers once, and now he's getting a divorce." Chance hoped his answers would be enough to satisfy Kat.

Kat eyed Chance, skeptically. "The woman still loves you, doesn't she."

"Maybe she did once, but not now. She knows I love you. I made that perfectly clear."

Kat sank deeper into the water, her gaze settling on the bathroom tile. "Were you together when you were away? In the cabin?"

"She was there." He cringed with the knowledge of how close he and Monique had come to going all the way.

"Did you make love to her?"

"I'll be honest with you, honey. There were times I wanted to, but purely out of frustration, when I didn't think I'd ever see you again. She pushed it a couple of times. She had a job to do. Philip wanted her to ruin our relationship. But I swear to you, we didn't go that far. I couldn't do that to you. All I thought about was how to get back to you."

He shifted to the bathmat, closer to her, and set the cup on the floor, then reached for her hand and kissed it, the moisture wetting his lips. "Don't turn away from me now, Kat. I love you too much. I need your support through this."

She leaned her head against his, touching him tenderly. "I need time to digest it all. It's happening so fast."

"We both do. But we both need sleep. We can think clearer in the morning on a good night's rest."

"I was so scared when I couldn't find you. I thought I'd lost you forever."

"I know, honey, but I'm home now." He kissed her, and the lavender's sweet scent lifted him into the realm of the last time they'd made love. Back then, she was so open and willing. "Will you come to bed with me? I want to feel you in my arms."

"I want that more than anything."

"I'll check on Stella, and give you some space." He lifted to a standing position and placed the cup on the tub's rim. He smiled. "I'll meet you in the bedroom. I love you, Kat."

She blew him a kiss, and tiny soap bubbles floated in the air.

Chance left her soaking and stepped out onto the porch. Though the sun was setting and casting a pink hue to a lingering streak of clouds, it was still hot and dry. His truck was coated with dust.

He waved to Stella, who was walking up from the barn with Zeke tagging along. When Zeke saw Chance, he took off running and charged up the stairs. Chance roughed up his coat. Zeke wiggled, whined, and playfully nipped at Chance's hands. Stella met them on the porch, and Chance swung an arm around her. "Are you ready to come in?"

"I guess, but tomorrow I'm going horseback riding with Rusty."

Chance opened the door, and Zeke bounded in first.

"Can Zeke sleep in my room tonight?"

"I don't know why not."

In the kitchen Zeke lapped up water while Stella poured herself a glass. She clucked her tongue. "Come on, Zeke." He trailed her to the living room where she turned to look at Chance. "Dad, are they going to come after you again?"

"Stella, I can promise you. You don't have to worry about that ever again. They got what they wanted."

"But you did all that work on your manuscript. It's not fair."

"I know. But what's important to me now are the people I love. As long as I have you and Kat with me, that's all that matters. I came too close to losing you both to ever regret handing over my work." He accompanied her down the hallway, and thought of Michel. His son mattered, too, and he couldn't rest until he knew the boy was in his care. He only hoped Kat could accept the idea of having his son added to their relationship.

***

Kat was snuggled in Chance's bed in one of his T-shirts, waiting for him to join her. She longed to show him how much she'd missed him. But it was hard for her to get past the reality that Monique had lain in this very spot, had lain with Chance. And now Kat had to get used to the idea of their having a child together.

Despite the ordeal they'd just been through, their relationship was fragile at best, given the fact they'd argued many times about her working so much and not wanting to stay with him in Rosswood. Being here now wasn't so bad, although she hadn't seen any of the townspeople, who would most certainly dredge up the past. But a child—Chance and Monique's child—brought up a tangled set of issues. Could their relationship weather this?

Kat had always been afraid of commitment. Before they'd launched into this long-term affair, she'd warned Chance. She'd told him he'd have to fight for both of them. With this astonishing turn of events, he'd have to don full metal battle gear.

Her mind was filled with a merry-go-round of what-ifs when he entered the room. He'd closed the door softly, in an effort to be quiet. Peeking above the covers, she watched him pull his T-shirt over his head, unzip and step out of his shorts. He went into the bathroom and gargled with mouthwash. The mattress sunk a little as he climbed in and lay on his back. She rolled to her side and laid her arm across his bare chest, anticipating his next move.

"Sweetheart," he whispered, "I'm so terribly exhausted. Can I just hold you?"

She cuddled up to him. "You were up all night. We both need sleep." By the time she'd finished her last sentence, his breathing had settled into a rhythm. So much had to be worked out, but for now it would have to wait.

***

When Chance woke, an inkling of light was peeking in from the corners of the blinds. The clock's hands lit up at 5: 30 a.m., sunrise. Kat was curled up with her back to him. They'd gone to bed early, and he had a good eight hours under his belt. Considering how much sleep he'd lost in the last two days, he could have used more rest, but dozing off this morning was the last thing on his mind. He was groggy enough that right now his only thoughts were of Kat and how much he wanted her.

He slipped off his boxers and scooted over until his body shaped to hers, like a perfect quarter moon. As he drew her into his sphere, she made a moaning sigh. He lifted her hair and kissed the nape of her neck. "Are you awake?"

She turned over with a half smile and sleepy eyes. "I am now."

He pulled her on top of him and yanked her T-shirt up so he could feel her softness. He slid her undies down to her thighs. Her breath was hot on his shoulder. She rewarded him with a passionate kiss. By now he was fully aroused.

The bedroom door creaked open. "Dad." The word had a sharpness to it, but Stella's voice wavered, as if she were about to cry.

Kat rolled off Chance, tugged her shirt down and her undies up while Chance felt around for his boxers. "What is it, honey?" he asked.

"I need to talk to you, now!"

"Can't this wait? It's early."

"No!"

Her frantic tone startled him. "Okay, but let me get dressed first. I'll only be a minute." After Stella had left the room, he said, "I wonder what this is about."

"Maybe she's had a bad dream about being locked up. She's awfully fragile."

Chance climbed out of bed and found his boxers on the floor. Before putting on the clothes he'd worn yesterday, he looked down at himself. "Well, that was enough to put a damper on things."

"Do you want me to come with you? Maybe I can help."

He cinched up his shorts and pulled his T-shirt over his head. "You stay here and keep the bed warm. I'll handle it. She probably needs reassurance." He leaned over Kat, swept her hair off her face, and kissed her. "I've never wanted you more." He wrenched the covers back. "You look so good right now." He ran his fingers down her belly.

She squirmed to get away. "Don't start anything you can't finish."

He groaned and threw the covers back over her. "I'll be back in a minute."

"Chance," Kat said, as he was walking toward the door, "there are a lot of issues we have to discuss."

The contentment he'd felt, just holding her, skittered away.

CHAPTER 23

Chance crossed the living room threshold, and Stella was nowhere in sight. He checked her room. The bathroom door was open, but she wasn't there. Nor was she in his study. He searched for her in the kitchen. Zeke wasn't in the house either, but the front door was ajar, and he found them both sitting on the porch in the cool morning air. With a blanket wrapped around her, she was slumped over, holding the paternity papers. Zeke circled around Chance. Chance commanded Zeke to lie down, then sat next to Stella.

"Where did you find them?" he asked.

"When I got up to go to the bathroom, they were in the hallway."

They had fallen out of his back pocket. How could he have been so careless? He wasn't ready for this.

"You and that woman had a stupid kid together. How gross is that."

"Stella, don't talk like that. He's your stepbrother."

"I don't want a stepbrother, especially if that woman is his mother. What about Kat? She has to hate this. I do. I hate you for this."

He'd known talking to his daughter would be difficult, but not this difficult. "Stella, honey, it happened a long time ago, before I even met Kat, before I came back to take care of your mother. I didn't even know about it until yesterday."

Defiant, she threw the papers on the ground, causing Zeke to spring off the porch and give them a hearty stiff. Satisfied they weren't doggie treats, he lay in the dirt and kept an eye on Chance.

Stella folded her arms. "I hate this."

Chance tried pulling her into his warmth. At first she resisted, but then she let go and allowed him to swallow her in a big hug. "I'm sorry, Stella. If I could take it all back, I would. I didn't know what I was doing back then. I was still the man in my novel who thought he loved Monique. But I can't undo the past. I have to go forward from here. We all do."

"Are you going to see him?"

Now was the clincher. She'd have to know the truth. "He's coming here to live."

"With her? How can you do that to Kat?"

"No, honey, he's coming here to live with me."

"Why?" Stella tried to pull away, but he wouldn't let her.

"Because Monique can't take care of him anymore. He needs to be with his father."

"Dad, you have me."

He wiped the tears from her cheeks. "You'll always be the most important person in my life. We've been through a lot together. You and I have a very special bond that can never be broken. But don't you think our hearts are big enough to embrace this little boy? He needs all of us—you and me and Kat—to make him feel wanted. He'll need his big sister. Can I count on you?"

"Jeez, Dad, he's at least fourteen years younger than me. He's just a baby. It's too weird."

The door opened, and Chance twisted around to see Kat in the doorway in shirt and shorts. She joined them on the step and reached for the papers. He put an arm around her, too, and now he had both his girls close to him. This was how it was supposed to be. Was there room for one more?

"Are you okay with this?" Stella asked Kat. "Because I think it's just creepy."

"It's a lot to get used to, but I'm trying."

"Hopefully, we'll all have time to adjust before it becomes a reality," Chance said.

"When is that going to happen?"

"I don't know, Stella. I'm waiting for a call."

"Do you have to go get him?"

"I won't know until Monique calls me. But I do know that I want him as far away from Philip's influence as possible, and so does she." Chance felt Kat's body tense. This wasn't going to be easy for her until Monique was in the background, although the child's mother would, no doubt, always maintain contact with him. Thinking about that likelihood only made Chance weary, and if they sat out here discussing the details, it would ruin their time together. What they needed most were a few days to relax and recover. "Why don't you two go riding this morning before it gets too hot?"

"That sounds like a good idea. What do you think, Stella?"

"Yeah, I'd like that." Stella rose, along with Chance and Kat.

Stella dragged the blanket inside, and Chance grabbed Kat's hand, preventing her from following Stella's lead. "You're the only woman I'll ever want. I hope you know that."

She peered up at him with her soft, chocolaty eyes. "I hope so, Chance. I really do."

"After we have a late breakfast, I'll send Stella into town with Rusty, and we can have some time together." He held her close and slid his hands down the small of her back. The feel of her body pressed against him sent him into sensual overdrive. "You better go in now, or I won't let you leave the house and Stella will have to ride alone."

The burros began braying, ushering Rusty from his cabin. Chance waved to him, then trailed Kat inside.

Stella had already slipped on her shirt and jeans and was roaming the kitchen, looking for something to eat. "Do you want me to fill the coffeemaker?"

"I could use some coffee. How about you, Kat?"

"Not if I'm getting on a horse." She left them to change her clothes.

In the fridge, Stella found an orange and dug her nail into its flesh, releasing a citrus scent. "Tell Kat I'll be down at the barn." Intent on peeling the fruit, she meandered toward the door.

"Stella?"

"Yeah, Dad?"

"Do we need to talk more about Michel?"

"That's like your middle name, isn't it?

"It's the French version."

"Hmm...I want to get back to work and back to my routine, so I can forget about everything."

"You won't be able to forget about Michel. He's not going away."

"I know. I'll just have to get used to it."

"Do you think you can do that?"

"Dad...right now I just want to ride Hazel."

"All right, honey. You go. We'll talk about this later." He had to remember not to push.

As soon as the door closed behind her, his cell phone rang. The caller was Monique.

"Yes, Chance, it is I. How are you?"

"About as good as can be expected."

"It has been difficult, I know. Difficult for me, also, to come to this decision I have had to make about Michel."

"Are you with him now?"

"Philip left me at the condo for a few days in order to talk to Michel and to make the arrangements. It is not easy for me, Chance."

"What have you decided to do? Do you need a few weeks to prepare?"

"I do not have that luxury. Philip is sending me on the assignment you and I were preparing for. I am to go with Carl. I must leave in a few days."

"The bastard doesn't have a heart."

"It is for the best. This way I have no time for regrets, and Michel will be safe with you."

"Do you want me to fly there to get him?"

"I want to be here, so I must ask you to come to Boston on Saturday. Can you do that? Otherwise, I will be gone on assignment. I must see Michel safely in your hands."

Chance gave a fleeting thought to Kat and Stella's feelings about his leaving so soon, but he felt he had no other option. "I'll be there, Monique. Now that I've come to terms with this, I'm anxious to see our son."

"*Merci*, darling. I will be waiting for you, as will Michel."

"Have you told him, yet? Does he want to be with his father?"

"Oh, yes, Chance. I am sure he does not understand everything, but he is excited to meet you and to see your horses."

"Do you think he'll want to come home with me?"

"Oh, yes. He has been wanting his father." She paused. "I wish things had been different between us."

"Monique, let's not go down that road."

"I know. But sometimes I cannot help myself. I will see you soon then."

"I'll call you when I get in Saturday night." Chance ended the call and noticed Kat standing nearby. Her face was drawn, and she looked as if she were making every effort to stay put. The instant he said her name, she bolted from the room. He ran after her and caught up with her in the bedroom. "Kat, I'm sorry."

She tossed her suitcase on the bed, then haphazardly flung underwear on top of shirts. He stationed himself between her and the bed, and she draped his shoulder with her nightgown. "This isn't going to work, Chance. I can't deal with all of this. It's too much. I'm not a saint."

"I don't expect you to be. But what do you want me to do? Monique is leaving town soon and wants me to come get my son."

Kat glared at him. "You mean yours and Monique's son, the child you had with her, the child who will always keep you two together in one way or another."

"What are you saying?"

"How do I know she won't fly into Seattle one day and show up at the ranch like she did before? And where does that leave me?"

"That will never happen."

"How can you be so sure? She'll want to see him. And she'll want to see you."

"She'll be Philip's wife, Kat. She won't be able to come here without his permission, and he won't allow that to happen. Besides, there will have to be rules of custody. Times and places will have to be arranged."

"Like I said, where does that leave me?"

"With me, honey. You'll be my wife."

Kat jutted her head back. "What?"

He slipped the nightgown off his shoulder. "Marry me." The harsh look she gave him wasn't exactly a comfort to him.

"That's your answer to the problem? 'Marry me' so I'll shut up?" She started for the door.

"Kat...that's not what I meant. I want you to be my wife."

"This isn't the time," she yelled back at him.

The front door slammed, and Chance sat on the bed, worn out. He felt as if he couldn't do anything right, couldn't satisfy anyone, not even himself. His arms and legs were steel weights. He was losing control. If he didn't handle this situation properly, he'd lose what was most dear to him.

Kat barged into the room, her face taut, not giving an inch. She pitched her nightgown into the suitcase, latched it shut, and carried it from the room. By the time he'd caught up to her, she'd already made it to the car. She heaved her bag in the back and slid into the driver's seat.

Chance stopped her door from closing. "What are you doing?"

"What does it look like I'm doing?"

"You can't leave now. What about Stella?"

"I'm too upset to explain things. Just tell her I got called back to work. Tell her Maggie is ill. Tell her anything. Just close the door."

"This is what you do every single time, Kat. You take off when things get tough."

"You have plenty to take care of. You can call me when you straighten your life out."

"Come to Boston with me. We can do this together."

"Then I'd have to face *her* again, knowing she still loves you. I couldn't take that."

"There's nothing to be jealous about. There's nothing between Monique and me. There never will be."

"Oh no? What about the son you have together?"

"I can't help that. Try to understand what I'm going through."

"Right now, I can't." She yanked the door shut and started up the engine.

Chance took a step back. With no energy to go after her, he watched helplessly as Kat drove off lost in a cloud of dust.

CHAPTER 24

Kat had made it across the mountains in record time. It was only sheer luck she hadn't been pulled over for speeding. The cooler temperature and cloud cover were a welcome relief. She could breathe again, in more ways than one, but she was still in a whirl of emotions.

Her anger had spurred her home, but the loneliness she'd felt once she'd walked into her own house was unbearable. She'd wandered aimlessly and at times felt Brianna's presence trying to come through, but Kat had been too upset to quiet her mind and tune in. Instead, she'd reached for the phone to call Chance but ended up calling Maggie, who was now on her way over.

When the doorbell rang, for Kat it was like *deja vu*. Only a short time had passed since she'd needed Maggie's advice. Maggie had always been Kat's grounding force.

Standing in the foyer in suit and hat, Maggie searched Kat's eyes. "This is big. I can tell. But I don't want you to say a thing until we get to my house."

"*Your* house. I don't want to leave here. What if Chance shows up?"

"From what you said on the phone, he has too much on his mind to care about you, but knowing the man like I do, I can hardly believe that. And anyway, if he can't find you here, he'll call you, or he'll call me. In any case, he'll find you. Now go pack a bag."

"Maggie, I don't want to go."

"Well, you have no choice in the matter." Maggie marched through the house with Kat behind her and found an unopened suitcase on the bed. "Good. You haven't unpacked." She hauled it from the room.

"Maggie..." Kat hurried after her.

Maggie spun around at the door and looked at Kat. "Consider this an intervention."

"An intervention for what? I'm not some addict."

"In my book you are. You're addicted to screwing up the best relationship you've ever had, and I'm not going to stand by and let that happen."

"He called you, didn't he!"

"Get your purse. I've got work to do, calls to make. Jim can take care of the office, and the rest I can do from home. You've been through too much to be alone right now, so let's go."

When Maggie was like this—a bulldog with a bone—no amount of reasoning would get through to her. Resigned, Kat snatched her purse and windbreaker and locked up.

All the way to the Ravenna District, a short distance away, Kat silently schemed on how to talk Maggie into turning around and taking her back home. But Maggie rambled on about one of Kat's clients, a man who had found fault with every house Maggie had shown him this week. She didn't know how Kat had the patience to deal with him. Kat tried to insert a sentence or two, but Maggie seemed bent on controlling the conversation. She knew Kat too well. No way would she give Kat any wiggle room.

Maggie parked in the alley and they walked in from the back. Her house, a renovated 1925 Colonial, with oak floors, french doors, and large rooms and windows looked like a picture in a magazine. Nothing was out of place.

Kat followed Maggie into the study, the only room that looked lived in, where Maggie unloaded her briefcase on a computer desk cluttered with work papers, magazines, and an empty coffee cup. "How do you keep anything straight?" Kat asked.

"I have my own special filing system, all in my head. Now if you move any of this mess, I would be utterly lost."

"I wouldn't think of it."

"I'll pour us some iced tea, and we can have a little chitchat." She laid her hat and jacket on a chair.

"Chance called you," Kat said when they were in Maggie's spotless kitchen.

Maggie presented Kat with a cold glass of tea. "Come with me." She walked out to the terrace that overlooked her fenced, park-like backyard, secluded with shrubs, perennials, and her prize-winning roses. Birds twittered in a tall maple tree. She sat in a wicker chair and motioned for Kat to sit down. "Ahh...now isn't this lovely? My gardener deserves sainthood."

"You've certainly done well for yourself."

"You know my story. I was one of the lucky ones. Been in the business for years and saved for rainy days."

"Is Rebecca coming back this year to rent a room?"

"She is, and I'm thrilled about it. She keeps the house clean, and I hardly hear a peep out of her. She's a good student. Goes to bed early. I couldn't ask for a better renter. This house is too big for me to rattle around in by myself." Maggie relaxed back. "So, are we done with the small talk?"

"What if I said no?"

"I'd say you were delaying the inevitable."

Kat took a long swallow of iced tea. Ever since Maggie gave Kat her start in the business, she'd been like a mother, always there when Kat needed a shoulder to cry on, always there when she needed help with anything, always there to offer advice. But today Kat wasn't sure she was up to listening to what Maggie had to say about Kat's relationship with Chance. Kat was in no mood to argue the reason why she'd walked away. "I know you talked to him."

"The man adores you, may I remind you. And in a very short space of time, you two have been through hell. As if the Rosswood incident wasn't enough, you've had to endure his and his daughter's abductions and now he's tossed a new kid into the mix. I wouldn't blame you if you wanted to wash your hands of Chance Eliason. I honestly wouldn't."

Maggie sipped her tea and peered out at the garden. "How do you like my new addition in the corner there?" She pointed to a rose bush that had roses whose petals were white with a broad red edge. "It's called Cherry Parfait. I couldn't resist. It really offsets the green of the shrubbery. I didn't have enough color in that area. Oh, and look at that Monarch butterfly."

"Do you want to talk roses and butterflies, or do you want to talk about Chance?"

"I think Chance is so much more interesting, don't you?"

"If you don't blame me for leaving, then why am I here?"

"I don't blame you, Kat, but I think you'd be making a big mistake if you left for good. You have a lot of unresolved fears, which, I might add, are understandable, considering what you've been through."

"I agree I'm still spooked about being in Rosswood, but now that I've stayed at the ranch, I think I could have worked through it."

"That's a good first step, but it's more than that. You're afraid of getting too close to Chance because you're afraid of losing him, like you did Brianna. You almost *did* lose him."

Kat lifted her feet up to the edge of the chair and hugged her knees to her chest. The possibility of losing Chance forever had indeed been gut-wrenching.

"You pull another stunt like this and you can kiss the man goodbye," Maggie said. "I don't know how much more he can take. He's been through hell, too, and he needs your support more than ever right now. He doesn't need you running off scared every time the going gets tough. That's not how good relationships work. You have to take the good with the bad."

Maggie took a long, needed breath. "When Harry was alive, back in the good old days before the cancer got him...what is it now, twenty years ago?...we used to argue until the sun went down, but we stayed put until we worked it out. That made for a good marriage. I wish you could have met Harry. A hard worker. A good provider. The love of my life."

"What about the child? Chance and I have barely been together nine months. We're just getting to know each other. I didn't
ask for this."

"At your age, dear, you're not going to meet up with many men
who don't have kids, and young ones at that. You found it in your
heart to love Chance's daughter, didn't you?"

"That's different."

"How so?"

"She's an adult, plus I'll never have to deal with an ex-wife or
an ex-lover in this case."

"So, that's what this is all about. Monique Bouvier. Now we're
getting somewhere. So, what are you worried about?"

"She still loves him. They were alone together in Maine. He
was tempted to make love to her. He told me so. And now they have
a child in common."

"I can imagine how that must feel for you, but think of Chance.
He almost lost his life. Then this woman from his past surprises him
with a child he never knew about, a child, by the way, whose early
years he happened to miss out on. And now you're threatening to
leave him. All of this in one week. Think of how *he* feels."

"But he'll have to see her again. She'll always be in his life."

"Of course, she'll want to see her kid. But that's only from
time to time. That's not every day of the week. She lives clear across
the country, for goodness sakes. In the meantime you and Chance
and that little boy can get to know each other and create a real bond
together. And also Kat, Chance loves you to no end. You can trust
him. He's never going to do anything to break that trust. In my book
he's the real deal." Maggie picked up her glass and stood. "Well, my
darling, I have work to do."

"Shall I touch bases with some of my clients? It seems like I've
been away from work for ages."

"I'd rather you relax and enjoy the flowers, and think about
what I've said. Tonight we'll order Thai or Chinese, then we'll cozy
up to the TV and watch a good movie and have popcorn. It'll be fun.

And if you want to talk some more, we can do that. Plan to be here
for at least a couple of days."

"A couple of days!"

"Get used to it. Jim's handling things. I'm working from home
until Saturday. So, for the next forty-eight hours, it's you and me,
kid." She squeezed Kat's hand. "Look at it this way. With Chance
you get a built-in family to love. Not like the crazy family you came
from. I'm sure the man has more than enough love for all of you.
Remember, you and I aren't blood relatives, but still you're like the
daughter I never had. I love you, you know."

"I love you, too. Is this what Chance told you to do? Keep me
occupied?"

"That was my idea. He's leaving for Boston tomorrow and
should be back Saturday night if all goes well."

"What do you mean, if all goes well? How do we know something won't happen to him when he's on the firm's turf? Those people will do anything, and can do anything."

"Chance didn't seem nervous about it."

"He wouldn't be. He's too focused on getting his son. What if
this is some kind of ploy? Is that why I'm here? In case something
goes wrong?"

"Don't start imagining things, dear. Those people have what
they want. I want you here so I can provide moral support until
Chance returns. It's as simple as that. Plus, I wanted to talk some
sense into you. Think about how great your little family is going to
be. Now, I have calls to make."

As Maggie walked away, Kat mulled over whether or not she
could accept a ready-made family, especially the youngest member,
especially if he resembled Monique. Being ensconced in Maggie's
home, in this cocoon of mama bear love that was always available to
her, Kat drank her iced tea and observed the towhees splashing in
the birdbath.

She closed her eyes and tuned in to the drone of the afternoon
traffic on the nearby thoroughfare. The noise lulled her into a medi-

tative state. In her mind's eye, she saw Brianna's face and felt comforted by her sister's presence, knowing Brianna would always be close, reminding Kat she could always get her own answers. All she had to do was listen to that still, small voice and feel the feeling it elicited.

The voice that came through now urged Kat to trust her feelings for Chance. Kat did love him, and she knew he loved her, but despite what Maggie had said, was their love for each other enough to keep their relationship from heading off the tracks?

More urgent, though, was her concern that Chance could possibly be stepping into another one of the firm's deceptive traps. As much as she wanted to know for sure, she couldn't settle herself enough to intuit the answer.

CHAPTER 25

Chance looked at his watch. It was almost suppertime. After Kat left, Stella had headed back to the barn and hadn't come up to the house when he called her for lunch. Later, Rusty informed him she'd gone riding by herself. That was two hours ago. Chance was concerned.

He changed into his jeans and boots. Outside, the sun was low in the sky, and the day's heat had eased. The wind had kicked up a little, swirling a tiny dust devil in the pasture. Down by the barn he found Rusty filling a water bucket. "Have you seen Stella?"

"Last I seen her she was riding toward the pines with Zeke in tow. That was a while ago, boss. She didn't want no company, so I just let her be. Do you want me to saddle up Jericho and go find her?"

"You can saddle him up for me, if you don't mind."

The burros had been trumpeting Chance's arrival, and he spent a few minutes patting the closest ones, smoothing their bristly hair. Now and then they'd swish their tails, fanning the flies.

Rusty led Jericho from the barn. Chance mounted the palomino and took off at a full gallop. The air, brushing his face, was hot and dry. Where pasture met pines, he pulled on the reins, easing the horse into a slow trot. He wove in and around the trees until in the far distance he saw Stella's horse. Zeke charged up to Jericho, then back to where Hazel was munching on a rare patch of green grass. Nearby, Stella was curled up on the ground. Chance's heart skipped. Assuming she'd fallen, he quickly dismounted and hurried to his daughter's side.

She peered up at him, sleepy-eyed. "What's wrong?"

"Are you all right? You gave me the worst scare. You've been out here for two hours."

She sat up, yawning. "I guess I fell asleep."

He settled in close to her on a bed of pine needles while Zeke circled around and nudged his shoulder. He gave the dog a pat. "It's peaceful out here, isn't it?"

"Dad, is Kat ever coming back?"

"Is that what's worrying you?"

"I like her a lot, and I don't want her to leave us."

"Oh, honey." This reminded him of the days following Meredith's death and of how he and Stella had clung to each other, trying to ease the pain. "Kat just needs time to process everything. She's gone through some very traumatic times. I wouldn't be surprised if she needed counseling to deal with it all. And remember, she's never had any children of her own. Now we're asking her to accept a situation she wasn't expecting."

"Do you mean Michel, or me?"

"I meant Michel. I know she loves you already."

"Did she tell you that?"

"Many times." He squeezed her hand and smiled. "But I hope you'll try to accept Michel."

"Before I fell asleep, I was thinking about him, and maybe it won't be so bad, having a little brother. But what happens if we get used to having him around and then Monique wants him back?"

"Everything was worked out legally so that won't happen. I'll have full custody."

"What about Kat? Is she going to be okay?"

"She's in good hands. Maggie's looking after her. We'll call her when I get back from Boston. Do you want to go with me?"

"Nah, I don't think so."

"I'm sorry this is happening so fast for you. For all of us, really. Unfortunately, it has to be this way. I wasn't given a choice."

Stella leaned into him, and he felt an overwhelming love for his daughter. The only positive thing that had come from Meredith's death was that his and Stella's relationship had blossomed, making up for all the lost growing-up years he'd missed with her. He wished he could have those years back.

He'd also missed out on Michel's early years. And that made him wonder if Kat would ever consider having a child. But then, wasn't he jumping ahead? He didn't even know if he had Kat.

"Dad?"

"Yes, honey?"

"I wish Kat was here."

"That makes two of us."

Zeke edged close enough to lick Stella's face. She hugged him around the neck. "You silly dog."

Chance stood and offered her a hand. She lifted up and brushed off the needles and twigs that had clung to her clothes and hair. Hazel reluctantly raised her head when Stella grasped the reins. Chance boosted her into the saddle, then mounted Jericho.

When they'd broken away from the pines, Chance raced Stella across the pasture. Zeke took off at full speed, but couldn't catch up until they'd slowed near the barn. Jericho pranced around Hazel. Both horses were breathing hard, their nostrils flaring, but seemed energized from the run.

Rusty helped Stella dismount and took the reins of both horses. "Your pa thought something bad happened to ya. You okay?"

"I fell asleep out there."

"Done that myself a few times. Sure is quiet in them woods."

"We're going to call it a day, Rusty. Would you mind giving the truck a quick wash? We'll be leaving in the morning."

"I thought you was staying till Sunday."

"Change of plans."

"Something to do with your lady friend?"

"Just business." Chance swung an arm over Stella. "Come on, honey."

Halfway to the house with Zeke trailing along, Stella asked, "Why didn't you tell Rusty about Michel?"

"That nosy ol' busybody will sniff it out soon enough."

Stella scampered ahead and let Zeke inside while Chance lingered by his old pickup, mulling its worth. For the past five years, the truck had been adequate transportation, an easy way to get around town. But things were changing. His family was growing. It might be time for a change. In his ideal world, that change included Kat.

If he'd had his way, he'd be with her right now, but he'd heeded Maggie's advice to allow Kat the space to come to grips with everything that was happening. He only hoped Maggie was right.

"Dad..." Stella called from the doorway. "You have a phone call. It's *her*."

Chance dashed into the house and grabbed the phone. "Kat?"

"I am sorry to disappoint you, but there is a change in plans."

"What now, Monique—are you going back on your word?"

"It is nothing like that. You see, Carl and I must leave town a day earlier than planned. Paulette is leaving for France today. That means there is only tomorrow for you to come for Michel. So, Philip is letting us come there on his private plane. We will be in Seattle at 3:00 p.m., your time. You are to come to the Seasons Hotel as before. Will you do that?"

"Of course I will, but isn't this too soon for the boy? A week ago he was ill."

"He is much better now."

"But you're pushing him on a man he doesn't even know. It might be too much stress for the boy. He hardly has the time to get used to the idea."

"Darling, your nerves are showing. One day sooner will not make a difference. Believe me, Michel knows you very well. You see, over the years I have talked about you many times. I have shown him your picture. I never said you were his father. I only spoke of you as a dear friend of mine. But now he knows the truth."

"Where does he think I've been all these years?"

"I told him you had a job that took you far away, but now he can spend all the time he wants with you. He is very excited to see you. He will love you, Chance. I know it."

Despite her upbeat tone, Chance could read the pain. "This will be difficult for you."

"There is no other way."

"Right...Philip."

"Do not blame Philip for everything. I think it is best for Michel. I cannot work the way I do and care for him also."

"Having been in the business, I'd have to say I understand."

"I must go, so promise me you will be there."

"I will. Goodbye, Monique." He hung up.

Stella stood close by. "What did she say?"

"I won't be going to Boston after all. They're flying to Seattle tomorrow." Chance felt a surge of excitement at the reality of seeing his son for the first time. "I don't even know what the boy needs. Maybe some boots and a cowboy hat for starters. We'll have to go shopping. What do you think?"

"Where are you meeting them?"

"At the hotel."

"The same hotel where they took me?" Stella's eyes widened with horror. "Dad, what if something bad happens to you?"

CHAPTER 26

Kat spent Friday morning helping Maggie with phone calls and connecting with some of her own clients. Maggie couldn't stop her. Kat had told Maggie she needed to keep her mind occupied. Tempted to call Chance, she'd let her finger hover over the call button, tried pressing it once, then hung up before he answered. Afterward, Maggie cautioned her to leave him alone, because he had enough to worry about without dealing with Kat's feelings. Kat thought about Brianna's last contact and for the moment settled down.

Around noon she called Ellen Davis to find out if she was satisfied with last Saturday's open house.

"I'm so glad you called, Kat. Did Jim tell you we may have a nibble on the house? I'm so excited. That means I'm one step closer to being with my lover boy."

"I've been out of town and haven't talked to Jim yet. I'm sure he's following up on it. When I go in on Monday, I'll make that a priority."

"Oh, goodie, I can hardly wait to get this horse out of the chute. Say, did you get the invitation to Libby's wedding?"

"I've been at Maggie's, and I haven't been home to collect my mail."

"The wedding is a week from Sunday. She'd love to have you and Chance come. They're having a small ceremony in a lovely rose garden at a mansion in town. I hope you can be there."

"I don't know, Ellen. So much is happening right now. We'd love to, but I'm just not sure. Chance needs to be with his daughter and..." She let her words trail off for lack of a better way to explain their situation. What could she say? She wasn't even sure their relationship was intact.

"Hey, all of you are invited," Ellen said. "Libby addressed your invitation to Chance, Kat, and family."

"That sounds positive, but I can't promise anything right now."

"Knowing my psychic friend, just by sending you an invitation, she already knows you'll be there. Mark my words."

"We'll see."

"Okey-dokey. But I'd bet on Libby's intuition."

"I'll be in touch, Ellen." After ending the call, Kat thought it uncanny that Libby had put Chance's name on the invitation. She must have intuited that he'd make it back safely. But why hadn't she reassured Kat? Kat shrugged it off as one of those perplexing mysteries about psychics.

Around two-thirty in the afternoon the doorbell rang. Kat was in the kitchen, her hands in soapy water. From her office Maggie yelled at Kat to answer the door. "You're closer," Kat yelled back.

"I'm busy, dear. Besides, I know for a fact it's for you."

Kat grabbed a towel and strode past Maggie's room, grumbling, "How do you know that?" Kat opened the door, and Stella stood there, smiling, catching Kat off guard. "What are you doing here?" She gave Stella a hug and noticed Chance's pickup idling at the curb.

"Dad wants to talk to you."

Kat couldn't have anticipated the excitement she felt, along with the feeling of peace that settled into her, the weight of despair lifting off like a helium balloon. She ran to the truck and slid into the passenger seat. Careful to spare the child's cowboy hat sitting between them, she scooted over and threw her arms around him.

He hugged her tight, then kissed her. "I was so afraid you wouldn't talk to me."

"I missed you too much. I'm sorry I acted like a baby. Forgive me?"

"There's nothing to forgive."

"Are you on your way to the airport?"

"I'm on my way downtown. My son is in Seattle."

"Seattle?"

"I don't have time to give you the details. I'm running late, but Stella can explain everything. Maggie said she could stay here while I'm gone."

Kat stole a quick kiss. "You must be terribly nervous. I can feel it."

"I can't begin to tell you. But I have to get going, honey."

"I know he'll love you. I love you."

"Why don't you come with me?"

She glanced at her capris and sandals. "I'd need time to get ready. Besides, I think this is something you need to do alone."

"You're probably right. I'll be back soon with Michel. Wish me luck."

"Come to my house when you're done. I'll have Maggie drive us over." Kat eased out of the truck. She shut the door and blew him a kiss. He smiled at her in that seductive way of his that could always stir her up. The man still had that effect on her.

Kat stood on the sidewalk in the sunshine, relieved she had Chance back in her life, but with the knowledge their relationship was changing. After watching his truck merge into the traffic, she went inside to talk to Stella.

Maggie and Stella were chattering in the kitchen. Maggie had made a pot of tea and had set out her Royal Winton teacups. "This calls for a celebration." She poured the Earl Grey.

"Did you call Maggie last night, Stella, and arrange to come here?"

"Dad did."

Kat zoomed in on Maggie. "Why didn't you tell me he called?"

"I wanted it to be a surprise. I didn't want you to run off and go hide somewhere."

Kat heaved a sigh. "Honestly, Maggie."

"Stella was just telling me Chance is meeting Monique and the boy at the Seasons Hotel."

"He didn't tell you that on the phone? I thought he was flying to Boston."

"Monique called him last night," Stella said. "They're flying here in Philip's private plane."

"Why the change in plans?"

Stella lifted a shoulder. "I guess she has to leave Boston soon. That's all Dad said. But I don't like that he's going to that hotel alone. It gives me the creeps."

"Maybe I should have gone with him," Kat said. "Now that I know he's going there, it concerns me, too."

"Now, girls," Maggie said. "I think you should trust Chance. He knows what he's doing."

"I don't know, Maggie. With everything that's happened to him, he has to be stressed to the limit. He's so excited about seeing his son I'm not sure he can think straight. How do we know Monique is telling him the truth? How do we know they won't do something awful to him? I wish he would have negotiated a different way of handling this." Kat could barely sit and drink her tea. She knew what the firm was capable of. Dwelling on Chance in that hotel room made all her fears rush back again and gave her no comfort at all.

***

The hotel's underground parking garage was nearly full. Chance circled around until he found a spot between a gold Chrysler and a black BMW. The garage was dark and cool with sunlight filtering in from the street level. He took the elevator to the lobby. Monique hadn't given him the room number but had told him to wait downstairs until she contacted him. Too anxious to sit, he paced in front of the stone fireplace with the small cowboy hat in his hands.

He checked his watch around five minutes past the hour. When two men in suits, the same two who had escorted him previously, came around the corner, he felt an underlying dread at accompanying them anywhere. Nevertheless, considering Monique's recent behavior toward him—helping him escape the cabin and return to Seattle—he figured he could trust her. He had the feeling that if it weren't for her intervention, Philip would have eliminated him a long time ago. He truly owed her his life.

Without a word, the two men took him up to the seventh floor and left him in a one-bedroom suite with a view of the Sound, a little less posh than the room he'd been in before, but nonetheless immaculately drawn in the hotel's taupe-and-marine blue color scheme. At first glance it appeared as if there were no occupants, but on further inspection suitcases were in the bedroom and a plastic figure of a horse lay on the floor. Chance picked up the toy and laid it on the nightstand. A flutter of excitement coursed through him at the reality of meeting the son he'd never known.

He left the bedroom and wandered toward the windows to catch a glimpse of the water, but stopped when the door opened and a little boy in tan slacks and a white shirt and blue tie walked in with Monique behind him. In person, he looked even more like Chance than in the photo, his black hair thick and wavy and his eyes an extraordinary aqua. He had Chance's Mediterranean complexion, and one side of his mouth tipped upward, the same as Chance's. The resemblance was uncanny.

The boy broke into a grin and marched up to Chance. "Are you my father?"

His heart bursting with pride, Chance glanced at Monique, then knelt and held out his hand for the boy to shake. The tender little hand was swallowed in his. "Yes, Michel, I'm your father."

Michel looked back at Monique. "This is my father, Aunt Monique."

"Yes, Michel, I know." Dressed more conservatively in fashionable trousers and a polished cotton blouse, she wiped the corners of her eyes.

As Chance stood up, Michel pointed to the hat Chance was holding. "Is that mine?"

Chuckling a little, Chance set the hat on the boy's head. "If you're going to ride horses, you'll need a cowboy hat."

"I want to show you my horses." He raced toward the bedroom.

"Michel, use the toilet first before you come out here," Monique yelled to him, then said to Chance, "He gets so focused on what he is doing he sometimes forgets to take care of the necessary things. You will have to keep after him."

"That's how I was when I was a boy," Chance said. "So, where's Philip?"

"He is in meetings today."

"And he trusted you to come here alone? Oh, but you didn't come alone, did you?"

"That is not for you to think about now."

There was an uncomfortable silence between them until Chance said, "This must be terribly hard for you."

"I am used to being away from him. I will miss him, of course, but knowing he is with you and you can provide a stable home for him is the best that a mother could hope for. You can call me if there are questions you have concerning him."

She handed Chance a manila envelope she'd carried in with her. "I have written down or copied everything I could think of, such as his medical history, his vaccinations, his birth certificate, and so forth. The custody papers are inside. Also, in there is the picture of me with Michel, the one I showed you before. I ask that you please keep this, and one day when he asks about his real mother you will show it to him and tell him the best way you can that I am his mother and that I always loved him in that way." She sucked in a quick breath and broke eye contact.

"You're acting as if you'll never see him again. You know I won't keep him away from you."

She nodded.

"I have a lot to thank you for, like helping me get back here alive."

"Oh, no, I owed you that, and more. After all, I kept Michel from you all these years."

"I'll do my best to take good care of him."

"I have no doubt of that, Chance. He is your flesh and blood. I know you will love him as I have. He already loves you." She hesitated. "I wish things could be different between us, but I know now that is impossible. But I must make my departure quick, or I will cry too much."

"I wish you would reconsider your choice to marry Philip. I don't see how that arrangement could be in your best interest."

"It is not a choice."

"I was right, then. You've done all of this for me, haven't you?" He felt a softening toward her.

"And Michel. That is all there is to be said."

Michel bounded up to Chance and held up two plastic toys. "You see, Papa, I have horses, too."

"Yes, son, and soon you will have a real horse, a palomino named Jericho."

His eyes lit up. "Aunt Monique, my very own horse. His name is Jericho."

"Yes, Michel. Your father treats you well. You will be spoiled in no time." She lengthened her arms. "Come here, my darling boy. I must go now."

He ran into her arms. "Will you visit me, Aunt Monique?"

"Ah...you will be so busy with your father and your horses you will not need me, sweet boy. But I will write to you and send you pictures of all the places in the world I visit. Now take your father's hand." When he left her side, she took a tissue from her purse and blotted her eyes.

"Chance, also in the envelope is Paulette's new address and phone number where she can be reached in Paris. If you have questions about Michel and you cannot reach me, she will have the answers. Also, he is in need of plenty of rest. He still gets tired from his illness. He needs to get stronger."

"Don't worry. I'll look after him."

"I am sure you will." She captured Michel in a hug and kissed him once more. "Be a good boy for your father, my little tomato."

"I am not a tomato."

"Yes, you are my juicy, little tomato, and I love you." She kissed him again.

He pulled away from her. "Aunt Monique..."

She rose and touched Chance's cheek. "Goodbye, darling."

His eyes softened with affection. "Take care of yourself."

She gave a quick nod, then fled the room, her perfume lingering.

With Monique gone, Michel's eyes widened, and he slipped a trembling hand in Chance's, as if the full impact of the situation were becoming clear to him. Chance was still a stranger, and for a moment Chance felt as discomfited as Michel. But then Chance realized he had to take control and be the father Michel needed him to be, even if at this stage of the game Chance didn't feel quite as though he fit the role. It would take time.

"Are you ready to ride in my truck?"

Michel peered up at him. "Are we going to see the horses?"

"First, I want you to meet your sister and a very important friend of mine. Would you like to do that?"

Michel nodded a yes, but not a very convincing one. "I have a sister?"

"That's right. Let's get your suitcases and be on our way." He tugged on the boy's hand, but Michel stiffened. Chance knelt and held him close. "I love you, son. I know right now you're scared. I would be too if all of a sudden I had to leave my home and my friends, and my Aunt Monique, but I'm going to make a good home for you, Michel. I promise. And soon you'll meet Zeke."

"Who is Zeke?"

"He's my golden retriever, and I'm sure he's going to love meeting you. Do you like dogs?"

"I never had a dog."

"Well, you have one now."

Michel smiled. "I would like a dog, Papa."

"Then let's get your suitcases."

CHAPTER 27

While Chance was picking up his son, Maggie drove Kat and Stella back to Kat's house and parked at the curb. "Keep me in the loop, my darlings."

"I wish Chance had called from the hotel."

"Me, too," Stella said.

"I know you've been through hell and you're both a bundle of nerves, but I'm sure it's going to be all right. When the boy gets here, he's going to love the both of you. I'd like to meet him when you've got everything sorted out."

"If all goes well, we'll definitely bring him over to meet you," Kat said. "After all, you've played a critical role in all of this." She squeezed Maggie's hand. "Thank you for being so understanding and also for keeping me focused on what's important."

"Any time, kid." Maggie twisted around to look at Stella in the backseat. "I'm glad I got to spend a little time with you. Michel is lucky to have you for a big sister."

"Thanks, Maggie."

Kat handed Stella the house keys. "Go ahead and open up. I'll be in in a minute." As Stella walked up the sidewalk, Kat said to Maggie, "She's amazing. I just hope she doesn't have any aftereffects from what she went through."

"You can help her get over that. You've had plenty of experience with those persistent fears. But maybe you should both go see Dr. Rosen. It wouldn't hurt."

"I know, Maggie. Maybe we'll both go together."

"With this little boy in the picture, you'll have to be flexible when it comes to Chance. You'll have some adjustments to make. It won't be all rosy."

"I know that."

"Then I want you to promise if you get cold feet, you'll come talk to me before you do anything rash. The man is going to need a little leeway. This is new to him, too. He's got two children to think about now." Maggie gave Kat one of her pointed stares. "What I'm saying is, it's not all about you. Don't put him in a box with no way out, all right?"

"Lesson learned."

"He loves you, Kat. I've never seen a man as devoted to anyone as Chance is to you. Give him time to integrate everything, as I'm sure he'll allow you, too. Now go see about Stella. You're going to have a nice family, you know."

Kat opened the car door. "You're my savior, Maggie. You always have been. I'm so lucky to have you in my life."

"Hey, kid, that goes both ways."

As Kat walked toward the house, she waved to Mr. Singleton. The sun was peeking out from behind a cumulous cloud. A gentle breeze cooled the afternoon air. Inside, she kept the front door ajar and for cross ventilation had Stella open the back door.

Kat wasn't sure when Chance planned on driving back to the ranch, but in case he chose to stay overnight, she took some sheets and blankets from the linen cabinet in the laundry room and had Stella follow her upstairs to help make up the two twin beds in the room facing the front yard. She moved boxes aside, so they could get through.

"I'm really nervous," Stella said. "I wish we would hear from Dad."

Kat opened the window to circulate the stagnant air. "We'll have to trust he's going to be all right, just like Maggie said." Kat thought better than to vent any more of her own worries, for Stella's sake.

After they'd tucked in the last sheet and pulled the blanket over, Stella sat on the bed and slumped down. "What if he doesn't like me?"

"Michel? Believe me, he's going to love you." Kat sat next to Stella but wouldn't voice her own doubts about the boy's opinion of her. She wasn't his mother. She wasn't even Chance's wife. She wasn't quite sure how she would fit in to this scenario.

Stella jerked to attention, then bounded to the window. "I thought I heard voices. They're here!" She hurried from the room.

Kat stayed behind to watch Chance coming up the sidewalk with a grip on his son's hand. Chance glanced up in time to see her and smiled. She left the window to greet them but hung back near the bottom stair where she could observe them, unnoticed. Chance was introducing him to Stella. Kat's fears about being reminded of Monique every time she looked at the boy instantly vanished. He was the spitting-image of his father.

"I never had a sister," he said in the sweetest way, his head cocked toward Stella.

"I never had a little brother, either."

"Do you have a horse? Because Papa says I have a horse and his name is Jericho."

Stella's expression was one of concerned curiosity. "I ride Jericho sometimes, but there's another horse named Hazel you can ride."

"But Papa says my horse is Jericho."

"Michel, you can ride Hazel, too," Chance said, jumping into the conversation.

Kat chuckled to herself. Chance was getting a quick lesson in juggling the attention of two children. She stepped into the room. "And who is this?"

"Kat, this is my son, Michel. Michel, this is Kat, the pretty lady I told you about."

"Is she my aunt, like Aunt Monique?"

"No, Michel. Kat is my very best friend in the world, and we'll be spending a lot of time with her. Shake her hand and say hello."

Michel hesitated until Kat held out her hand. He shook hands with her, then ran back to Chance. "I miss my Aunt Paulette and my Aunt Monique."

"I know you do, son."

"I'd like to get to know you," Kat said. "But first, would you like some orange juice?"

"Yes, please."

"I'll get it." Stella wandered into the kitchen with Michel traipsing after her.

Kat let out a breath. "I feel so awkward."

"*You* feel awkward. Right now, I feel like I have two left feet. I was gone when Stella was that young. This is all new to me."

"You're doing just fine. He seems happy when he's around you. And I think Stella will be a real help. He's taken to her right away."

"He'll take to you, too. Just give him time."

"I'm not so sure."

"Come here." He pulled her into a hug. "Kat, honey, I want you more than ever."

"I was worried about you. I didn't know if the firm was pulling some sort of trick."

"To tell you the truth, I was apprehensive myself, but it all worked out. I have my son now." He looked toward the kitchen. "I don't hear their voices. Let's go see where they went." Chance took Kat's hand and led her through the kitchen. He looked beyond the mudroom and found Stella and Michel sitting together on the back step. "Looks like they're getting along."

"I told you she'd be a big help."

"Now where were we?" He embraced her again. "Why don't you come to the ranch with us? I'm sure Maggie will understand."

"I really need to spend time at work. Maybe after a week or so I'll join you. Besides, I think you and Michel need some bonding time without anyone else around."

"You're probably right. Stella wants to go back to work, and he and I will have the time alone."

"At least stay the night. You don't want to fight the Friday afternoon traffic. We made the beds upstairs."

He pressed her close. "I want to hold you forever."

Just as she reached up to kiss him, Michel and Stella walked in. Kat tried to step back, but Chance wouldn't let her.

"You better get used to this," Stella said to Michel. "They're an item."

Michel looked at Stella, puzzled. "What is an item?"

***

Later that evening in Kat's SUV after they'd all eaten at the Spaghetti Factory, Chance drove along the waterfront so they could see a ferry docking. The sun's rays reflected off the evening clouds, offering a tangerine sky. On the way back, he drove past the Space Needle. In the backseat next to Stella, Michel was chattering away and taking everything in. By the time Chance turned off the car's engine in the alley behind Kat's house, the boy had fallen asleep.

"I'm afraid I've worn him out," Chance whispered as he lifted him from the car. "Monique warned me he needed his rest after being sick all week. Fine father I am."

"I'm sure he'll bounce back after he's had a good night's rest," Kat said.

After taking the house key from Kat, Stella ran ahead and unlocked the door. They all filed through the mudroom, Chance turning sideways, careful not to bang Michel's knees in the doorjamb.

"Where's he going to sleep?" Stella asked.

Chance looked at Kat, resigned at spending another night apart. "If the beds upstairs are made up, he and I can sleep up there. If he wakes, he'll probably need to know I'm nearby."

Stella peered at her brother's limp body. "He's cute when he's like this, all floppy and drooly, and quiet, too. He sure talks a lot."

"Why don't you and Michel sleep in my bed," Kat suggested, "and I'll sleep upstairs with Stella?"

"I have a better idea," Stella said. "I'll sleep upstairs with him, and you guys can sleep down here. If he wakes up, I can handle it. He knows me now."

Chance didn't wait for another suggestion. He lugged Michel upstairs, avoiding the creaky steps. Along with her backpack, Stella hauled up one of his suitcases that had been brought in earlier. Together, they carefully removed his shoes and trousers. He woke for a moment and called out Monique's name, then curled on his side and went back to sleep.

"We'll let him sleep in his shirt. We don't want to wake him." The room was warm from the day, but a light breeze drifted in from the opened window. Chance covered him with a sheet. For a moment he stared at the boy, proud to have his son with him. "Stella, thanks for staying with Michel and also for making the effort to get to know him. It means a lot to me." He gave her a hug and a kiss. "Remember, you're still number one. I love you, honey."

"I love you, too, Dad. Now go on. Kat's waiting for you."

"I'm sorry about what happened to you, Stella. I worry that you'll have flashbacks about it, or it will affect you in some other unpleasant way. Are you sure you won't change your mind about staying at the ranch with us this week? I know your boss will understand if I talk to him."

"Dad, I'll be all right. It was just good to be with you and Kat for a while. But I'm ready to go back to my apartment and get back to my normal routine. Honestly, I'll be okay."

"But promise me, if you have a hard time during the week, you'll call Kat. Stay with her if you need to."

She pushed him toward the door. "I will, Dad. Now go. Michel wore me out today, and I want to get some sleep."

Downstairs, the house was quiet. The lamp had been switched off in the living room. Chance searched for Kat and found her in bed. The freeway hum sounded in the background. The paling light from outside was enough for him to detect her shapely figure under a thin sheet. He disrobed and climbed into bed. He grabbed for her at the same time she grabbed for him, and they breathed a collective sigh.

Chance wasn't about to let this moment slip away, either by sleeping or talking, or by a child's tiny, questioning voice. Though he was weary from the day, the feel of Kat's body touching his, hot and sticky from the heat, awakened his senses. He inhaled the smell of her, sweetly subtle, like honeysuckle on a warm summer's day. He roamed her neck and chest with hard, wet kisses. His hands slid over her skin. He couldn't wait. He wouldn't. Hungering for more, he pressed into her. He was more aggressive than usual, but she offered herself eagerly and rewarded him with tender words and satisfied sighs. He gave her everything he had, and the unmerciful tension, built up over the last few days, finally eased.

He rolled on his back, spent. "We needed that, didn't we?"

She nestled close, her arm across his midline. "I know I did."

He lay silent, feeling the peace of being with Kat and contemplating the future. "Kat?"

"Yes, Chance?"

"It seems so surreal, having my son here with me, but I feel so inept at caring for a six-year-old."

"We're going to be quite a pair then, because I can't help you. I've never had kids, so I'm flying blind."

He swept her cheek with the back of his hand. "Do you want one of your own?"

She pulled back. "Are you crazy? I'm too old for that now."

"Forty-one isn't too old. Lots of women have children later in life."

"I've been way too busy. I've never really considered it before."

"Before now? Kat, would you ever consider having my child?"

"Whoa, Chance. Aren't we putting the horse before the cart? We're not even married, but even if we *were* married and wanted a child, right now Michel needs your full attention."

"I know, but we can imagine it, can't we?"

"Imagining is one thing."

He tickled her neck with his tongue. "How about getting in some more practice for when the time is right?"

***

In the morning Kat sneaked into the bathroom, careful not to wake Chance. He'd woken her early. At first she'd felt his lips, his warm breath on the back of her neck, then his hands exploring. She couldn't resist him. When it came to sex, the man was insatiable. He could be gentle or forceful, depending on his mood, but he always seemed to read how she liked it. He had a sixth sense about that. He totally satisfied her in every way. In sex and in temperament, they were well-matched. She only hoped from this day forward they could love each other enough to ride out the blustery winds that would come along to test them. Michel was an unexpected squall.

When she returned to bed and tried to inch in, she realized Chance was looking at her. "I woke you, didn't I?"

"I was awake and waiting for you to come back. I wanted to feast my eyes on you. Come over here." He tugged her into his arms. "I can't get enough of you."

"Chance, look." She nodded toward the doorway.

Michel was leaning against the doorjamb. His hair stuck up in places. His shirt was wrinkled and hung over his spindly legs. Chance reached for his boxers. Kat scrambled into her T-shirt and undies.

"I didn't see you when I woke up, Papa."

"Where's Stella?"

"She is sleeping." Michel leaned against Chance's side of the bed. "I was afraid."

"Come here, son." Chance moved over, as did Kat, making room for Michel to climb in. "Is that better?"

Michel nodded. "I had a bad dream."

"What was it about?"

"I dreamed Aunt Monique went far away, and I never saw her again."

"Well, Michel, she did go far away to work, but I'm sure she'll be back, and one day she'll visit you. She told me so."

Michel lifted up and looked over at Kat. "Are you my papa's girlfriend? Aunt Monique and Philip are friends, too. I like Philip. He plays with me and brings me toys. Will Philip visit me?"

"I don't think so," Chance said rather abruptly, and Kat was sure he was working to suppress his feelings. "Philip is very busy now. But that doesn't mean he doesn't like you. I'm sure Aunt Monique will tell him all about you."

"You'll be busy, too, on your father's ranch." Kat hoped the change of subject would help Chance out of this uncomfortable conversation. "There are donkeys and horses. And there's a man who works there. His name is Rusty. He knows all about ranching and riding horses."

"Kat's right," Chance said. "We'll have lots to do and new people to meet."

"Will you visit us there?" Michel asked Kat.

"I sure will."

"Why do you want Kat to come to the ranch, Michel?"

"Because she makes me think of Aunt Monique," he said as Chance and Kat exchanged bewildered looks. "And then I am not so sad."

CHAPTER 28

On the ranch, Chance had spent the whole week with Michel. He'd taken him into Rosswood and introduced him to some of the residents. He'd sat him on Jericho and walked him around the pasture. Michel had fallen in love with the burros and had helped Rusty with their care: feeding them treats and extra hay, making sure they had fresh water. He'd giggled at their strange trumpeting brays.

At his age, Chance never thought having a six-year-old around could be so satisfying. But by the end of each day, he was as tired as Michel. Chance had to coax him with promises of pancake breakfasts just to get him to sleep in the guest room, because every night Michel would argue for sleeping with Chance. There was a fine line between healthy discipline and giving him whatever he wanted.

Monique had phoned once to speak to Michel and also to make sure Chance was giving their son his medicine. Chance wished he could avoid having any contact with her, but since Michel was her son, too, he had to take the calls.

In the evenings after tucking Michel in bed, Chance would call both Stella and Kat. Stella had adjusted well to her normal routine and had spent a couple of nights with Kat. Kat loved the company and also seemed genuinely pleased at the excitement Chance felt about being with Michel. She'd been working hard all week to make up for her absence and hadn't had time to think about coming to the ranch. But he'd had time to think about her and how much he'd missed her. He'd been looking forward to heading back to Seattle for the weekend. They'd been invited to Libby McGraw and Kipp Reed's wedding.

When they arrived at Kat's house, Chance carried a suitcase and sport jacket up the sidewalk. Tagging along, Michel was dressed up in shirt and tie, his cowboy hat perched on his head. Stella and

Kat were on the porch, Stella in black jeans and one of Kat's silky shirts and Kat in a pale yellow linen suit.

"Papa, why do I have to wear this tie? It's too hot."

Chance stopped and whispered to him, "Take off your hat, like a gentleman, and go hug the girls."

"But I want my hat on."

"After you give them a hug." Chance removed the hat for him, and Michel stomped up the steps.

Before Michel had a chance to do anything, Stella grabbed hold of him. "Hey, little brother, what've you been up to all week?"

"Feeding the donkeys. And Papa showed me how to ride Jericho."

"Michel, what about me?" Kat motioned him over.

He gave Kat a quick hug, then looked toward his father. "Now can I have my hat back?"

Chance propped it on his head. "We're being a bit testy today."

"Papa, what is testy?"

"Never mind."

"Come in, you two." Kat ushered them inside and hung Chance's jacket on the coatrack.

"Look what I can do." Michel grabbed the suitcase from Chance and started dragging it toward the living room, but Chance caught him in time to keep him from marring Kat's hardwood floors.

"We have to leave in an hour," Kat said. "Have you eaten lunch?"

"We stopped on the way, but I know Michel is thirsty, and he needs to use the bathroom."

"Stella, why don't you take Michel to the bathroom, and get him a glass of juice or water."

As soon as they'd left the room, Chance pulled Kat into the corner of the foyer and backed her against the wall so she couldn't escape his affection. She didn't resist. "You look so good," he said. "I can't stand being away from you any longer. You have to move in with me."

"Chance Eliason," she said between kisses, "if I didn't know you any better, I'd accuse you of wanting a built-in babysitter."

"You know that's not true. But I *will* admit this is harder than I thought. These days I have to sleep longer than usual. I'm feeling like an old man."

"Well, you don't act like an old man. I had proof of that last weekend. You wore *me* out."

"And you can bet I'll do it again. If we were alone right now..."

"Well, we're not, and we have a wedding to go to, may I remind you. So, how's he doing?"

"Pretty good. He had a couple of episodes where he asked about Monique and Paulette. He cried a little."

"It's a big change."

"Now we're learning who the boss is. I think he's winning."

Michel came around the corner. "Papa, are you kissing your girlfriend again?"

"That's right, young man. You better get used to it."

"Why? Because you are an item?"

Kat exchanged an amused smile with Chance.

***

The wedding ceremony of Libby McGraw and Kipp Reed was about to take place amidst the flourishing gardens of the historic Covington Mansion in Harbordale. In the parking lot, Chance had a brief fatherly talk with Michel about being on his best behavior because in the first place, as Chance reminded him, that was the reason he'd been allowed to wear his cowboy hat.

Stella took Michel's hand, allowing Chance to take Kat's. They stepped into the lush yard where a long aisle separated two sets of white wooden chairs. At least seventy-five guests were in attendance, all facing a colorful line of rose bushes on either side of a canopy. Nearby, a string quartet played Mouret's "Rondeau." Beyond the roses were a grouping of chairs tucked under tables spread with white clothes. The late afternoon sun, now past its peak, provided a relaxing warmth. A gentle breeze stirred the branches of the surrounding trees.

They were barely on time and were seated in the back row. Chance filed in first, followed by Kat. Michel scooted in next but complained he couldn't see, so Stella, who had taken the aisle seat, traded places with him. They'd been settled ten minutes when the quartet launched into Pachelbel's "Canon in D." Heads swiveled toward the rear, then everyone stood. Stella prompted Michel.

Kelly, Kipp's seven-year-old daughter, clad in a deep pink dress, led the procession, dipping her hand in a basket and sprinkling rose petals along the way. Her golden curls bounced on top of her shoulders. Kipp and Libby followed, Kipp in a summer suit and Libby in a pearl pink sheath with matching short-sleeved, waist-length jacket. Up ahead, waiting on either side of the canopy were Ellen, in a dress the color of Kelly's, and Charlie, in a light-colored suit. A woman minister stood between them.

After the bride and groom had passed by them, Kat whispered to Chance, "She's beautiful, isn't she?"

Chance pictured himself and Kat strolling down the aisle one day, although in his imaginings Kat would be wearing a white wedding gown. He couldn't help wondering if her thoughts harmonized with his. After they sat again, he gave her hand a squeeze.

During the ceremony, he was having a difficult time keeping his mind on the minister's words. He was a bundle of nerves. He slid his damp palms over his slacks. Kat glanced at him, curious.

He waited for the right moment, and just as Kipp and Libby were exchanging vows, Chance slipped his hand in his coat pocket, pulled out a small black box, and presented it to Kat. She stared at the box, then tipped her head, questioning. He nudged her to open it. Inside was a diamond engagement ring. He leaned in so only she could hear. "Will you marry me?" Her mouth dropped open; she was speechless. Lest she refuse him, he slipped the ring on her finger and hid the box away.

Stella gave Chance a thumbs-up. Michel, who had been squirming in his seat, squeezed past Stella and Kat to get to Chance. Chance lifted him onto his lap. Kat gazed at the ring.

When the string quartet started playing "The Wedding March" by Mendelssohn, and the bride and groom turned to face the crowd, Michel touched Kat's ring. "Papa said not to tell."

Stella whispered to Kat, "Say yes, please?"

Knowing how volatile Kat's emotions were, Chance wasn't at all sure what her reaction would be. Hopefully, their time apart, albeit under dreadful circumstances, had been a blessing in disguise. Hopefully, the experience had been a positive test of their love for each other. And hopefully, Kat had discovered how much she actually cared for him.

Kat, who seemed pleasingly shocked, held her hand out for all of them to see, glanced at Chance, and nodded a yes. Her acceptance gave Chance a deep sense of relief.

They shared a quick kiss. Stella gave her a warm hug. Michel, on the other hand, seemed more curious about the little blond girl up front, who was burrowing in between the bride and groom. He slid off Chance's lap and returned to his seat.

Everyone stood to watch Kipp and Libby, holding hands with Kelly, march back down the aisle, all three faces beaming. As Libby approached their row, she winked at Kat.

Intrigued, Chance whispered, "What was that about?"

"Beats me." But Kat was grinning.

Guests gathered around as a modest amount of pictures were taken of the wedding party. A three-tiered cake with cream frosting and gold trim was brought out from the mansion and cut into serving slices. The quartet played softly in the background.

Instead of a bridal bouquet, Libby had an orchid pinned to her jacket. In lieu of throwing a bouquet, she made an announcement that, although there was another potential bride among those in attendance, her best friend would be the next in line and pinned the orchid on Ellen's dress. Ellen beamed at Charlie, and his face turned a healthy scarlet.

With the ceremony officially over, most of the guests meandered toward the refreshment table, mingling along the way. Stella walked ahead with Michel. Chance had an arm around Kat's waist.

"When did you have a chance to buy this ring? You couldn't have bought it in Rosswood. The town is too small."

"Michel and I stopped at a jewelry store in Seattle before we got to your house. That's why we were a little late. You wouldn't back out, would you?"

"Do I have a choice?"

"It's bad luck to say no at a wedding, but honestly I didn't know if you would say yes, considering what's happened."

"You mean Michel," Kat said. "He's a part of you, Chance, and I love all of you. I know it will be an adjustment, but I'm willing to try. We'll have to consider the logistics, though."

"I've thought about that already," Chance said, "and I'm open to selling the ranch and moving to Seattle if that's what you want."

"Don't be so hasty. To be frank with you, I'm getting tired of working so hard. Maybe we can compromise somehow."

"I'll discuss any possibility, Kat, as long as I have you with me. I don't want to be apart from you, but we can take it slow if you want to."

"I'm not sure I want to take it slow."

"Whatever you want, honey. Just keep the communication open." He kissed her cheek. "I love you, Kat Summers."

Michel ran up to Chance and grabbed his free hand. "Come on, Papa. Let's get cake."

Ellen and Charlie walked up to them. "This must be Chance," Ellen said, looking him over. "You struck gold with this one, lady."

"Don't embarrass the man," Charlie said.

"He can take it." Kat grinned, peering up at Chance.

After the formal introductions, Kelly skipped up to them. "My daddy and Libby got married today, and Libby is my new mommy."

"She's going to make a wonderful mommy, too," Ellen said.

Michel stepped forward, puffing his chest out. "My daddy is getting married to her." He pointed to Kat. "And she is going to be my new mommy."

Kat latched onto Chance's arm. "Oh, boy, the reality is just sinking in."

"You wouldn't back out, would you?" Ellen asked.

"There's no way I'm letting her back out."

"Are you two really getting hitched?" Charlie asked, and Chance held up Kat's left hand, so they could examine the ring.

"That's a beauty." Ellen looked at Charlie. "Take note, big boy."

"Hey," Charlie said, "you've just raised the bar, my man."

"Sorry about that," Chance said, "but when it comes to Kat, I can't help myself."

Stella wandered over, and after introductions herded the children to the refreshment table for cake. Kipp and Libby walked up to the group, holding hands, and Ellen introduced them to Chance. Both Chance and Kat offered their congratulations.

"I knew you'd make it back," Libby said to Chance.

"So that's what the wink was about."

"I had a feeling."

"Why didn't you clue me in when I had my reading?" Kat asked.

"The answers come when they come," Libby replied. "That's all I can say. I do know you've both been through hell and back. I wish I could have prevented that, but sometimes things need to play out just as they're supposed to so we can gain a deeper understanding and in the end a deeper caring for one another."

"I felt that all along," Chance said.

Libby touched Chance's hand, her eyes intent on his. "You're a sensitive, perceptive man. I know you'll take good care of her." She turned to Kat. "It looks like you'll be following in my footsteps as a ready-made mom. We'll have a lot to share."

"If Kat's anything like Libby," Kipp said to Chance, "you're in for a wild ride. You'll never get away with anything."

Chance laughed. "It's already been a wild ride, believe me."

"The six of us will have to get together and go out to dinner sometime," Ellen said.

"That sounds about right," Charlie chimed in.

"We better keep mingling," Libby said. "We're so glad you all could come. And I'm thrilled everything is working out for you. Let us know when the wedding is. We'd love to be there."

"That goes for us, too. But we won't be having a shindig like this." Ellen looped arms with Charlie. "As soon as I get my house sold, I'm taking this big hunk to the courthouse, right Charlie?"

Charlie winked at Ellen. "That's about right."

Michel ran up to Chance. "Come on, Papa. We got you some cake."

"In a minute, son."

"We're heading up to the Straits for a few days, and then Kipp and Kelly are moving in to my house," Libby said to Kat, "but when we get settled, I'll call you."

"I'd like that."

Chance took Michel's hand. "All right, son, let's get some cake."

***

That night, after Stella and Michel were upstairs in bed, Chance and Kat sat quietly snuggled together on the couch. Chance slipped his hand under her robe and caressed her thigh. "Penny for your thoughts."

She extended her arm and admired her ring. "If we hadn't had that stupid argument that day, you never would have left so abruptly, and none of that terrible stuff would have happened. I feel so badly about it."

"Don't," he said. "If we *hadn't* argued that day, maybe *this* wouldn't have happened." He held her hand and circled the diamond with his thumb.

"Life can be crazy and unpredictable and chaotic."

"That's true. But sometimes chaos can turn into something quite beautiful."

The patter of feet could be heard across the upstairs floor, then down the stairs. Michel appeared first, followed by Stella. "Someone can't sleep," she said. "Too much sugar."

Chance beckoned them over. Michel climbed on Chance's lap, and Kat made room for Stella in between her and Chance.

Michel leaned forward so he could see Kat. "Are you my mommy now?"

Kat looked to Chance for an answer, and Chance immediately thought of Monique's request to one day tell Michel the truth about her, that she was his mother and not his aunt. But now was not the time. "Son, when Kat and I get married, Kat will be Stella's new mommy, so she'll be your new mommy, too, and the four of us will be a family."

"Yeah, Michel. Kat rules." Stella raised her arm to make the point.

Michel pointed to the ceiling, copying Stella. "Kat rules."

Chance smiled. "I couldn't agree more."

Other books by Candace Murrow
available in e-book and paperback

ROSE FROM THE GRAVE

Ever since her sister Brianna's untimely death, strange phone calls and ghostly visions have haunted Kat Summers. Weary and grief-stricken, she returns to the sleepy town of Rosswood to dispose of Brianna's property and to gain closure. Instead of the relief she seeks, she uncovers disturbing secrets about Brianna's life and encounters suspicious characters that cause her to question Brianna's ill-fated suicide. On Kat's quest for answers, she confides in Chance Eliason, a rancher with secrets of his own, who has more than a passing interest in Kat. Can Chance convince this fiercely independent woman to open her heart again before the truth about Brianna leads Kat into an unexpected trap?

VISIONS OF HOPE

Left with emotional and physical scars from an abusive marriage and breast cancer, psychic Libby McGraw has no desire to opt into another relationship, especially a relationship with a skeptic of the paranormal, a way of life quite normal to Libby. As fate would have it, mysterious visions draw Libby into the life of Kipp Reed, a skeptic who has moved back to the Pacific Northwest to quell the memory of his young daughter's disappearance. Once it becomes clear that Libby holds the keys to finding his daughter, Kipp is drawn to Libby for answers, and together they depart on an unpredictable journey of the heart.

THE DAY MEL QUIT DREAMING AND OTHER STORIES

An eclectic group of stories dealing with the disappointment of lost hopes and dreams. In coping, some of the characters move on, hoping for better times ahead; some face difficult challenges; and some simply accept their fate. Several of the stories are edgy, but all are spirited and entertaining. Eight stories. Quirky characters.

www.candacemurrow.com

Made in the USA
San Bernardino, CA
07 August 2013